A Killer of a Case

A McCall / Malone Mystery

Glenn Harris

I0607132

First Edition 2022

www.glennharris.us

Front Cover design: Cathleen Rehfeld

Cover / interior design: Matthew Wayne Selznick / MWS Media

A Killer of a Case

CHAPTER ONE
THEN

Something was wrong with the doll.

It looked okay on the outside. The frilly pink dress was clean and neatly in place. The blond hair was carefully combed. The shiny plastic skin was without any dust or blemish.

But inside, something was broken. The doll wouldn't sit up straight, slumping to the side no matter what the little girl did to fix it.

She trembled as she tried one more time and then gave up with a sniffle. She set the doll on a shelf, in one corner leaning against the wall. The rest of that shelf held her schoolbooks.

Maybe Daddy wouldn't notice. Daddy didn't like things that were broken. It could be bad.

She climbed back into bed, lay on her side, pulled her legs up, and clutched a pillow to her chest. She wished her mother hadn't died.

Apart from the doll, her room was perfect as always: her toys put away, her bed made, her little desk clean. The books on the shelf all straight. Just the way Daddy liked it. Except for the doll. She wished she had a sister, or even a brother. Someone.

She was half-asleep when she heard the first shout. She was wide awake when she heard the second and realized that it was not Daddy. Who could it be and why was he yelling? There was never anyone in the house but her and Daddy. Was Daddy gone? Had he left her alone with a strange man in the house? But the stranger was clearly yelling at someone. Daddy? Was he in trouble? What would she do if he was in trouble? She had no phone in her room and he would never forgive her if she brought the police into the house.

She eased herself off the bed onto the floor so that she couldn't be seen from her doorway. She held her breath as she heard more shouting, including Daddy now, and then things breaking.

She closed her eyes tight. Oh, this was really bad.

Then, abruptly, it was quiet.

Really quiet. There was total silence, except for the susurration of her own shallow breathing as she listened for something, anything, to tell her what had happened, what *was* happening.

After what seemed like a very long time, she raised her head to peek over the bed at the doorway. No one. Nothing.

Slowly, slowly, she edged around the end of the bed and crept across the room to the hallway. Still no sound other than her own breathing. She moved to her left, as silently as she possibly could. That was the nearest way out, but also the direction the sounds had come from.

She got past the first open doorway, Daddy's bedroom, without any problem. The second open doorway, the bathroom, without any problem. Then she reached the living room, where the front door was.

All the shades were pulled, blocking most of the early morning light. But all she had to do was cross the room and go out the front door. What she would do then, she wasn't sure, but she knew something bad had happened in here and she wanted to be out there.

She dashed for the door.

And tripped over something halfway across the room, going down on her knees hard. She couldn't help crying out before she scrambled to her feet and looked down to see what had tripped her.

Even in the dim light, she could see it was Daddy. Lying in a pool of blood. In all her eleven years, she had never seen so much blood. She froze in place, making no sound, not even breathing.

Her breath returned in a gasp as she detected movement out of the corner of her eye. Someone else was in the room. After a moment, she forced herself to look up.

Then she began to scream and, on some level, never stopped.

CHAPTER TWO
NOW

"Morty has been kidnapped!"

The wail exploded into the room the second I answered the agency main line. I'd seen on the display it was our old client Agatha Pepper and put it on speaker so that my wife and partner could also say hello to her.

Apparently we were going to skip the niceties.

"Ms. Pepper! Agatha!" I interrupted a second, even more prolonged wail. "This is Clint and Devon is here, too. You're on the speakerphone. Tell us what happened."

"I just told you! Morty has been kidnapped!"

Ms. Pepper was an elderly retired librarian and Morty was her hefty and equally elderly beagle.

Malone leaned in and I could tell she was suppressing a grin so it wouldn't be in her voice. "When and where was Morty kidnapped, Agatha? And do you know who did it?"

"It was three hours ago! Three hours! And Rodney has only just told me!"

"Ah," I said with no surprise at all in my voice, "the dog was taken from Rodney." Rodney was Agatha's ne'er-do-well and not-very-bright nephew who was recently written into her will after trying to kill her several times. Long story. "Maybe we'd better get the specifics from him," I continued.

"You can't! I've thrown him out of the house! And out of the will, as soon as I can get to it. Irresponsible twat!"

Malone stepped in again. "Take a deep breath, Agatha, and stop yelling. As calmly and clearly as you can, tell us what you know of what happened. We can't go out and find Morty with no information."

Malone and I made eye contact, which was not that easy when we were both rolling our eyes. I'd joked a couple of months ago about getting into the business of pet-finding, but I hadn't expected the reality.

We listened to our old—and apparently new—client take a couple of breaths. "Rodney took Morty for a walk this morning, as usual. He stopped in a delicatessen for a snack or a coffee, I don't know, and left Morty tied up outside, just for a minute, so he says." Another deep breath, followed by a small sob. "Morty was gone when he came out."

"And that was about three hours ago? So, eight or a little after," Malone confirmed.

"Yes."

"Which delicatessen?"

Agatha and Rodney Pepper lived in Lake Oswego, one of the richer suburbs of the Portland metro area. I didn't think there were very many delicatessens there.

"The Lake Oswego Deli, of course!"

Of course.

"Did Rodney see anyone suspicious?" I asked. "Or maybe a vehicle fleeing the scene? Anything like that?"

"Not that he mentioned." Another stifled sob. "I confess I didn't give him much chance to talk after it became clear that he'd lost Morty."

"Do you have any idea where Rodney is now? We need to talk to him."

"Oh, he's probably in back."

"In back?"

"There's a small cottage at the back of my property here. That's where he usually goes when he's afraid of me."

"Aha. Well, we'll come out to interview him for further details as soon as possible and of course we'll also check out the deli to see if there were any witnesses."

"Please hurry. God knows who has Morty or what is happening to him."

"We'll be there as soon as we can," my partner assured her.

"All right. And if I get any ransom calls in the meantime, I'll take notes."

"That's good, Agatha. We'll see you soon." Malone stood to reach across the desk and end the call. "Good thing we don't

4

have a lot on our plate right now," she said as she sat back down. "How the hell are we going to find a kidnapped beagle?"

I shrugged, having no more idea than she did. "We've got to give it a try. You know Agatha dotes on Morty. She'd be devastated if he were gone forever. Plus, I'd hate to see her convicted of Rodney's murder. I'm sure she still has that handgun of hers, especially now that she's famous for it."

Malone swiveled her chair a little to look down on Stark Street and the Monday morning busyness of Portland's downtown. "Yeah, we've got to save the dog to save the two humans." She grinned. "Plus, we'll be getting our per diem to investigate a dognapping. Let's get going."

But it was not to be. We were just getting to our feet and I'd opened my desk drawer to retrieve my Smith and Wesson when there was a very soft knock on our door. It opened slightly and stopped.

"Come on in," I called as I closed the drawer again.

The door swung the rest of the way to reveal a small young woman, maybe late twenties, rail thin, with pale complexion and almost white blond hair—an adult waif who looked like she would twang if you flicked her with a finger.

She stood in the doorway wearing a light jacket over a prim, knee-length green dress and clutching a small leather purse.

"Can we help you?" I inquired.

"Are you the detectives?" Her voice was as frail as her frame.

I stood up and gestured for her to come further in. "Yes, I'm Clint McCall and this is my partner Devon Malone. What can we do for you?"

She didn't move, just looked from one of us to the other. "I want you to find out who I am."

CHAPTER THREE

I exchanged a quick glance with Malone. "I think you'd better have a seat," I said to the young woman.

She made her way across the room to the visitor's chair nearest me and carefully settled herself, sitting very straight with the purse positioned squarely in her lap. She seemed to be waiting for us to speak first.

So I did. "You don't know who you are?"

The corner of her mouth twitched as if there might be a smile back there somewhere. Or possibly a grimace. "Well, I know that my name is Sylvia Ralston, that Sharon and Jeffrey Ralston were my adoptive parents, and that I write cozy mysteries under the name Lynn Hanna. What I don't know is my original name, my birth parents, or what happened to make me forget all that."

"Wow" was all I could think to say for a moment.

So Malone took over. "Maybe you'd better start at the beginning, whenever that is. How far back do you remember?"

The woman seemed to relax slightly. "Twenty years. I was found unconscious in an alley here in Portland, near the downtown area. I had a variety of injuries, evidence of abuse both sexual and physical. When I finally came to, after several days in a coma, I remembered nothing. Not who I was or where I'd been or what happened. Nothing. They estimated that I was ten or eleven years old."

Sylvia Ralston did not look like a rich woman, so I figured I'd better jump to the bottom line before we got too far. "Two decades is a very long time. Trying to find out what happened that long ago could be a lengthy and very expensive process with no guarantee of success."

Again there was that twitch. "I was put in the foster system after I got out of the hospital, of course, but less than a year later I was adopted by the Ralstons who had no children of their own.

Lucky for me, they had plenty of money. My father, my adoptive father, developed a number of computer games that were very successful. Now that they have both passed, I've inherited a sizable fortune."

"How did they die?" asked Malone.

"My mother died of cancer four years ago and my father in a car accident almost a year ago."

"Did no one ever report you missing?"

"No. No one. There were no missing person reports that could have been me."

"And you never tried to find out about your true identity before now?"

She sighed. "No. No, I haven't. It's complicated. I always got the subtle but strong message from my adoptive parents that they didn't want me to look. I don't know why. But I grew up with that and it's taken me almost a year to get past it even now that I'm entirely free to do as I choose."

"You were entirely free when you turned eighteen." Devon Malone was not one for subtlety.

The young woman shrugged it off. "Like I said, it's complicated. Jeffrey and Sharon Ralston rescued me from foster care—where I was *not* thriving, to say the least, and provided me with love and education and material well-being. I went from nothing to everything overnight thanks to them and I never wanted to go against them."

I took a turn. "Have you done any checking of your own? Adoption records, old friends of your adoptive parents, anybody?"

She shook her head. "No, that's why I'm here. I'm not up for it even now. I want to go back to my writing and leave it to the professionals." She looked at Malone, sitting on the other side of our partners desk with her shoulder-length brunette hair and all-black leather outfit including kickass boots. The contrast between the two women was pretty extreme. "You two are married as well as partners, right?"

"You've done your research," replied my wife.

"Yes, I have. You were a police officer in Tigard and then a detective who worked on missing persons cases here in Portland." She transferred her attention to me. "And you were a Pulitzer-Prize-winning journalist and then professor—with a fourth-degree black belt, I understand."

"Very good," I responded.

"And now you're partners in this detective agency."

"Yes."

She looked from me to Malone and back, maybe wondering what the svelte and mid-thirties Malone was doing with the slightly stocky, slightly balding guy in his mid-fifties. "So. Will you take my case?"

Or maybe that.

Malone and I exchanged our own look across the desk. We couldn't pass it up. "Of course we will," I told Sylvia Ralston as I pulled another drawer open. We can do the paperwork and get started if you're prepared to give us a retainer."

"I have my checkbook right here."

And now we had a lot on our plate.

CHAPTER FOUR

The past two months, since the latest rescue of my daughter and her boyfriend in August, had been relatively quiet. Just the normal routine of cheating spouses, disappearing creditors, and larcenous employees. Our one ongoing case of any urgency was a downtown jewelry store that wanted their security evaluated and enhanced. It was urgent only because they'd recently been robbed and they were extremely nervous about being hit again.

It shouldn't be that hard, I thought, to add in the search for a kidnapped dog and the identity of our new client. The latter would probably just be a lot of research, most of which would be done by others anyway.

My daughter Colleen and her boyfriend Hoke, by the way, seemed to have a clearer focus since their last adventure. At the moment, in fact, they were both fully and gainfully employed: Colleen was the assistant stage manager at a reputable downtown theater and Hoke was working for a construction company that was a regular client of ours. I held out some faint hope that they'd both stick with it.

In a further half-hour or so of paperwork and interviewing, we learned among many other things that Sylvia Ralston had never been married and didn't currently have a boyfriend. Then we sent her on her way to gather any records and notes she could find from around the time she was found, treated, and placed in foster care. The door closed behind her as I sat staring at the remarkably hefty check she had left in my hand. Malone drew my attention by standing and retrieving her Glock from her desk drawer.

"If you're done drooling," she said, "we need to head for Lake Oswego. We still have a dog to find and Ms. Pepper may have shot Rodney by now. I'm surprised she hasn't called to see what happened to us."

"Indeed." I stashed the check and paperwork in the middle drawer, got my Smith and Wesson from the side drawer, and followed my partner out of the office.

Since Morty did not require much advance planning, we mostly discussed the Ralston case as I drove us to Lake Oswego in my Subaru Outback.

Along the way, Malone called Portland Police Lieutenant Mike Whitehall, my long-time friend and her former colleague, to ask if he could track down any report on the discovery of Sylvia Ralston in that alley twenty years ago. He said he'd try, but it might take a while. He hadn't entirely forgiven me yet for involving him in the extralegal violence two months ago. While he didn't mention it, I knew it might add a little more delay.

Nevertheless, it allowed us to feel we'd started the research on Ms. Ralston's case before we delved into the dognapping.

It was a little past noon as I drove up Agatha Pepper's tree-lined driveway to her front portico. The three-story home was almost large enough to qualify as a mini-mansion. For a retired librarian, Ms. Pepper had done quite well financially, probably because she was even more intelligent than she was eccentric. Which was saying a lot.

"I hope she's planning to feed us," my partner muttered as we bailed out of the car and climbed the three steps to the porch.

The door opened before we could knock and there she stood, looking very much as she had when she'd first come to our office: classic little old lady, wearing a colorfully patterned muumuu that fell almost to her ankles, a bright red ribbon holding her white hair in a long ponytail.

The biggest difference was her drawn and worried countenance. She'd been happy and excited to hire private detectives because someone was trying to kill her. A missing Morty, on the other hand, was serious business.

"At last!" she cried. "I thought you'd never come." She anxiously motioned us inside.

We hadn't been in her home before and we found ourselves

in a large foyer of muted colors with what looked like an actual crystal chandelier hanging from a twelve-foot-ceiling. There was a broad staircase to our left, an archway leading to a large sitting area ahead of us, and a closed door to our right. Very close to a mini-mansion, indeed.

The living room to which our client escorted us was much more in her style—colorful cushions on colorful couches with colorful drapes and wall decorations. It was a little like walking into the largest candy store I'd ever seen.

"Sit, sit," she urged us to the nearest couch, which happened to be deep purple with bright green cushions. "Tell me what you've done so far." She lighted on a bright yellow chair nearby and bounced a little. I was already beginning to wish I had some Dramamine.

I held up both hands placatingly. "We haven't done anything yet, Agatha. As I told you on the phone, we need to talk to Rodney and get as many details as we can about what happened then check out the deli."

"And then?"

"Well, hopefully we'll get a lead somewhere in there." I glanced around the room, squinting slightly. "Rodney's not here?"

Agatha Pepper huffed. "Must you talk to him?"

"Of course."

"All right." There must have been a pocket somewhere in the folds of the muumuu because she produced a phone and tapped it, then put it to her ear. "Rodney? Are you in the cottage?" She listened a moment. "No, I don't forgive you, but I need you in the house. The detectives are here to review your many failings." She shoved the phone back into her garment and we waited.

It was about three minutes later that we heard a door open and close somewhere in the back of the house, followed by footsteps hurrying in our direction. Rodney Pepper duly appeared in the archway.

He too looked about the same as when we'd last seen him: younger than his thirty years, with tousled brown hair above a round face with deceptively innocent blue eyes and a small silver earring in his left earlobe. He was stocky heading toward hefty, wearing a white tee shirt, blue jeans, and tennis shoes.

He glanced at us but focused on Ms. Pepper. "I am so sorry, Aunt Agatha."

"Piffle. Get in here, sit your butt down, and start making up for it."

He scuttled—there was no other word for it—to the nearest free armchair and perched on the front edge. He looked at us, then dropped his gaze to the floor. "What can I tell you?"

"Start at the beginning," Malone told him, "when you left the house with Morty. Every detail. Don't leave anything out."

He looked up again. "You'll be able to find him, won't you?"

"We'll do our best," she responded with some asperity. I recognized the tone: hamburger deficient.

"But we need your help, Rodney," I jumped in.

"Okay. Well, I always take Morty for a walk first thing after breakfast. That's what we did this morning. We left between seven and seven-thirty and took our usual route."

"Which is?" That was my partner.

"Five blocks east on this street here, then five blocks north, then ten blocks west, then five blocks south, and finally back home."

"Where is the deli in all that?" I asked.

"About the middle of the ten blocks west."

"What's the name of the street?"

"I don't know. I've never paid any attention."

"Ookay. Well, what happened when you were at the deli? Every detail."

He closed his eyes as if trying to picture it all. "I tied Morty's leash to the bike rack out front as I always do. I went inside. There was a guy behind the counter and no other customers...oh, and I think there was an employee out front, sweeping the sidewalk. Yes, there was. I ordered my coffee, paid, came back out...and Morty was gone. There was no one in sight, on foot anyway."

"What happened to the person sweeping the sidewalk?" my partner asked.

Rodney thought about it. "I don't know. Maybe he came back inside while I was getting my coffee—or maybe he went around back for something."

That needed some further investigation, right there, but I had another question. "Are you sure you didn't see anyone else or anything unusual? Think. Take your time."

He took his time, eyes closed again, sweat beading on his forehead. "Well...I think there was a girl...."

"A girl?" That was Malone.

"A kid, that was walking by while I was tying Morty's leash to the bike rack."

"What did she look like?"

"I don't know. She was a girl, young girl, maybe twelve or fourteen, dark hair, short."

"She was short or her hair was short?"

"Hair. She was average size, I guess."

"How was she dressed?"

He made a face. "Shit, I don't know. Dark clothes. Pants, not a dress. Some kind of top. I don't know."

I exchanged a glance with Malone. We weren't going to get anything else. I stood up and looked down at Agatha who had been quiet throughout our questioning of her nephew except for the occasional snort. "We'll do our best to find Morty," I said.

She scooted forward in her chair and glared first at me, then significantly at Rodney. "I just hope we all survive this misadventure." I didn't think she was talking about us or Morty. From the way he paled even further, I don't think Rodney thought that, either.

CHAPTER FIVE

It was after one by the time we left Agatha's house and my partner was near starvation coma, so we headed for the Lake Oswego Deli. Food first, questions second.

The place turned out to be very nice, as one would expect in Lake Oswego: large, airy, well-lit, and sparkling clean with a menu consisting mostly of options for people on a variety of health kicks.

Alas, no hamburgers. In fact there were very few choices for people like Malone who hated health kicks. She finally settled on a sandwich of whole-grain bread with grilled chicken breast and grilled veggies. No mayonnaise. No cheese. Very unhappy partner.

I told the guy behind the counter to make it two, in the spirit of solidarity. Besides, I thought it looked kind of good.

The counter man appeared to be in his twenties, with a big friendly smile and healthy glow. Maybe five-ten, one eighty, with his hair cut so close to his scalp that I couldn't tell what color it was. I watched him as we ate our very healthy meal at a corner table. He didn't strike me as a dognapper or accomplice.

A young woman had appeared from the back as we were sitting down and started wiping down the tables and carting away dishes left behind. The lunch trade was mostly gone, only one other couple and a singleton still lingering.

There was another guy in the back, preparing the food, but I hadn't gotten a good look at him yet.

Malone wolfed down her sandwich despite sneering at it first and I finished soon after. We returned to the counter with our IDs in hand.

The bright smile dimmed a little as he looked from one ID to the other after we introduced ourselves. "Jeez. Private investigators. Is there a problem?"

"There was a guy in here early this morning to get a coffee," I said. "Thirtyish, stocky, blue eyes, silver earring...."

"Oh yeah, I know who you mean. He comes in most every morning. Did something happen to him?"

"No," Malone replied, "but something happened to the dog he was walking. It was taken from the front of your shop while he was in here."

"Oh. I'm sorry about that, but we didn't.... He hired two private eyes to find his dog?"

"Yes," I conceded a little grudgingly. "We're trying to track down the dog." *McCall and Malone, Pet Detectives.* "He said that one of you was out front sweeping the sidewalk while he was in here."

He glanced over his shoulder. "That would have been Charlie. He always makes sure the outside looks okay, front and back, before we get a lot of customers."

"Could we talk to Charlie?" Malone inquired.

"Sure." He glanced around. "It's plenty slow this time of day." Again over his shoulder, "Charlie! Some folks need to talk to you out here." He turned back around to us. "Charlie's my brother. We own this place together. I'm Jason Federici."

The young woman had wandered over and joined Jason behind the counter. She looked to be late teens, slender with reddish blond hair. "And you are?" I asked her.

"Annie. Annie Boritz. You guys are private eyes looking for a dog? Did I hear that right?"

"Yes," I said again, perhaps a little tersely. "Did you see anything that might help?"

"What time was it?"

Jason answered. "It was around seven-thirty, before you came in, Annie."

Meanwhile, Charlie had joined us. He could have been a carbon copy of Jason, who grinned when he noticed my reaction. "Twins. Can you tell?"

"What's going on?" inquired Charlie.

I explained once again what we were doing there and what

we wanted to know. I conceded once again that, yes, we were two private investigators looking for a damned dog.

"Well," said Charlie, "I remember the customer and I remember him tying the dog's leash to the bike rack, but I went around back to check that the alley was clear right after that. The dog was still there then."

"Did you see anybody besides the customer?"

He gave it a few seconds thought. "I don't think so." Another few seconds. "Wait a minute. I do remember somebody. There was a kid walking by as I headed around the corner, a young girl, teenager. I've seen her around the neighborhood but I don't know who she is."

"What does she look like?" asked my partner.

He shrugged. "Kind of a goth look, really short black hair, kind of spiky, dark pants and top. Tall for as young as she looked. A gangly girl, if you know what I mean."

"I know who that is!" Annie spoke up, then blushed. "I mean...I don't actually know her, but I've seen her around and we've said hello. I think her name's Beck or maybe Becky. Something like that."

"No last name?" I asked.

"Nope. Sorry."

Malone focused on Charlie. "You're sure that you saw her as you were going back to the alley?"

"Yeah, she was coming down the sidewalk as I headed around the corner."

There didn't seem to be anything else to discover from this crew, so I paid for our lunches, left our office number in case they saw the goth girl or the dog, and we stepped out onto the sidewalk. The sky was looking a little gray and the breeze was chilly. Mid-October in the Pacific Northwest.

"Why did you want to know exactly where Charlie was when he saw the kid?" I asked my partner as we walked to the car.

"Rodney said he saw a girl who looked like that walking by as he was going into the deli," she replied across the top of the

Subaru as we were opening our respective doors. "And Charlie saw her as he was heading around back, after Rodney was inside," she continued as we settled in and fastened our seatbelts. "They both seem pretty sure about the time, so if it was the same girl she must have walked by twice. Why would she walk by twice in such a short time?"

We looked at one another as I turned the ignition key. "Huh. I think we need to find and have a chat with Beck or Becky," I said.

CHAPTER SIX

I pulled into my assigned parking spot in the lot across from the office. I beeped the door locked and headed for the corner, only to realize that Malone was hanging back.

I turned and looked at her. She appeared a little put out for some reason. "What?"

"You go on to the office. I'm going to stop in the Home Run for a few minutes. I need a second lunch."

I tried not to laugh in her grumpy face. "Don't hobbits do something like that? Second breakfast, second lunch?"

"I don't know. I'm not a fucking hobbit. But I am still hungry."

I didn't dare chuckle. Grumpy face had become hostile face. "No problem. See you soon." I grinned only after I was across the street and approaching our entrance.

Our office is at the corner of Third and Stark, in an old two-story commercial building on the northeast edge of downtown Portland, Oregon. Downstairs is Previously Owned Books, operated by our landlords. The single stairwell, dimly lit with fading and chipped white paint over plaster, leads from Stark up to the second floor. The McCall-Malone Detective Agency is the first door on your right. Across from us is our attorney Sam Bitterly. Down the hall on the right is our insurance broker Raymond Witkowsky, with our accountant and hacker/researcher Eleanor Ivory across from him. A small telephone survey operation and the public restroom shared by all the offices completed the floor.

It was a convenient location, not only because so many support people were right there, but because the Home Run Sports Bar, serving my wife and partner's favorite hamburgers, was across the street.

I settled on my side of the partners desk and checked for messages. The desk sits in front of the double window that looks out on Stark. Besides the desk and the visitor's chairs, there's a couch, a coat rack, a small counter off in the corner that holds a mini-fridge, coffeemaker, and miscellaneous dishware.

There were no messages of pressing interest, voice or email. The snail mail that I had collected on the way up was even less interesting and went straight into the wastebasket.

I looked at the phone, my computer, out the window at the building across the street, and wondered how long it would take Malone to have second lunch. We hadn't heard back from Mike Whitehall, but it felt like I should be doing something for the check I'd been handed this morning.

So I decided to head down the hall to see if our accountant-researcher-hacker was in her office. You want to find obscure stuff on the internet, you want that lady doing the search. And I had to suppose anything on the web that could help us with a kid who showed up in an alley twenty years ago was going to be pretty damned obscure.

The upper half of all our office doors is a pane of frosted glass, with the name of the occupant in bold black letters. I knocked on the door that said Eleanor Ivory Accountancy and got an immediate "Come in!"

Eleanor was behind her desk and focused on her PC as I entered. She glanced up at me, smiled, and gestured at one of her visitor chairs. "Hey, Clint. Give me a minute. I'm just about finished with this form."

I sat in the well-padded chair, much more comfortable than ours, and waited. Eleanor was looking good. She'd recently turned forty, a few years older than Devon, five-nine with long blond hair and the body of a fitness magazine model. Her lips are slightly too full and her nose slightly too small for classic beauty but they worked well enough together with the wide violet eyes. She was wearing a conservative—for-her knit top. I couldn't see the rest, but it was probably a knee-length skirt.

My old friend and fellow black belt used to be quite the party girl, but several serious misadventures in recent years had settled her down a bit. She'd had a serious boyfriend for almost six months now and more regularly worked out in the dojang that I rented along with Mike Whitehall and several other black belts.

She hit one final key and I heard her printer start up as she swiveled to face me. "What can I do you for? Something mildly illegal but for the greater good, I hope. It's been a little boring around here."

I laughed. "I don't know about mildly illegal but it might be more than mildly difficult. We have a new client, Sylvia Ralston, who basically wants us to undo twenty years of traumatic amnesia."

Eleanor squinted at me. "Say what?"

"Long story short, twenty years ago, around the age of eleven, she was found in a downtown alley here in Portland with injuries and no memory of who she was or what happened. She ended up adopted by some good people with ample resources, but now she wants us to find out who she really is and what happened to her."

"Wow." I could see her brain was already ticking over. "That's something. Why now?"

"Apparently her adoptive parents discouraged her from trying to find out, but now that they've both passed and she has plenty of money for the investigation, she wants to do it."

Eleanor had pulled over a notepad and started writing. "So her name, now anyway, is Sylvia Ralston. And she's, what, around thirty?"

"That would be a good guess. Maybe late twenties."

"Is she married? Kids? What does she do for a living?"

"No husband or even boyfriend, apparently. Ditto kids. She's an author. She writes cozy mysteries, whatever those are, under the name Lynn Hanna."

Eleanor's pen froze and she looked up at me with wide eyes. "Lynn Hanna? The Enchanted Bookstore series? Really?"

I shrugged. "She didn't mention any titles. You've heard of her?"

"I've read all her books! I'm a huge fan!"

"Well. Small world."

"Not so small. She sells a *lot* of books. She's really very good. I can understand why she has plenty of money."

"Plus, her adoptive father made a fortune developing computer games."

"Huh. Wow again. And she was abandoned in a damned alley twenty years ago? That's terrible but...this is going to be so much fun. I assume I'll get to meet her."

I grinned. "I'll make sure you do." Nothing like a highly motivated researcher, I always say.

The pen started moving again. "Okay. What else can you tell me about her? And what do you want me to focus on first?"

CHAPTER SEVEN

Malone was back in the office when I returned from my meeting with Eleanor.

She looked up as I entered. "Bathroom?"

"Eleanor. I've got her started on researching Sylvia Ralston." I took my place opposite my partner. "She's a fan, apparently. Says Ralston is a big deal in her genre. What is a cozy, anyway?"

Malone sat back and nodded. "A cozy mystery is a murder mystery most often set in a small town, featuring a female amateur sleuth who usually owns something like a bookstore or bakery shop. She has quirky friends and at least one cat or dog, also quirky. There are no bad words, no sex, and no graphic violence. There are, on the other hand, usually recipes."

I looked at her and did my own squint. "That's pretty specific. How the hell did you know that? Don't tell me you're a closet fan."

She chuckled. "Hardly. But I Googled it while eating. I also Googled Lynn Hanna. Ms. Ivory is correct that she's a best-selling author. Or so her website claims."

"Huh. Well, Eleanor wants to meet her and is planning to stock up on books to be signed."

"Hopefully all that enthusiasm will produce some research results."

"That is my hope." I took a gaze out the window. "You know, it strikes me as odd that Sylvia Ralston seems so tense and vulnerable if she's a best-selling author. She must do book tours, interviews, things like that all the time."

"Doesn't mean she's not shy. People do what they have to do. Also, those things are very different from hiring two private eyes to dig up your own dirt."

"True. Though she doesn't know it's going to be dirt."

"She was found in an alley as a child, sexually abused, badly injured, with apparently permanent amnesia, Clint. It's going to be dirt."

I picked up the phone. "Well, now that I have Eleanor on the case, I'm going to give DHS a call and get them started on looking for her foster care records. Given that we're talking twenty years ago, I imagine it will take a while."

The Oregon Department of Human Services handled foster care statewide. The perky young woman who took my call confirmed that no one from two decades past was still at any of the local offices and that not all the records from those days were digitized. However, she was sufficiently thrilled to be talking to a private detective that she promised to try her best. I hung up without a lot of optimism.

It was nearly three thirty by that point. Neither of us could think of anything else to do for Sylvia Ralston right away. We were still hoping to have some inspiration about Morty before having to go searching for a random goth girl possibly named Beck. A ransom call or note would be good. The dog simply turning up would be even better.

Anyway, it was too early to go home. There was no paperwork to catch up on. The phone wasn't ringing. Malone wasn't hungry again yet. So we headed over to Morton Jewelers to continue our evaluation of their current security set-up.

Ninety minutes of chatting, note-taking, and then driving later, we pulled into the driveway of our house, Malone parking her Jeep behind my Subaru Outback.

Our house, which had been my house long before I met Malone, is in what's known as the Hawthorne District of Portland, on 37th three doors from the Marrakech Theater on Hawthorne Boulevard. It's a fairly nondescript house, built back in the '50s, the original wood siding currently painted a light green and the windows trimmed in white. There's a small open yard in front and a larger fenced one in back. It's fine for us and the cats.

Yes, there are cats, tortoiseshell sisters Stella and Maxine, also mine long before Malone appeared in my life. Stella is a sleek and multi-toned tawny troublemaker while Maxine is a chubby, gentle, gray and white ball of fluff.

They greeted us at the door, complaining as usual about the extreme neglect and starvation they had to endure while we were at work.

"I'm feeling grumpy," Malone announced as we changed into casual clothes for the evening. I was sitting on the edge of the bed, taking my shoes off, and looked up at her.

"We've got some good frozen dinners," I said. "That would be quick."

She snorted. "I'm not talking about food. It's frustrating that things are so slow while I feel like we should be doing a lot. The Ralston case is really interesting—and then there's Morty. He's out there somewhere, hopefully still okay.... He's an old dog. He's not going to be happy with any new tricks."

She plunked herself down beside me. "And there's not much we can actually do for either client. At least not for sure."

I took her hand and squeezed it. "I know, but we do already have Eleanor and Mike and DHS looking for background that we'll need to move forward on Ralston. And we can head back to Lake Oswego first thing in the morning to start canvassing for the goth kid. We might get lucky."

"Yeah, yeah. We might."

"So," I said, standing up, "let's go fix something to eat. Then we'll just relax for the evening and be raring to go in the morning."

She stood. "Yeah, yeah."

We headed for the kitchen and the microwave.

A few hours later we settled ourselves in bed. The evening had been quiet and our interactions desultory. I'd not been very successful in cheering up my partner. I tried again as we lay facing one another.

"We have cats," I noted. "Maybe Lynn Hanna will write a cozy mystery about us."

Another one of those snorts. "Nah. It wouldn't be us without cursing, sex, and graphic violence."

I laughed. "I guess that's true. Plus, you can't cook, so no recipes."

"You can't, either."

"Yeah, but I'm not supposed to."

More like a hiss this time. "Fucking sexist pig." She rolled over, presenting me with her stiffened spine.

So much for cheering her up. And there went the sex. At least I avoided the graphic violence.

CHAPTER EIGHT

We decided over breakfast to head straight for Lake Oswego. Ms. Pepper and Rodney had both texted us during the night and we wanted to be able to immediately reassure them we were on the job.

Speaking of the night, it turned out my wife wasn't seriously pissed after all and I for one ended up pretty cheerful.

We took Malone's Jeep simply because it was the vehicle nearest the street. Normally we drove both cars to the office so we'd have separate transportation if needed during the day. Our plan this morning was to swing back by to get my Subaru after doing whatever diligence we could for our elderly client.

At a little past eight-thirty, Malone was just turning left onto Hawthorne and I had my phone out to call Agatha and tell her we were going to be in her neighborhood soon. The phone's ringing beat me to it. I glanced at the display and was surprised to see it was the number Sylvia Ralston had given us. I swiped the screen and put the phone to my ear. "Ms. Ralston?"

"Mr. McCall, where are you?" Her voice was breathy and tremulous.

"In the Hawthorne District. Are you okay?"

"No! I've been threatened!"

"What do you mean? Who threatened you?"

"I don't know who! There was a note pinned to my door early this morning. No signature. Just the threat!"

"What kind of threat was it?"

"They threatened my life!"

My partner had been following my side of the conversation closely and I motioned to her that she should take the next corner and go around the block. "Okay," I said to Ms. Ralston at the same time, "I want you to head for our office and we'll meet you there. Be careful...."

"I'm already at your office, standing in front of the locked door! I didn't even think to call you before I rushed down here. I wasn't thinking...."

"Well then, I want you to go down the corridor to the office that says Eleanor Ivory Accountancy on it. Eleanor is our accountant and should be there by now. Explain who you are and that I told you to shelter with her until we get there. She's more than just an accountant. She's very fit and has a second-degree black belt."

"Okay. Okay, I'll do that."

Another minute or so and we were back in front of our house. Less than sixty seconds after that, I was backing out of the driveway to follow my partner downtown. It was about a twenty-minute drive in Tuesday morning traffic and I checked in with Eleanor to make sure she was indeed at work and had our client safely at hand. She was and she did.

It was right on nine a.m. when we hurried across Third Street from the parking lot and took the stairs two at a time. We went straight down the corridor to Eleanor's, where I knocked and got a "Who is it?"

"It's Clint and Devon."

"Come on in, then."

Eleanor was behind her desk and Sylvia Ralston in one of her visitor chairs. Our accountant was looking a little tense and our client was looking a complete wreck. I sat down beside Sylvia Ralston and Malone took up a position to the side of the room where she could watch the door.

I reached over and laid my hand on Ralston's arm. "How are you?"

She jolted even though she'd seen it coming. "Not good."

Might as well get right to it; she was in no mood for small talk. "Do you have the note with you?"

Turned out it was already clutched in her hand. She shoved it at me and I practically had to pry her fingers off it. I uncrumpled the small sheet of white notepaper as Malone stepped closer to read over my shoulder.

It was typed in all caps: FIRE THE PRIVATE EYE. LET IT BE. LIVE YOUR LIFE—OR LOSE IT.

Wow. I looked up at our client. "Who knows that you've hired us?"

She threw up her hands. "That's just it! Nobody! I haven't talked to anybody about doing this! How could anyone possibly know?"

Good question.

"You sure you didn't mention it in passing to a friend?" Malone followed up. "Maybe went out to have a drink with somebody and...."

"I don't drink," Ralston interrupted, "and my best friend is probably my editor—whom I've seen twice in the last decade or so. I'm not a people person."

"Well," I said, "in that case we have to think about who we've told. It's probably a good assumption that no one has been following you around for twenty years in case you got curious about your past." I focused on Eleanor. "Have you done much research yet? Gotten into any databases where you could have triggered an alert?"

She shook her head. "No, nothing. I did a couple of preliminary Google searches, but I haven't found anything worth clicking on yet."

I thought for a moment and then stood. "Okay, we'll get out of your hair then. Might as well continue mulling this over in our own office. One thing: Is there a way for you to know if you've triggered an alert as you continue to research?"

She shook her head. "That requires all kinds of special software I don't have—and even then it doesn't always work."

"Well, keep detailed records of what links you do click on, just in case."

"Will do." She looked at Sylvia Ralston. "And you take care."

CHAPTER NINE

Back in our own office, Malone and I settled at the desk and this time Sylvia Ralston took the visitor chair closest to my partner.

"Only the three of us, Eleanor, and Mike Whitehall know about this investigation," I said as I reached for the agency phone. "I need to call Mike."

"Who's Mike Whitehall?" Ralston asked my partner as I hit the speed dial.

Mike answered on the first ring and skipped the hello. "I just put the request in a few minutes ago, Clint. I should have whatever report exists for you later today. I was tied up with two separate homicides after we talked yesterday. Didn't get to it."

I went with it. "No problem, Mike. Just thought I'd check in. Talk to you later." I hung up.

"The alert, if there was one, wasn't triggered in the Portland PD system. Mike just put in the request this morning."

"What else could it have been?" asked Malone. "Something had to have triggered an alert, unless whoever it is has a psychic available."

"What about the note itself?" chimed in our client. "Could you check for fingerprints?"

"Probably not worth it," I replied. "We've all handled it and you had it crumpled up in your hand. Forensics would be lucky to get a smudge that didn't belong to one of us."

We were all silent for a moment.

"If there was an alert on our client's DHS records after twenty years," Malone said thoughtfully, "and it triggered a threat in less than twenty-four hours...then this is very important to somebody who's got a lot of clout."

"The government?" I speculated. "National security?"

Sylvia Ralston was looking pretty pale and tightly wound

again by this point. "Jesus. I was just a little kid. What the hell is going on? What the hell *was* going on?"

"That's what you've hired us to find out," my partner responded, looking a little dubious about my latest idea. I didn't blame her.

"Whoever they are, they aren't all-knowing," I went on. "The note referred to a private eye, singular. If it was DHS, I wouldn't be surprised if the enthusiastic young lady I talked to attached my name to her request—as an explanation or just because it turned her on that she talked to a private cop." I thought for another moment. "Maybe the note writer was guessing that the only reason a private investigator would request those records is that he was hired to do it and no one would hire him to do it except Ms. Ralston here. The response, the threat, was so incredibly fast. And more than a little iffy. That says panic to me. Feds dealing with national security aren't going to panic because some woman in Portland, Oregon, has hired a private investigator. They certainly aren't going to threaten her life the next day in a typewritten note pinned to her door."

"Okay," Malone said, "I buy all that. Not the government. So who the hell could it be?"

"I have no clue, but I guess finding a clue is part of the job now."

"What am I going to do in the meantime?" Ralston asked tremulously. "I live alone in a little cottage on a quiet South Tabor Street. Not exactly high security."

"That's right out at the end of Hawthorne Boulevard," Malone noted. "We live in the Hawthorne District."

"Can I stay with you?"

I caught my partner's cringe. "No," I said firmly, "I don't think that will work, but...let me make a call."

Daisy Mansfield picked up on the second ring, the background noise telling me she was in traffic somewhere. Daisy was another one of my friends who shared rent on our dojang downtown. Like all the black belts with whom I shared the space, she loved to play detective on my behalf when I let her.

"Clint!" she greeted me. "Hang on. Let me find a place to pull over. This damned thing is hard enough to drive in downtown traffic without talking on the phone at the same time. Plus, it's illegal, right?"

I held up a finger to Malone and Ralston, just to let them know there was a pause.

It was more like a full minute of soft muttering and cursing before my friend apparently got her Jaguar settled.

"Okay, guy, what can I do for you? Are you in the dojang wanting an opponent?"

"No, I'm in the office with a client who needs a place to stay temporarily and some protection."

"Whoo hoo! I'm only a few blocks away right now. See you soon!"

"Who was that?" our client asked as soon as I hung up.

"A good and trusted friend of ours, a young woman named Daisy Mansfield who has quite a substantial home in Lake Oswego and helps us out with our cases sometimes."

"Is she...like, a bodyguard or something?"

"Not by profession. She's only twenty-one but is independently wealthy and also a third-degree black belt. Like I say, she's worked with us before. She's got plenty of spare bedrooms, to say the least, and no one could possibly know you're staying with her."

Plus, her location only about a dozen blocks from Agatha Pepper would be convenient for us as we tried to coordinate cases.

Our young friend showed up about ten minutes later, a little out of breath. Blond, beautiful, and super-fit, she was wearing a lightweight slacks and top combo that matched her blue eyes. "Hey, guys," she greeted us as she swept in the door, "Since I already had a parking space, I decided to walk." She crossed immediately to our client, with a big grin on her face. "Hi, I'm Daisy Mansfield and I guess I'll be your protector for the next little while."

After a moment of hesitation, Ralston shook her hand, introducing herself and then sitting back self-consciously.

Daisy frowned. "You look familiar."

"Well, you might have seen me on the back of a book cover, I suppose. Do you read cozy mysteries?"

The frown was, after a few seconds, replaced by amazement. "My God! The Enchanted Bookstore. That's one of my favorite series! You...you're her!"

Ralston blushed and offered a little smile. "Yes, I'm also Lynn Hanna."

Another damned fan. I exchanged a look with Malone. I didn't know about her, but I was beginning to feel culturally deprived.

CHAPTER TEN

"Well," my partner said after the two women had left, "those two certainly hit it off."

Daisy was driving Ralston to her cottage and then to Daisy's place in Lake Oswego. Our client was fine with it because, she said, she could write anywhere. As for us, we had told Daisy only that Ralston had been threatened and shouldn't be at home alone right now, leaving it up to Sylvia to share more if she chose.

I was about to make some comment about needing to visit the library one of these days when the main agency line rang and the display indicated it was Agatha Pepper. I hit the button for the speakerphone. "Good morning, Agatha." Malone grimaced and said the same.

"What's good about it?" our client practically screeched. "Rodney and I have been walking the streets looking for Morty everywhere. We've hardly eaten or slept. Well, I haven't. My worthless nephew has done both. But...you know what we haven't seen?"

"No," I responded a little contritely.

"You two! What are you doing? Why aren't you out here looking for my dog?"

"We have a lead," I said, thinking fast. "Witnesses at the deli did see a young girl acting a little suspiciously at the time Morty disappeared. We're looking for her." Well, walking past twice could be suspicious and we were planning to look for her.

"A girl? A child? Who was she?"

"We don't know yet. The deli waitress thought her name was Beck, or Becky. Short. Black, spiky hair. Tall and gangly. Wearing dark clothes. Maybe early teens.... Ring any bells?"

"I don't know anyone like that. Why would a little girl take Morty? What are you doing to find her?"

"We don't know it was her who took Morty, but she might

have seen something." Still thinking fast. "We know it's terribly important and we're going to put a whole team on it."

"A team?"

I noticed my partner looking just as bewildered as our client sounded.

"Yes, we have a number of people that we use for surveillance and searches like this. They'll be able to give it much more time and attention than Malone and I can right now."

"Why can't you and Devon do it?"

"Well, we have another client, a young woman with amnesia who is being threatened. I'm afraid that has to take priority. But our backup people will find the kid who might be able to help with Morty. I guarantee it." I hoped.

Silence from the other end for a moment, then a sigh. "I guess a young woman in danger has to take precedence over a missing dog.... But get your darned team on it, will you?"

"We will. Right away."

She hung up.

Malone, who hadn't said a word since "good morning," was looking at me like I had two heads. "What team?"

"We can use the black belts," I said. "We're already using Daisy. We might as well tap the rest of them. There's no big risk in canvassing for a teenage goth girl."

"I guess not. It would have been ideal for Johnny and Hap, if they weren't RVing across the country."

"And I think they're serious about their total retirement this time—or, at least, their wives are."

"Okay, okay. That doesn't give us a very big team, does it? We've already given Eleanor and Daisy their assignments. Mike isn't going to take time off from solving homicides to look for a kid who might be a dognapper. That leaves...."

"Carmen Gonzales, Roger Arbuckle, and Bobby Brewster." All third-degree black belts, Carmen was a 38-year-old veterinarian, Roger a 53-year-old retired Army colonel, and Bobby, who was in his 30s, a corporate lawyer and Mike

Whitehall's domestic partner. One way or the other, they all seemed able to find time to play detective.

"That's not bad."

"I'll make sure they're all in the dojang this evening and have a little meeting, sort out some kind of schedule depending on their availability."

"And you can get in some sparring at the same time. You don't want married life to soften you up."

I faked a fair indignation. "Ha. You want to come along and spar with us for an hour or two?"

She grinned. "I have my own exercise routine. Don't worry about me softening up."

I grinned right back. "My dear, that is the last thing I would ever worry about." I picked up the phone to call Carmen Gonzales.

CHAPTER ELEVEN

Tuesday afternoon was devoted to following up on the research we'd already set in motion.

Along the way, I had the additional inspiration of recruiting my friendly nemesis, TV reporter Alison Roberts, to check news archives for anything that might be of interest—in return for the promise of a scoop, of course.

Alison at twenty-seven already had her own show, a late evening mix of soft features and breaking stories called "Inside the News"—on Channel 11, the city's one independent (i.e., least viewed) channel. Not a small portion of her success was due to her coverage of the McCall-Malone Detective Agency, its adventures and shoot-outs and screw-ups. Also, it didn't hurt that she's five-nine with shoulder-length black hair and a thin, wiry build, just the type that TV cameras find attractive.

So then we were waiting on Eleanor, Mike, the young woman at DHS, *and* Alison. Mike was the first to come through, about mid-afternoon. "I just sent you the file," he said. "And you owe me. I had to send a second request and then go downstairs in person before I could pull the damned thing up. It was mislabeled or something—and apparently the records division is currently understaffed. Anyway, it should be in your agency email now."

I thanked him, hit a couple of keys, and opened his email. "Mike sent the police report," I told my partner and she started clicking away as well. Within moments, we were both reading it on our screens.

It was pretty straightforward. On a Friday in late June, twenty years ago, a good citizen called 911 to report a bleeding and unconscious female child in an alley off of Fifth near Taylor. Officers Timmons and Burkowitz responded, along with EMTs. The child, shoeless and dressed in ill-fitting shorts and top, was treated at the scene, then transported to the emergency room.

Timmons and Burkowitz canvassed the area but could find no pertinent evidence or witnesses.

It was determined that the child had suffered a severe concussion in addition to several broken bones and evidence of repeated sexual assault. The case was assigned to Detective Sarah Stevens of the sex crimes unit. The child was in a coma for several days and awoke with no memory of who she was, where she came from, what had happened to her. Further investigation yielded no clues and no missing person report matching the child's description was ever filed. The final notation was that the case remains open but not active.

"Well," Malone said after we'd both finished reading, "that was not a goldmine of new information. I guess we should try to track down Detective Stevens if we can. I don't think she was on the force when I was. Retired, maybe."

She was still researching Detective Stevens when Eleanor Ivory rapped on the door and stuck her head in. "You got a minute?"

"Sure." I waved her in and Malone stopped clacking on her keys. "Whatcha got?" I asked as Eleanor settled in a visitor's chair.

"Well, I'm not sure. First off, I've got nothing on Sylvia Ralston that hints at where she came from or who she was originally. Everything says that her amnesia is total and probably permanent. She might as well have come into existence twenty years ago."

"Okay," Malone responded, "so what do you have?"

Eleanor paused as if marshaling her thoughts. "Her adoptive parents. Mr. and Mrs. Ralston. I got into some of their financial records and they're a little hokey."

"Hokey?"

"For a number of years there was money coming in from a Swiss bank account. A lot of money. Going as far back as I can track and ending about ten years ago."

"And, of course," I said, "you can't identify the account holder."

"Nope. That's the whole point of having a Swiss bank account."

"How much money are we talking about?" Malone asked.

"Ultimately, about a hundred grand a year."

"Wow," I said. "That is a lot of unidentified money. Ms. Ralston said her parents were wealthy, that her father was a very successful game developer.... Could this be income from the games? Was it monthly income?"

"No, the payments were annual. I doubt it was from the games. He had local business accounts that show those costs and income. The accounts are complete and legit, as far as I can tell. And he was doing fine there—a little more than a million in his best year."

"So up until a decade ago they were getting a hundred grand every year that they didn't really need from an anonymous Swiss account."

"A hundred grand at most. It looks to me like it was increasing some every year."

"But then it stopped ten years ago."

"As far as I can tell. That, or started going into a different account I haven't identified yet."

"Well," my partner said, "that is a conundrum."

"No kidding," I agreed. "Anything else?" I asked Eleanor.

She shook her head. "No, sorry. But I'll keep looking in between my own clients. Fortunately this is a down time in the tax biz." She'd gotten to her feet as she was speaking and, with a wave, left the office.

I looked across the desk at my wife and partner. "And what do we make of that?"

She gazed out the window a few moments. "I don't have a clue." Another long gaze, then the focus on me. "But I do have a thought: ten years ago could have been around the time that Sylvia Ralston turned eighteen." She held up a hand when I opened my mouth. "Just a thought."

"An interesting one, certainly," I conceded. "At least this new information gives us a couple more questions. Not only who was paying them, but what were they paying for?"

CHAPTER TWELVE

I was still mulling over those questions when I stepped out onto the highly polished dojang floor that evening.

After Eleanor's revelation, the remainder of the afternoon had been quiet. Too quiet. Nothing from Mike, Alison, or DHS. We speculated about those payments to the Ralstons. Something to do with coding? Specifically with the games he developed? Maybe it was blackmail? We checked in with Ms. Pepper. No dog, no ransom demand. We set a meeting with Sylvia Ralston for tomorrow morning at Daisy's home at nine. That was about it.

So I had some frustration just waiting to be taken out on the friends who greeted my arrival. Bobby, Carmen, Roger, and I were all wearing the white outfits that in Korean are called "dobaks." (And it's a "dojang" rather than a "dojo" because Taekwondo is a Korean martial art.)

We all greeted one another formally with bows and I took my place, as senior black belt, in the front of the room to lead the zazen (sitting meditation) and warm-up. Even though we were there for a meeting, we never missed a chance to work out. The talking would come after the sparring.

So, once our spirits were settled and we were warmed up, I took on Roger while Carmen sparred with Bobby. Every two or three minutes, I signaled that we should rotate to another partner. By the end of an hour, everyone had sparred everyone else a number of times and we were all drenched in sweat. There had been no serious injuries. It felt great.

After a quick warm-down and showers, we gathered again in our street clothes, sitting cross-legged on the floor.

I have to confess that, after the build-up, my fellow black belts were a bit disappointed to learn that they'd be canvassing a Lake Oswego neighborhood looking for a goth teenager who might be a dognapper or witness to a dognapping. Bobby and

Carmen, after a minute or two, were amused at the prospect. Roger, on the other hand, had to be convinced that this was an appropriate activity for a middle-aged retired Army colonel with a third-degree black belt. It occurred to me that I wouldn't want to be the goth girl if he was the one who found her.

I was still soothing his mild irritation as we left the dojang together, maybe five minutes behind Carmen and Bobby. We descended the stairs from the second floor of the old warehouse and after we stepped out onto the sidewalk I locked the door behind us.

It was a little after nine p.m. and the immediate area around the corner of Second and Pine was quiet. No traffic. No pedestrians. At least I didn't see any pedestrians. Roger was a different story.

He nudged me as we were about to separate and head for our cars. "Across the street," he said softly. "Your two o'clock."

I looked, but all I saw were patterns of light and shadow against the commercial building on that side. "What?"

"There was a guy, a person, who stepped back into the shadow just as I saw him. He's not moving. You think it's worth checking out?"

Normally, of course, it would be no big deal that a random person was standing across the street from the dojang, regardless of the time of day. But I had been in the private detection business for a long time and had accumulated a lot of enemies. Roger knew that, so his question was a good one—and I agreed.

"Yeah, let's check it out."

We were only halfway across the street when the person broke from cover and took off up Second. I could see that it was a male and that he was fast, probably young. Roger and I were both in our mid-fifties. Very fit, but neither young nor anywhere near that fast. We stopped and watched him disappear in the distance.

"Trouble?" inquired my friend as we turned back toward our cars.

"Could be," I said, "or it could just be a kid who didn't want trouble. Good catch spotting him over there, though."

We parted ways then, but I kept an eye on my rearview mirror as I drove home. Didn't see anyone suspicious. The lurker downtown was, as we'd speculated, probably just an innocent bystander who didn't want to be hassled.

Still, I was uneasy.

CHAPTER THIRTEEN

When we arrived at the office the next morning, we already had a plan. Well, a small set of contingencies. If we didn't get anything of real interest from Eleanor, Alison, Mike, or DHS by nine, we'd focus on finishing the security job for Morton Jewelers. We were going to lose the client pretty soon if we didn't pay them more attention.

Initially, it was looking good for the jewelry store. No emails or voicemails, notes tacked to our door, nothing. Not even anything from Ms. Pepper yet—probably because I'd called her last evening to tell her that our "team" would be on the job this morning. She thanked me, but sounded like she was in terrible spirits. Morty had been missing for forty-eight hours now.

Then, at quarter to nine, we got a very odd call from Alison Roberts.

"Who is this Ralston person?" she asked abruptly.

"I explained that already. A young woman who has had traumatic amnesia for the last twenty years and has hired us to establish her original identity and determine what happened to her."

"No, I mean who is she now? Is she someone important? Someone with a shitload of clout? Or maybe the ability to hurt someone with that kind of clout?"

I'd switched Alison over to the speakerphone as soon as I recognized her voice and Malone was looking just as mystified as I felt. "The woman writes cozy mysteries under a pseudonym. I don't think that's going to hurt anyone with any kind of clout."

"What's a...oh, never mind. There's something weird about the woman."

Malone finally spoke up. "Other than the fact that she doesn't know who she is?"

"Oh, hello, Devon. You guys have never met my boss, have you? The station owner and manager, Warren Macintosh?"

"No," I said and Malone nodded in agreement. "We've never met him. Why?"

"Because he just called me into his office to tell me that there are far more important stories than this one and I should devote my time where it counts. There was a strong implication of 'or else.'"

"Okay," Malone responded. "So you've got a boss who's uptight about your journalistic priorities."

"You don't understand. The last time I was in his office was when I was hired. His background is financial management. He's never had any particular interest in my little news and feature show. He's one of those people who has people for that. There's something about your Sylvia Ralston that pushed his button. The man was sweaty."

"Sweaty?" That was Malone again, looking like she couldn't decide whether to be amused or concerned.

"He had little beads of sweat along his hairline, such as it is...in an air-conditioned building, in October."

"Maybe he has a condition."

"For Christ's sake, Devon, I've seen the man around often enough to know he doesn't normally have flop sweat. I think you guys need to take a closer look at your client. And I mean who she is now, not who she was then."

"All right," I chimed in, "point taken. So. You're not going to be able to help us?"

"Are you kidding? Macintosh just lit up this story with a damned floodlight—and just because I started a standard search. How he even knew that, I have no idea. But now I'm all over it—on the down-low, of course. Let's keep each other posted."

"We'll be interested to see what you come up with," I said. "And thanks for the call."

"You're very welcome." She hung up.

My partner and I just sat there staring at one another for a moment. "What the hell was that?" Malone finally asked.

"I don't have the slightest idea. Let me give Eleanor a call."

"Oh, I'm sure that will explain everything."

"Hush." I hit the speed dial. "Eleanor? Clint."

"Yo."

"Have you had time to do any more research on Ralston?"

"I'm still at it, but I haven't found anything more yet."

"In all your research, have you seen anything in connection with her that might make a local mover and shaker uneasy?"

She had to think a moment. "That's an interesting question, but no, nothing like that."

"I guess I'm not surprised. Well, keep an eye out and let us know if you find anything."

"Will do."

I said goodbye and hung up.

"That was short and sweet," Malone said as I hung up. "She's got nothing, right?"

"Nothing new. Certainly nothing that would explain the reaction of Alison's station owner. We need to have another meeting with our client, do a little subtle probing. See what we see."

"You want to do that now? We've still got Morton Jewelers to worry about."

I sighed. "I know. But I'm getting a strong feeling that Sylvia Ralston is going to be a much bigger deal than she first appeared."

Malone nodded. "I've got the same feeling. Think about it. Something triggered the threat she received. Mike had unusual difficulty tracking down the police report. And now Alison is warned off after she does a simple search in the news archives. With Eleanor and that woman at DHS also pursuing it, bells may be going off all over the place."

"Shit. You're right. Now I'm even more worried." I gazed out the window a moment, trying to sort out my thoughts. "I wonder if...."

The main agency line interrupted me. I saw on the display that it was Mike again. "Maybe this is something," I punched on the speakerphone. "Hey, Mike."

"How about you guys meet me for an early lunch at the Home Run?"

My partner and I frowned at each other. Not that we wouldn't enjoy a lunch with our friend, but Mike had never before called in the middle of a work day to suggest lunch, much less without saying hello first. Much, much less when he was still pissed at me. Something was up.

"We can do that," I agreed. "Devon is always up for an early lunch. Any special reason?"

"Eleven?"

"That's fine, but...."

"Talk to you then." He hung up.

Malone and I sat there looking at each other.

"What the hell is going on?" she finally asked.

"Apparently we're going to be asking that a lot," I replied.

CHAPTER FOURTEEN

We had about an hour before our new lunch date, so I completed what I'd started to say before Mike called. "I wonder if Sonny would be available to cover the security job for us?"

Malone pursed her lips. "I don't know. She's pretty busy with wedding preparations—and she's licensed in Nevada, not in Oregon."

"If she was our contractor, it would be kosher."

"It would also be expensive. You remember what she said her rates in Las Vegas were? More than ours."

"How about I give her a call, see what she says? We can't do a good job for Morton the way things are going."

"Oh shit. Give her a call."

Sonny Sampson was a former Las Vegas private investigator who'd come to Portland in pursuit of the gangster who ultimately kidnapped my daughter and her boyfriend. In the course of helping us out with that crisis, she met and fell in love with my old friend Veronica Fortune, who owns a coffee shop around the corner from my house. After finishing some important business in Vegas, she'd moved to Portland and was now preparing to marry Veronica.

I had no idea if she'd have the time or inclination to take on a job right now, but it was worth a try. At least no one would be shooting at her.

She answered her phone immediately, asked me to wait a minute while she pulled over, and we exchanged greetings. "How busy are you?" I then asked.

She laughed. "Not too bad, really. We've decided to keep it simple—just close friends, in the Pen and Pastry, probably right after the New Year. Think you can make that?"

I laughed in return. "Yes, I'm sure we can be there. Look, we're in the middle of developing an enhanced security set-up and protocol for a downtown jewelry store. We pretty much have the evaluation done but haven't made any recommendations—and suddenly we've got a case that's looking much more complicated than we thought it would be. Does your expertise cover developing security plans and would you be willing to help out?"

There was a moment of silence. "My regular rates?"

"Well, this is Portland, not Las Vegas—a lot fewer high rollers. Plus, you'd be an unlicensed contractor. We're about halfway through the job. How about half our total fee?"

Another moment after I told her how much that would be. Then: "Tell you what, send me a copy of your evaluation. Then this afternoon I'll go check out the store for myself, tell them I'm one of your people, and see what I think. And what they think, for that matter."

"Sounds good. Let me know." She agreed and I ended the call.

"Okay," I said to my partner as I turned to my keyboard. "That's taken care of. Maybe. She'll visit the store this afternoon after she looks over our evaluation—which I am sending to her at this moment. At least they'll hear something from us today and maybe the job will be off our backs."

"I hope so," Malone responded. "And I hope Mike doesn't ruin my lunch."

One thing you can say for my wife and partner: she's got her priorities.

CHAPTER FIFTEEN

The ambience of the Home Run Sports Bar is casual. The color scheme is warm golden yellow rather than fast-food orange. There are booths along three walls and a bar along the fourth, with tables spread across the open floor space and at least one big flat-screen high-def TV visible from every seat.

Homicide Lieutenant Mike Whitehall entered looking very much like a man who was going to ruin our lunch. He spotted us in our booth right away and grimly weaved his way through the tables in our direction.

He slid in beside Malone and nodded to each of us. Mike is extremely fit as you'd expect a fourth-degree black belt to be, six three of solid muscle with short-cropped brown hair. He's also way smarter than the average cop and openly gay. He's almost always relaxed and on top of the situation no matter what it is.

Today appeared to be an exception.

"Let's order first," he said. "I need some sustenance."

Malone grinned at him, clearly trying to lighten the moment. "You sound like me."

He just nodded again, so I motioned for a waitress and we placed our three identical orders: hamburger special with fries and a beer.

"So," I said to Mike after the waitress had departed, "are you going to wait until after we eat or spill it now?"

He took a breath and almost shrugged. "I'm still trying to make sense of it," he began. "I got called into Captain Melman's office and told to back off on the Ralston cold case. No point, current cases to pursue, yada yada. I asked him how he even knew I'd been digging into those files and all he would say is that it came from higher up. Much higher up, apparently." He looked from me to Malone and back. "What are you guys into?"

"We have no fucking idea," Malone answered him. "Sorry it

got Melman on your case, though. I never worked with him when I was on the force, but I heard he's an asshole."

Mike shrugged at that.

"You know your department," I said to him. "Any guesses where it came from? Have you run into anything like this before?"

The waitress arrived with our food before he could answer, but it took her only a few moments to transfer our plates and beers to the table.

After taking his first bite, Mike focused on me. "To answer your second question first, I have been warned off lines of inquiry a few times in my career. Lots of people have leverage; it happens." He took another bite, chewed and swallowed. "But the timing on this one.... It was a matter of minutes after I found the file—which I almost didn't find in the first place— and emailed it to you. That is a brand-new level of hinky in my experience."

Another bite, another swallow, a swig of beer. "And, given all that, I couldn't even guess the answer to your first question. The Chief? The Mayor? The goddamned President of the United States? I don't know."

We all contemplated that in silence for a few minutes as we plowed through our lunches. Malone, as usual, was finished first and addressed Mike as she sat down her empty beer mug. "Did you know Sarah Stevens?"

"Who?"

"Sarah Stevens. She was the lead detective trying to identify our client when she was found in the alley. Her name was in the report you sent us."

"Ah. I just glanced at it before I sent it to you. Which reminds me that I want to take a closer look at it when I get back. It's on my own damned PC, so that shouldn't send up any signals. But...Stevens...Stevens. Yeah, she was Captain Stevens when I joined the force and she retired soon after. I can't say that I got a chance to know her at all. She had a good rep."

"And you have no idea where she is now."

"Nope."

"And you can't even try to track her down."

"It probably wouldn't be a good idea."

"We can put Eleanor on it," I said. Noticing my partner's glare, I added, "We have better things to do than internet research."

Mike agreed that that was a good idea and left to return to the Justice Center. Malone and I stayed put for a few minutes, an extra beer for each of us and an extra side of fries for Malone.

"So," she observed as she munched away, "Sylvia Ralston receives a threat almost immediately after you call DHS. Alison Roberts is called on the carpet right after she checks the news archives. Now Mike has been told to back off just after he retrieves the old police report for us." She picked up her latest last fry and contemplated it. "I think the first priority is to meet with our client again. If she can't tell us anything, we need to tell her how this is shaping up. And we can check in with Agatha while we're in Lake Oswego." She sighed. "Two unhappy clients. I'd rather have a third beer."

CHAPTER SIXTEEN

"Somebody's put alerts on all my files? What does that even mean?"

Sylvia Ralston sat back in her padded rocker so abruptly that I was afraid it might overturn. She and Daisy had greeted our arrival in good spirits and, after the usual offer of coffee or tea, which we declined, our hostess left the three of us in the spacious living room to chat privately. Our client had just finished enthusiastically describing the sunroom she'd been using for her writing and I hated to bring her down this way.

"Well," I answered her, "it means that someone is electronically notified when the file is accessed. What does it mean that all these alerts are on files concerning the young girl found in an alley twenty years ago? We have no idea yet. Do you?"

"I...I don't.... Can you trace the alerts?"

"Good question. Maybe so, but in each case the person who accessed the file has been told by a superior to back off and do nothing further on it. They'd get no cooperation in trying to do a trace."

Our client had paled to a dead white and sunk farther into her rocker. "This is unbelievable. What could it mean?"

"Most likely," Malone responded as she shifted in her well-cushioned straight-back chair, "it means that it's very important to someone, somewhere, that your original identity and/or what happened to you not be brought to light."

"Where have these alerts been found?"

"So far," I said, "the Portland Police Department and the news archives of an independent TV station for sure—and probably the foster care records at the Department of Human Services. We haven't confirmed that last one yet, but we called them first, not long before you received that threatening note."

"I got threatened by the Department of Human Services?"

"No, I don't think so. But that may have been the first time whoever it is was alerted that someone was looking for your information. If they assumed it was you or an agent of yours, the note was your message to back off. It fits with the other responses."

"I'm completely bewildered."

"Join the club," Malone muttered.

I changed tack. "In connection with something else we've learned," I began, "were you aware of any sources of income your parents had besides your father's game development?"

Ralston frowned and shook her head. "No. My mother didn't work and that was what he did for money. Why do you ask?"

"Because your parents were receiving an annual substantial payment from an anonymous Swiss bank account."

She shrugged. "Maybe he licensed the rights to some of his games to somebody in Switzerland. How much were the payments?"

"Steadily increasing and topping out around a hundred thousand dollars."

"Wow. But what could that have to do with who I was originally or what happened to me?"

"Maybe nothing, but apparently the payments began when the Ralstons adopted you and stopped after you turned eighteen."

"Really? I.... That doesn't make sense. Dad didn't really hit it big with his games until I was fifteen or sixteen. Why would somebody...?"

"Exactly. And, on the other hand, what could the payments have to do with you?"

"I don't know."

"Is it possible," Malone chimed in, "that someone was supplementing your parents' income *because* they adopted you?"

Our client stared wide-eyed at my partner. "Someone *paid* them to take care of me? No!"

Malone waved that away. "I'm not saying that, but we don't know yet who your biological parents were or why you ended up as you did. Maybe your bio parents were even richer than the Ralstons and there was some reason they couldn't care for you, or needed to hide you."

"After they left me sexually abused and injured in an alley?"

"No, I'm not saying that, either. There are lots of possible scenarios. You were kidnapped and they only tracked you down after the Ralstons were in the process of adopting you. They couldn't take you back because you would have been in danger if you were with them...."

"This is sounding more like a movie than real life."

"It could be anything," I said, "but obviously something bad happened and the payments need an explanation. We'll keep working on it. Meanwhile, did you come up with the records we asked you to find? Anything in your possession about your time in the hospital or foster care?"

Her shoulders slumped. "I looked. I looked through my parents' old papers and my own. I couldn't find anything from that time."

"Nothing?"

"Not a single piece of paper. I told you my parents didn't want me looking into it. I guess they didn't want me coming upon anything by accident, either."

I looked at Malone. "We've got to give DHS another call."

She nodded agreement and then we all sat there in silence for a moment, everybody with more than enough to process. "Anything else?" Sylvia Ralston finally asked.

There was nothing we could think of, so we said our goodbyes and headed for Agatha Pepper's house.

CHAPTER SEVENTEEN

Rodney Pepper opened the front door, apparently no longer relegated to the cottage out back. He was excited for a moment when he saw us, his eyes darting around our feet, but then he realized there was no Morty with us.

He scanned our faces, looking a little sick. "Morty isn't...."

"We have no news, good or bad," I interrupted. "We just wanted to check in with Agatha. Is she here?"

He stepped aside. "Of course. Come in."

He led us through to a comfortable little sitting room that we hadn't seen before. It had a working fireplace and Ms. Pepper was sitting next to it, staring into the glowing coals. She turned and, like her nephew, had a brief moment of anticipation when she saw us; then she settled back again, looking a little fearful. "What is the news?"

"None, I'm afraid," I said as we settled on a nearby wingback settee. Our seat was bright green. Her armchair was bright yellow. She was wearing her usual colorful motley. Thank goodness the walls and rug were muted. "Our team is out there looking for a possible witness. We were in the neighborhood, anyway, and wanted to check on you."

She looked up in bird-like inquiry. "In the neighborhood? For something besides Morty?"

"Yes," Malone answered her. "We have another client staying in a house near here. Do you know Daisy Mansfield?"

"Is that your client?"

"No, it's her house where the client is staying. It's just a few blocks from here."

Agatha brightened a bit. "Oh, I see her at neighborhood get-togethers sometimes. A nice young woman." The brightness faded and she stared glumly into the fireplace.

"We'll find Morty," I said, wishing I believed it as much as I wanted her to.

"I hope so." She didn't look away from the coals as she spoke. "I don't know what I would do without Morty. He's been my only companion for so many years. He's been my rock."

Rodney, who had maintained a silent vigil next to our settee, cleared his throat. "I'm here now, Aunt Agatha."

Her head turned slowly until she was focused on him, her expression unreadable. "You're more of a slippery slope," she finally said, and turned back to the fireplace.

"Let me make a call," I said, pulling out my phone. "Check on how our team is doing."

Assuming the three "team members" were spread out over the neighborhood, I chose to call Roger as the senior member. As it turned out, they were together.

"We've got a good lead," he told me, after I said hello and explained we were calling from Agatha Pepper's house. "Bobby and I are currently surveilling a teen activity center on the east side of town, a fair hike from that deli, but possible. Anyway, Carmen talked to a kid who said a goth girl named Beck hangs out at this place. Carmen's inside right now, looking to see if this Beck is there or if anyone knows where she lives."

I was already on my feet. "Give me the address. We're on our way." He did and I gave Malone a thumbs up. "Our people think they may have found the witness," I told Ms. Pepper.

She clapped her hands and jumped up, looking exactly like a bird hopping from its nest. "That's wonderful! Bring Morty home!"

"We'll do our best," I said over my shoulder as Malone and I headed quickly for the car. It felt good to have a clear direction on one of our cases, at least.

CHAPTER EIGHTEEN

Lake Oswego does not cover a large area, nor does it have heavy traffic, so it took only five or six minutes to drive to the address Roger had given me.

The Lake Owego Teen Center turned out to be a pleasant, one-story brick building occupying about a quarter block. We easily found a parking space and walked up to Roger and Bobby, who were standing across the street from the center watching the main entrance.

"Hey, guys," I said. "Carmen is still in there?"

"Yeah, I don't know what's taking her so long," Roger answered.

Malone nudged me and pointed. "That probably explains it."

Carmen Gonzalez was just exiting the building accompanied by a tall young woman dressed all in black with short, spiky, dark hair. It appeared that our witness had indeed been found. I hoped she would have something useful to tell us.

And did she ever. Carmen broke the big news before she even reached our group: "She has Morty."

Apparently her companion was just realizing that she was about to confront a rather large group. Her heavily made-up eyes—"kohl," I think they call the stuff—went wide and she stopped just short of the curb.

Carmen tugged on her arm. "Come on, Beck. I told you I had some friends out here."

The kid stepped slowly up onto the curb, her eyes jumping from Roger to Malone and back. I guess the big old military man and the leather-clad tough chick were more striking than the gay attorney and the middle-aged balding guy.

Malone stepped up. "You have the dog."

The girl almost stepped back into the street. "Yeah," she said sullenly, "I have the dog."

"Why?"

"That's...a little hard to explain."

"Well, let's start with: Where is the dog?"

"At my house."

"So your parents are in on this?"

Even more sullen now. "No. My dad's long gone and my mother is...doesn't know the dog is there."

"How could she not know the dog is there? How big is your house?"

"Not that big. You'd have to meet my mother."

Malone nodded and stepped back. "Sounds like a plan. We'd love to meet your mother."

The teenager, already a little pale compared to all the black she was wearing, went significantly whiter. "No!" She reached out and grabbed my partner's arm. "I'll go get the dog. Bring it to you. We don't need to involve my mother in this."

Malone calmly removed the kid's hand from her arm. "Sorry, kiddo. You're underage, you stole somebody's pet, and now you're caught. At the very least, your mother gets involved. The police may get involved as well."

"Oh, shit."

Malone made a come-along gesture. "Let's go."

Carmen squeezed the young woman's arm one last time and looked at me and my partner. "You don't need me for that, do you?"

"No, of course not," I replied and gave her a smile that took in Roger and Bobby. "You can all get on with your lives. Thanks for helping us out. Great job."

Roger nodded. "Keep us posted."

"Will do. We'll let you all know when Morty is home safe and sound. And thanks again."

The three friends dispersed, presumably heading for their cars, while we escorted our young dognapper to my vehicle.

"Your name is Beck?" Malone asked as we walked along.

"Rebecca. People call me Beck."

"Last name?"

A slight hesitation. "Canham."

We reached the Subaru and I opened the rear door. "Okay, Rebecca Canham. Get in and direct us to your house."

She stopped with one foot in the car. "Who are you people? Is this really about the dog? How do I know you aren't perverts?"

"We're private investigators," I said, "hired by the dog's owner to track him down." I just knew she was going to say something about pet detectives, but she didn't.

Instead: "Can I see some ID?"

A sensible request, all things considered, so we pulled out our IDs. She examined them carefully, handed them back, and—still somewhat reluctantly—settled herself in the back seat of the Subaru.

It took us a good five minutes, just sitting there at the curb, to get her address out of her. She really wanted to go get Morty and bring him to us, but that was not on. Her mother needed to be made aware.

The house was only about three minutes away, halfway between the activity center and the deli. It was very modest by Lake Oswego standards, a blue-tinted ranch-style with a slightly weedy yard and an elderly Ford pickup sitting in the driveway.

The three of us traversed the cracked brick walkway up to the front door and Beck Canham opened it without the use of a key. I entered behind her, wondering if the mother was confident or careless.

It turned out she was neither. More like semi-conscious. And not at all sober. We would not, at this time, be making her aware of much.

We'd followed Beck through the somewhat grungy and more than dusty house to a kitchen that featured out-of-date appliances, dishes piled in the sink, the odor of very old pizza, and a woman—maybe thirty-five, maybe forty—slumped at the small Formica table wearing a ratty gray bathrobe. She roused herself to glare at us over the empty shot glass held loosely in her left hand. The whiskey bottle sitting next to it was also empty.

"What the fuck?" she inquired blearily.

Beck moved to one side and gestured grandly at the woman. "Mr. McCall. Ms. Malone. Rowena Canham. My mother."

It was late afternoon, probably close to five, and this woman was still in her bathrobe, drunk out of her mind. Now I understood the kid's reluctance to bring us home. Also how the dog could be here without Mom knowing.

We didn't even bother to say hello. I looked at Beck. "Where's the dog?"

She stepped toward a door leading to a hallway off the kitchen. "Come on."

We followed the kid out of the room as Rowena Canham's head sank slowly toward the table. The second door on the left was closed but we could hear the snuffling and scratching before we got there. Somebody was hoping rescue was at hand. Or at least dinner.

The kid opened the door and there was Morty, quivering with excitement. He made it to Malone first and she crouched down to pet him as I glanced around. The room was unexpectedly clean and neat, quite unlike the rest of the house. The bed was made, the little desk appeared organized. There were books on the shelves, as well as a small collection of dolls. I noted a comfortable looking dog bed in the corner, with food and water dishes—neither empty.

Beck Canham had created her own little home within the house and she was caring properly for the dog. So what was the story here?

"Why did you take him?" I asked as my partner stood up and reached for the leash that was hanging over the back of the desk chair. "And how did you get all this set up without your mother knowing?"

A shrug. "The first is hard to explain." Then a little grimace. "The second is easy. Rowena is always drunk or stoned. She doesn't know whether I'm here most of the time."

"Okay. So you...what, took the dog for company?"

"No, that's not it." She looked down at Morty and then up

at me. "Can I come along when you return him? Maybe I can explain it to Ms. Pepper. At least I need to apologize."

By this time Malone had the leash attached. I exchanged a look with her and we both kind of shrugged. "Okay," I said to Beck Canham. I didn't much want to leave the kid with her totally sozzled mother anyway.

Rowena Canham was not even aware that we passed back through the kitchen. "Is there anything we can do for your mother?" Malone inquired as we let ourselves out the front door.

Beck sighed. "I don't know what."

With that, we headed down the sidewalk to the car, Morty trotting happily along by our side and me contemplating something odd that had just occurred to me.

Beck Canham did not say "the owner" when she asked to come along. She said "Ms. Pepper." She knew all along whose dog she had taken.

CHAPTER NINETEEN

I hadn't called ahead because I wanted the pleasure of seeing our friend Agatha's reaction. It was worth the wait.

Luckily, Ms. Pepper was the one who opened the door this time. She was dressed casually in an incandescent pink muumuu. I watched her eyes meet mine, then glance over to Malone and frown slightly at Beck, but all that was in the first second or so. Then she looked down at the snuffling near my feet.

With a squeal and a huge smile, she eased as quickly as she could down onto her knees and embraced Morty—who in turn tried to make up for two missed days of face licking.

"Aunt Agatha! What...." Rodney stopped in the middle of the immense foyer behind her and looked like he might collapse himself. "Oh, thank you, God," he said to the high ceiling.

He rushed forward to help Agatha to her feet, help that she definitely needed since she wasn't letting go of Morty.

"Come in! Come in!" she said, still grinning madly. "And thank you! Thank you so much!"

She looked back at Beck as she led us into the larger living room where we'd first met. "Is this young lady one of your people? Is she the one who found Morty?"

It took a moment for us all to settle, Beck between me and Malone on a couch with Agatha Pepper in a chair directly across from us, Morty on her lap, and Rodney standing beside her. I noticed that Beck seemed a little mesmerized by all the colors popping around the room. "No," I said then, "she's the one who took Morty."

Ms. Pepper's bright smile dropped immediately into a frown as she eyed the young woman. "You kidnapped my dog? Why did you do that?"

I felt Beck Canham take a deep breath. "Because I wanted to meet you."

I hadn't seen that coming. I looked at Beck, who was blushing furiously. Beyond her, I could see my partner looking as surprised as I was. Of course, I was even more dubious than I was surprised.

"If you just wanted to meet Ms. Pepper, why didn't you knock on the front door? Why did you steal her dog—and then keep it for two days while she worried herself half to death?"

"I'm sorry. I'm really sorry. It was a stupid idea. I was going to return Morty today anyway. I thought that if I was the one who found your lost dog, you might...."

"Might what?" Agatha inquired after a long pause.

"I don't know. Might...might like me."

Agatha sat forward, still frowning but more in bewilderment than condemnation. "I don't understand."

Another deep breath to the left. "I was hoping we could be friends, that maybe you could be...maybe like my grandmother. Sort of."

At that Agatha sat back and looked at the young woman appraisingly. "And what is your grandmother like?"

"I don't know. That's the point. I never knew any of my grandparents. I never knew my father. And I might as well not know my mother. My life is for shit, honestly."

Still appraising. "And?"

"Well, I guess I was hoping you could be my bright spot."

"Bright spot?"

"I read that somewhere, that everybody needs a bright spot in their life. I wanted it to be you."

"Why? Why me?"

"I read all the stories about you. Saw all the videos. I knew about Morty and your gun and your nephew and the TV series and...all of that. How could anybody not want you for a grandmother?"

The silence must have gone on for a full minute as Agatha, Rodney, Malone, and I all exchanged looks.

Finally Agatha summed it up. "Well, if that doesn't beat all."

"I'm sorry," Beck said yet again and slumped back into the couch.

It felt to me like time to end the awkwardness, so I stood. "I think we should give you some time to be with Morty and make sure he's all right but, first of all, do you want to press charges?"

She raised the hand that had been petting the dog in question and waved that away. "No, of course not."

"Okay." I glanced down at the still-slumped Beck. "Then I guess we'll take Beck home and let you all have your evening."

The hand gestured for me to pause. "Leave the young lady here," she said. "My driver can take her home later.

She and I need to have a chat."

Malone was also on her feet by this time and we gave each other the side-eye, but...what the hell, the client is always—or at least quite often—right. Again I looked down at Beck, who was now sitting up straight with an expression that was somewhere between wary and excited. "You okay with that?"

I think she may have bounced a little. "Sure. Sure, that's okay."

"Good," announced Agatha Pepper firmly as she made her way to her feet after setting Morty on the floor. "I'll escort you two to the door," she said to us. "You just make yourself comfortable," she said to Beck, "and I'll be right back."

I noticed as we left the room that Morty was crossing to Beck. It occurred to me only then that nephew Rodney had not said a single word since addressing the ceiling upon our arrival. He continued to stand vigil next to the chair.

"Thank you so much, again," our client said as we reached the front door. "And that team of yours, too, whoever they are. Who are they, by the way, and will I have a chance to thank them one of these days?"

"Perhaps so," I told her. "They're really just friends of ours who provide this kind of backup now and then. Civilians, not professional private investigators. Remember, I already mentioned that Daisy Mansfield was one of them."

She thought for a moment and then grinned. "I do! You

said she's providing a safe place for another client of yours so she couldn't join in the search."

"Right."

"Well, you all do have interesting lives. I love it."

"You're doing okay yourself," Malone said with a grin of her own.

"Indeed I am."

I looked at my watch as we got into the car. "It's after five. No point in going back to the office. You want to eat out somewhere to celebrate the successful conclusion of at least one case—however weird the conclusion may be?"

"Sounds like a plan." She belted herself in. "I'll tell you something else that sounds like a plan. I'm going to run a background on Rowena Canham because I'm curious how a raging alcoholic affords even a small house in Lake Oswego. Then I'm going to call a buddy of mine at Child Protective Services tomorrow and have a chat about the woman."

I started the car and pulled out. "Don't make things worse."

"I'm not sure they could be but, no, depending on what's going on there I'll see if I can get the woman some kind of help. She's got a pretty good kid, I think, apart from the whole stealing dogs thing."

"I'd love to be a fly on the wall for that 'chat' between her and Ms. Pepper."

"I'll bet we hear all about it eventually." She reached over and put her hand on my arm. "But meanwhile, we need to focus on Sylvia Ralston. I think that's going to turn out to be way more weird than this one."

CHAPTER TWENTY

Thursday morning we'd heard nothing further from my young friend at DHS and we could hardly confront Captain Melman about his motives for pulling Mike Whitehall off the cold case, but we *could* go talk to a TV station owner/manager to get his thoughts on Sylvia Ralston.

So far everybody was being warned off. If nothing else, I wanted to see for myself what that looked like.

We headed for the Channel 11 offices as soon as we'd confirmed there was nothing urgent on voicemail or email. The Subaru was temporarily blocked in by another car, so we took Malone's Jeep. I figured that even with my heavy-footed partner driving, it would take twenty minutes or more to get through Thursday morning traffic to our destination just off Columbia Street beyond the 405 freeway, so I took the opportunity to settle in for a short snooze.

Which was soon interrupted by a sharp jab at my left arm. "What?" I muttered as I came around.

"Don't look now, but we've got a tail."

I cocked an eye over at the side mirror. We were on a major street and there was plenty of traffic behind us. I saw nothing that stood out. "What makes you think so?"

"The fact that I just went three blocks out of my way, including several pointless jigs and jags, and it's still back there."

"Really?"

"You snored through the whole thing."

"I don't snore." Examining the side mirror again. "Which one?"

"See a gray SUV in our lane two cars back?"

"That's it, huh."

"Yep. And now that you're awake I think I'm going to see about switching roles. There's a short street with a couple of good alleys coming up on the right. Hold on."

"Oh boy." I made sure my seat belt was tight. Malone loved these opportunities. I was grateful to live through them.

The right turn began sedately enough, then halfway through Malone punched the accelerator and the Jeep slewed the rest of the way with, thankfully, no one coming in the other direction. We were halfway down the short street and making another squealing turn into an alley within five seconds. I had twisted in my seat, both to watch the corner behind and to avoid seeing what was ahead of us. I didn't glimpse our tail before the corner disappeared from sight, so he (or she) would turn the corner and see no sign of us. Meanwhile, Malone had hit the brake and was also twisted around, looking out the back window.

It was maybe ten seconds later that a gray SUV sped past the end of our alley.

Malone slammed the Jeep into reverse, accelerated back into the street as I prayed that the SUV had no one following it, and charged in pursuit of our pursuer.

Apparently the plan was not to be subtle.

He—the profile I'd glimpsed certainly looked male—clearly had no question about what was going on. He accelerated around the corner at the end of the street and down the next block toward another major thoroughfare. And a red light.

Somehow he managed to blow through it and across two lanes of fairly heavy traffic without getting hit. From the cacophony he left behind, I gathered that at least several cars that slammed on their brakes weren't so lucky.

My partner hit our brakes and drowned out the other noise with some very creative cursing.

We sat there for a minute, until she ran out of expletives, and then proceeded on to Channel 11 as if nothing had happened. We didn't exchange a word until she'd pulled into a parking space near the building. She was probably recovering her temper and I was certainly recovering my breath.

She started to open her door and shut it again, turning to me. "I think we're in the middle of something really big," she said. "Did you see that fucker? How close he came? He was just tailing us, for God's sake, but he was willing to risk his life rather than be caught."

"Yeah, I wish we had some clue about *what* we're in the middle of."

She opened her door again. "Well, let's go see if we can get one."

CHAPTER TWENTY-ONE

The double glass front doors of the two-story commercial building opened into a small lobby with a single receptionist, a small dark-skinned woman wearing a pale lavender suit and a gentle smile.

"Welcome to Channel 11," she said as we approached the desk.

"Hi, my name is Clint McCall and this is Devon Malone. We're private investigators and we'd like to talk to Warren Macintosh."

The smile faded a little. "Oh. Well. Do you have an appointment?"

"No, but we're hoping he'll have a few minutes he can give us. It's about a case we're working on."

"Ah. I see. Hm. You'll have to check with his secretary about that. His office is on the second floor, in the back." She pointed. "You can use those stairs there. Don't open any door that has a red light on; that would be an on-air studio."

"Understood. Thank you."

"I guess only employees get to use the elevator," Malone muttered as we started up.

"Considering how worn these steps are, maybe only the big boss gets to use the elevator."

"The whole place could use a paint job, couldn't it?"

"Eh, it is a small, independent station. Probably not rolling in cash."

The hallway at the top of the stairs did not undermine my speculation. There was a thin, frayed carpet that ran the length of it and otherwise it was utterly devoid of decoration—not even the photos of on-air talent that you'd usually see. Three doors on the right, two doors on the left (one with a red light) and a door at the far end. We headed for that one.

And discovered where all the money was going. This

reception area was anything but bare: plush carpet, well-upholstered chairs and couch, quality art on the walls, and a highly polished desk with a highly polished blonde sitting behind it.

She looked up from the monitor she'd been studying. "Can I help you?"

We again introduced ourselves and asked about taking a few minutes of Warren Macintosh's time.

"Gee, private detectives," she almost gushed. "Oh, sure, I think he's free." She picked up her handset and pushed a button. "Mr. Macintosh? There are two private investigators here to see you. Uh, their names are...Clint McCall and Devon Malone. Really? Uh, I mean, of course, sir. I understand."

She hung up looking a little embarrassed. "I was wrong. Mr. Macintosh is very busy right now and can't see you."

"When will he be free?" Malone asked. "We're happy to make an appointment."

The blonde's neck was blushing bright pink by this time. "I, uh, I'm afraid he said that he wouldn't see you."

"Period? Ever?"

"I'm afraid so."

"Okay, then," I said. "Thank you for your time."

"That was interesting," my partner observed as soon as we'd closed the door behind us.

"Not least because he asked our names before making us persona non grata. Let's see if we can find Alison around here. Get her take on what just happened."

It took a few minutes, but the friendly receptionist downstairs tracked down Alison Roberts for us and called her to meet us in the lobby.

She appeared a little flustered, wearing a tan pantsuit, white blouse, and tennis shoes. She was five-nine, with shoulder-length black hair, a thin, wiry build, nose a little narrower than most and mouth a little wider, but always camera-ready and usually steady as a rock.

"What are you guys doing here?" she kind of half-whispered as she came up to us and gestured that we should step farther away from the front desk.

"We wanted to have a chat with your boss to see what he might know about Sylvia Ralston," I replied.

She winced. "My boss. You mean the big boss? Mr. Macintosh? What did he say?"

Malone snorted at that. "That he was too busy and never wanted to see us, according to his secretary."

"Oh. Wow."

"He seemed to react to our names," I said. "Did you mention us in connection with your archive search? Say anything about us when he got on your case?"

She shook her head vigorously. "No. No. Nothing. Of course he might know your names because I've covered you on my show lots of times. But the last thing I'd tell him is that I was using company time and resources to help you guys."

"Interesting," Malone said again. "You'd think he'd be curious about what we wanted, especially with all the ratings points we've added to his late-night schedule."

"Unless he somehow knew what we wanted," I observed.

My partner looked at me, at Alison, back at me. "Now that would be *really* interesting."

CHAPTER TWENTY-TWO

I called my young friend at DHS as soon as we were back in the office, just after ten, no tail having been apparent on the way back. She was very apologetic and assured me that she had done her very best, but the files on the child who became Sylvia Ralston were missing. Probably misplaced, she said. That was not my best guess, but I didn't try to correct her. I just hung up and told Malone about our latest dead end.

"Crap," was her response as she kept tapping away at her keys and peering intently at her monitor.

"What are you doing?"

"Running a background check on Rowena Canham." She tapped and peered some more, then hit one final key and sat back with a grunt. "Our databases don't have much. Certainly nothing about how she could afford even a hovel in Lake Oswego. She's got a sheet, mostly vagrancy and prostitution, a couple of petty thefts. No mention of child neglect or endangerment, which surprises me."

She turned to the keyboard again. "I think I'll email my buddy at CPS and see if he has anything, then point him in that direction if he doesn't. Meanwhile..." She grimaced as she typed. "I guess I'll see if our hacker down the hall can find any financial resources for this woman."

I didn't say a word. Malone was never going to enjoy appealing to Eleanor Ivory for help because—I supposed—the woman pushed one of her buttons. That was the extent of my understanding.

As soon as she was on her way, I dialed Mike's number. He picked up on the second ring. "Lieutenant Whitehall."

"It's Clint. I just wanted to give you a heads up that you're not alone in being warned off the kid found in an alley twenty years ago. The DHS records of her foster care are missing and

Alison Roberts got called on the carpet for checking the news archives for coverage from back then."

There was a long moment of silence on the other end. "And that fits with some information that I've learned," he finally said.

"What do you mean? I thought you were going to leave it alone."

"That's what I'm supposed to do, yeah, but I did find a way to do some roundabout checking on Captain Stevens. I thought maybe if I could find her, you guys could get in touch with her and have a chat. She moved to Moab, Utah, after her early retirement."

Which reminded me that I was going to have Eleanor check on the original investigator and forgot. Oh well. "And?"

"And she then disappeared."

"She's not still in Utah?"

"I have no idea. As far as I can determine, she's dropped entirely off the map. No current address, no credit card activity, no current driver's license, no medical records.... On the other hand, no death certificate or missing person's report. She's gone underground, figuratively or maybe even literally."

"Wow. How did you discover all that without tipping Melman?"

"A friend in another department, in another state. He's not going to rat me out."

"Good job. Given all this, what do you think could possibly be going on?"

"I don't know. Somebody, two decades later, is still monitoring inquiries about a little girl found in an alley—and it's somebody who can reach into my department, a local TV station, the Department of Human Services, and who knows what else? That's a real somebody. But what is it they're worried about? That's the question."

"Well, the obvious answer is that they don't want to be pinned with the assault and abandonment of a child—and, if they're this concerned and this connected, they must have a lot to lose."

"I don't know. Going to all this trouble for twenty years to protect yourself? Why didn't they just take out this Ralston woman a long time ago? That would be a lot simpler and cheaper."

"That would be another crime that might lead to them. And she hasn't caused them any trouble until now."

"I guess you're right. So. You got any ideas how to find out who 'they' are?"

"We're working on it."

He laughed. "Ah yes. The investigation is ongoing. Well, let me know if you come up with anything we can take action on. Somebody to arrest would be good."

I hung up just as Malone was coming in the door. "That was quick," I said.

She settled into her chair. "I gave her the name. Told her what I wanted. We don't do girl talk. Who were you talking to?"

"Mike. He says Sarah Stevens retired, moved to Utah, and disappeared."

"Disappeared?"

"No current address, no credit card activity, no current driver's license, no missing person report, no death certificate. Just gone."

"Surprise, surprise. Another dead end."

"Yeah."

She looked at her watch. "Let's adjourn to the Home Run."

I looked at mine. "It's barely eleven o'clock."

She stood and gave me a gimlet eye. "I'm hungry. My brain needs a beer and a burger. Thinking calories."

I had to laugh. What the hell. We weren't doing anything else right now. "I never heard of thinking calories," I said as I locked the office door behind us.

"Thinking hard burns more calories even than exercise. Didn't you know that? And we definitely need to do some hard thinking."

CHAPTER TWENTY-THREE

Forty-five minutes of speculation and theorizing at the Home Run gave us exactly zilch. I think the whole thing was simply a ploy to get an early lunch. The only plan we had as we returned to the office was to follow up with Eleanor and CPS to see if they had any new information.

I hadn't even managed to unlock the office, however, before Alison Roberts appeared behind us at the top of the stairs and hurried in our direction. Her hair was in disarray, her jacket flying open, and she had a possible smudge on her blouse—definitely not her normal, put-together, ready-for-air self. A big change from just an hour or two ago.

"What's going on?" I asked as she stopped next to us. By then I had the door unlocked. "Come on in."

She followed us in without answering my question, or saying anything else, and then plopped herself on the couch rather than in one of the visitor chairs. We had both taken our seats by then and swiveled around to stare at her.

She took a deep breath. "I've been fucking fired."

"What?" I exclaimed. "When? Why?"

"What did you do?" Malone inquired more or less simultaneously.

Alison chose to answer my partner. "I think it's more what you did."

I jumped in before Malone jumped down her throat. "Why don't you start at the beginning and tell us what's happened. You've been fired?"

She sat a moment and I could see her pulling herself together. She took a calming breath. "Well, technically, my show is on hiatus and I'm on leave. But that's probably just until the station's lawyers do the proper paperwork to can my ass."

"They give you a reason?" asked Malone.

"Not really. They don't have to, to put me on hiatus. I imagine that's what the lawyers are doing: coming up with a reason that sounds valid." She glared from one of us to the other. "But we know why. Because you guys showed up after Macintosh told me to leave it alone."

"Did Macintosh personally give you the news?" I asked.

"No, he doesn't get his hands dirty like that. Gray Wallerby, who's the news director and my immediate boss, is the one, but he made it clear it was coming from the top. Gray is one of the good guys. He seemed almost as devastated as I was."

"I'm sorry."

She groaned. "Clint, you couldn't have known this was going to happen." And threw up her hands. "*Nobody* could have guessed that I'd be out of a job just because I went looking for some twenty-year-old coverage of a kid found in an alley." A beat. "But I'm still pissed at you."

"Understood."

"And I want an interview with Sylvia Ralston."

"No," Malone answered quickly. "We have her in a safe place and we're not giving anybody access."

"I get first dibs when she's available. Whatever she's got you—and me—involved in, my gut tells me it's big. If it's big enough, I could move to one of the major locals or even the network." She peered at me and then at Malone. "You owe me. First dibs."

I'd been thinking while she bartered with my partner. "What's your news director's name again?"

"Gray Wallerby."

"And you say he was upset about having to give you the notice?"

"Maybe more upset than I was. Of course, I was still in shock."

"Then maybe he'll talk to us even if Macintosh won't."

"And risk getting fired himself? I don't think so."

"There's no risk if Macintosh doesn't know he has talked to us. Do you know when he gets off work? Where he lives?"

"No." She stopped to think for a minute and looked at her watch. "But he'd be going to lunch soon and I know where he usually goes."

"Any chance Macintosh would be there?"

She laughed. "No. No chance. It's way below his pay grade."

I stood up. "Then let's go see if we can have a chat with Mr. Wallerby."

A couple of minutes later we hit the sidewalk, three abreast, me in the middle, heading for the parking lot. The air was clear and chilly, the traffic sparse for this time of day downtown.

For some reason, I glanced over my shoulder at the street behind Malone who was on my left. There was a black SUV coming up slowly in the lane nearest us, the passenger side window open and someone's elbow hanging out. Just then the arm began to straighten.

"Gun!" I yelled and tried to grab both women at once.

Malone was already dropping into a crouch and going for her weapon, so I missed her and ended up basically tackling Alison to the sidewalk as I heard several familiar-sounding pops, along with the whine of ricochets, followed immediately by the roar of acceleration.

I quickly disentangled myself from a whimpering Alison and pushed up into my own crouch next to Malone. "You okay?" I asked.

"I'm fine." She holstered her weapon and we both stood. "The asshole took a left before I could get the plate."

I took a quick glance around to confirm there wasn't a second shooter. One lane was blocked by a car that had stopped and people for a block around were slowly standing upright again, most of them with phones in hand. I could already hear a siren approaching.

Satisfied that there was no further threat, I turned to help our friend to her feet. She was holding her elbow that looked pretty badly scraped. "Sorry for taking you down so hard," I said. "Any injuries besides your arm?"

"No, I'm okay. Better than being shot. Thanks."

Traffic was moving again, though a number of people were still in place looking at us, half of them probably making videos to post on social media.

The sirens were almost on us. "We might as well stay put," I said to Alison. "The cops will be here in just a minute and will want statements."

"Damn!" she responded vehemently.

"What? You have someplace you need to be?"

"No, that's exactly the problem. I don't. Damn, damn, damn. This would have been the lead on my show today!"

CHAPTER TWENTY-FOUR

The next hour or so was more than somewhat chaotic. The first officers on the scene isolated the three of us and spread out to both check for any injuries to bystanders and to ensure that the shooter was long gone. Luckily, no bystanders had been hit.

I didn't know the detective who arrived about two minutes later. (We were only a few blocks from the Justice Center, after all; in fact the shooter had turned in that direction and probably driven right past it.) Malone knew him, though they greeted one another as acquaintances rather than friends.

He began taking our statements, noting the few details I could offer about the black SUV—not much beyond the facts that it was black, an SUV, and either brand new or very well cared for. I could tell him that the shooter was a white male and that another person, race and gender unknown, had been driving. Malone and I could both testify that the vehicle had turned left on Third. That was about it.

Alison had been on the sidewalk throughout the incident and gave her very short and uninformative statement while her bloody arm was being treated by paramedics. By that time the media had shown up, including someone from her own station that I didn't recognize. She finished giving her statement to the detective, then borrowed my key in order to flee upstairs and hide in our office. "If I can't make air on my own show, I'm not going to do it on theirs," she muttered in parting.

We stayed put to talk to the media. Not that we were much more excited about it than Alison was, but we knew the routine. If we didn't talk, speculation about our silence would be part of the story and we didn't need that kind of grief. We portrayed ourselves as simply being in the wrong place at the wrong time, victims of a random drive-by. Nothing to do with any of our cases. Some of the less experienced reporters might even have believed us.

"It could be true, you know," observed my partner as we finally headed up the stairs to our office. "Random drive-bys do happen."

I glanced over at her as we reached the second floor. "Do you think it *is* true?"

"No. Hell, no. We've got something by the tail. We just don't know what it is, yet."

We entered the office to find Alison slumped on the sofa with tears streaming down her face. Malone walked right past her and sat in her own chair. She might have sneered slightly as she passed. I didn't know what to do, but figured that simply walking by was not my best choice.

I stepped over to the sofa and leaned down to put a hand on Alison's shoulder. "Take your time," I said gently. "We know you're upset. That's okay."

She jerked upright, displacing my hand. "Okay?" she practically screeched. "I've been fired, publicly embarrassed in front of my colleagues, and someone tried to shoot me! There's nothing okay about any of that!"

"You don't have to worry about that third one," my partner said drily. "It was us they were trying to shoot."

Alison threw up her hands. "That's just great! I'm sure they would have felt bad if they hit me!"

"Eh. Probably not."

I gave the poor kid's shoulder another squeeze and headed for my own chair. "Like I say, take your time, take a deep breath. We're safe now. But," I added as I sat down, "we do need to figure out our next move."

We were all silent for a minute, during which Alison seemed to calm a bit. In fact, she was the one who broke the silence. "So...are we all in this together now?"

It took me a moment to catch her meaning. "If you're asking whether you get to tag along and cover our investigation for some future publication of yours, that would be a no. And I don't think you're in any danger. We're the ones turning over rocks and we're the ones who will take the risks."

I noted that my partner and beloved wife had raised her hand. "Yes?"

"I think she should tag along for a little while."

That surprised me. "Okay. Why?"

"Because the only open avenue is Channel 11. We can't talk to DHS or Captain Melman and I don't think Sylvia Ralston knows anything she isn't telling us. So we need to talk to this Wallerby guy—and we're more likely to get him to talk if Alison is with us." She focused on the woman in question. "Do you know where he lives? When he gets off work?"

"He usually leaves the station around six. I don't know where he lives, but the Internet can probably tell us. Or the phonebook."

"Okay. Let's all drop by his house around seven-thirty. See what he has to say if he's home."

Alison stood up. "I'll meet you there. I need to go home myself for a while. Get my head together. Take a shower. Feed my dog. Is that all right?"

"Certainly," I answered. "You're not obliged to help us at all."

"Oh, I want to. And I want the story." With that, she crossed the room and opened the door. "I'll give you a call at seven to make sure we agree on where we're meeting."

With that, she was gone.

CHAPTER TWENTY-FIVE

It was a little after three at that point. We had no inquiries from possible clients, no messages or calls to return. No new ideas about the Ralston case and no idea who was shooting at us. Or even if we were the intended targets.

So I called Sonny Sampson to see how Morton Jewelers was coming along. It sounded like she was in her car when she answered. We exchanged greetings, then there was a pause while she found a place to pull over.

"I was going to call you in the morning," she said. "I've just about got this wrapped up."

"You've already provided them with a plan?"

"Their operation is very similar to a jewelry store I did security for in Vegas. All I had to do was modify that plan a little, for a slightly smaller staff, and write it up. I just finished what I think will be the final meeting. They seemed happy with it. I was going to wait until they'd slept on it before I called to give you the good news, but here you are."

"That's great. Assuming they don't have a problem after they've slept on it, shoot us your bill tomorrow."

"Will do—and, speaking of shooting, I saw on the news that you guys had an incident. You both okay?"

"Yeah, they didn't hit either one of us or the woman who was with us."

"Any idea who or why?"

"No, and no."

"Well, give me a call if you need backup. Veronica's taken over the wedding planning and is having a good time with it, so all I have on my plate right now is getting licensed in Oregon. I won't try to set up an agency until after our honeymoon."

"Where are you planning to go?"

"We haven't decided yet. Not Las Vegas."

I laughed. "I can understand that. Well, take care. I'll call if we need you."

The agency main landline was ringing as I hung up. "McCall-Malone Detective..."

"Dad!"

It was Colleen.

"Are you and Devon okay?"

She had obviously just seen the news.

"We're fine."

"Who's shooting at you now?"

I was getting tired of that question. "Honestly, we have no idea. We're working on it. How are you guys doing?"

"Oh, we're fine. Hoke is still getting used to waking up and going to work every morning. I don't have to be at the theater until early afternoon most days, so I'm still sleeping in. But you guys.... You guys be careful, okay? Let's get together for a visit soon."

"Sounds like a plan, *after* we determine who's shooting at us and why."

I could hear my daughter's grin. "That would be fine. Hoke and I would definitely like to avoid future kidnappings and shoot-outs."

"Another good plan." I noted that Malone was on a call now, as well. "I'd better get going. You guys take care."

"You guys, too."

I hung up and looked inquiringly at my partner. "I'm on hold with CPS while they track down my friend," she answered my unasked question. "I thought I'd check if she had anything on Rowena Canham yet."

"Ah. In that case, I think I'll wander down the hall to see if Eleanor has found anything on her." At least it was something to do while we remained clueless about the Ralston case.

Luckily, Ms. Ivory was free. Even more luckily, she'd come up with some possibly interesting connections (after trying to pump me for more information about one of her favorite authors). I was headed back to the agency office in less than ten minutes.

I opened the door to find Malone leaning over the desk and staring out the window. I could tell from her body language that something was wrong. A quick glance at the window itself told me the glass was intact, so not another shooter. "What is it?" I asked as I closed the door behind me.

"A drone." She practically spat the word.

I joined her in looking out the window. "A drone?"

"Hanging right outside the window here, looking at me."

"Whoa. Are you sure...?"

"I'm sure. It wasn't just going by. It wasn't delivering a pizza to somebody. It was equipped with a camera and it was pointing in here. When I stood up and stared back at it, it took off."

I sat down. "Wow. It reminds me of the time the bad guy set up long-range listening equipment in the building across the street."

Malone sat as well, looking sour. "Maybe we should check for that, too. One way or the other, we're going to have to be careful and circumspect from here on."

"Circumspect?"

"Hey, I can use five-dollar words."

"I thought they were twenty-five-cent words."

"Inflation." She grinned for a second, but then turned serious again, staring out the window. "I'm thinking the question is, City, state, or federal?"

"What do you mean?"

"Obviously we've pissed off some powerful, connected people—or at least one of them. Records disappearing. Cops and reporters warned off and even fired. Which makes me think that Mike really better not pursue this anymore. Drive-by shooting. A fucking drone. All within a couple of days of the first inquiries we made. That's a fast and very heavy response to what we—and Sylvia Ralston—thought would be strictly innocent research questions."

"That's true. Okay. Careful and circumspect it is. But it should be safe enough to compare notes about Rowena Canham. I seriously doubt she has any drones or listening equipment in play and Eleanor did come up with a name."

Malone took a breath and turned from the window back to me. "Butch Faron, by any chance?"

"Yep. What did your CPS buddy have to say about him?"

"Just that Canham once provided his name as an emergency contact. That was all they could tell me. Did Eleanor get more than that?"

"She did. It turns out Butch Faron, despite being a known drug dealer and professional thief, is a big user of social media. He doesn't advertise his crimes, of course, but he does claim that Rowena Canham is his girlfriend and that he's paying her bills."

"He's a dealer and thief?"

"Eleanor and I gave Mike a quick call. Faron is apparently good at what he does: often brought in for questioning, less often formally charged, and never convicted."

"So he's probably doing well financially. That explains where Canham's money is coming from. I wonder what his relationship is with the kid?"

"She didn't mention him, so maybe there isn't one."

"Or at least not one she wants to mention."

"A good, even if worrisome, point. Maybe we should check that out."

"Maybe." She stood again and opened the desk drawer to retrieve her Glock. "We can think about that some more after we're home. I need to get out of here."

CHAPTER TWENTY-SIX

I eyed Malone across the table over our microwaved meatloaf and macaroni dinners. "You're the one who wanted to find out how Canham could afford to live in Lake Oswego," I said. "The case is already done. We found and returned Morty."

She took a healthy swig of red wine. "I know, I know. I was curious. And I can understand your concern about Beck in that environment, but she has survived for a lifetime so far and we might not if we don't figure out who's trying to kill us and why."

I sipped my own wine and gave it a moment. "Okay. We table it, but we don't put it away. Agreed?"

"Agreed."

My cell phone rang and I almost ignored it because we'd been getting calls from the media ever since the shooting hit the airwaves. We hadn't answered most of them and had no comment for those we did. But I checked the display and, in one of those instances that prove the universe doesn't object to coincidence as much as I do, it was Agatha Pepper. So of course I answered. She was calling about Beck Canham.

"Hang on, Agatha," I said. "I'm going to put you on speaker so Devon can also hear this." I did so. "Now, what about Beck? She hasn't bothered you or Morty again, has she?"

"No, no, not at all. She's a sweetie—or, I should say, an interesting young woman. You don't like to be called 'sweetie,' do you, Beck? I just wanted to call to tell you...."

"Wait a minute." Malone leaned forward. "Were you just talking to the girl? Is she there at your house again?"

"That's what I'm trying to tell you. I'm going to mentor her!"

My partner and I looked at each other. She clearly didn't know what to say, any more than I did. "Mentor?" I finally managed.

"Yes! Isn't that a wonderful idea?"

I almost told her to start at the beginning, but this was Agatha Pepper we were talking to. God knew where she thought the beginning might be. So... "Um. How did that come about?"

"Hang on a second."

I heard her asking Beck to go in the other room and shut the door. A moment later she was back on the phone. "Well, I was really taken with her when she was here, even though she was Morty's kidnapper. Thought she had real potential. So I had my driver take me to her house for a visit and, oh lord, such a horrible situation. Her mother, if you could call her that, was drunk out of her mind and the place was dirty and, well, you met her mother and saw the place, didn't you?"

"Yes."

"Okay, so you'll understand that I needed to get her out of there. Her mother didn't object. Hell, she wouldn't have objected if I'd put my gun to her head."

"You didn't...."

"No, of course I didn't. Like I say, her mother barely knew we were there or that we were leaving with her daughter."

Malone was still focused on the phone. "You're not planning to...keep her, are you? You can't just take the woman's daughter away from her, no matter how crappy a mother she is. Besides, I already brought Rowena to the attention of Child Protective Services, so they're going to want to know where Beck is."

"And I'll be happy to tell them. Look. I've got barrels of money and only Rodney to spend it on—and I can certainly do better than that. I won't keep Beck here, not all the time, and I'll do what I can to get her mother some kind of treatment or whatever, but I think I've got a real shot at helping this young woman find out who she really is and what she can really do. What better way to spend my final years? Better than a gun-shootin' granny TV show, if you ask me. Of course, we could still do that, too."

"Okay," I finally said. I noticed Malone was having a thought.

"Has Beck said anything about a guy named Butch Faron?" she asked.

"No. Is that her boyfriend? Just a minute; let me ask her. I think she's still in the next room. Hey Beck, get back in here! Do you have a boyfriend named Butch Faron?" There was a long moment of silence. "She just went dead white and left the room again. So...not a boyfriend."

"He's apparently her mother's boyfriend and not a good guy at all. I was hoping Beck had somehow avoided him."

"How not good?"

"Really bad, by all reports."

"Well, he'd better not come around here. I'll put a bullet in his butt. I'd better go make sure she's okay. I just wanted you guys to know she was in good hands."

She hung up. I looked at Malone. Malone looked at me.

"Wow," she said, "what are the chances *that's* going to go well?"

CHAPTER TWENTY-SEVEN

As planned, Alison Roberts called at seven to confirm Gray Wallerby's address. We met her there a half-hour later, keeping a careful eye out for tails and shooters on the way. His house, a nicely maintained ranch style, was the last one at the end of a two-block dead-end street on the far west side of Portland. Everyone on his block had garages and apparently used them, since there were plenty of parking spots available.

This being mid-October, it was already dark and I could see lights on in the house as Alison joined us at the bottom of his walkway.

"Is he married? Kids?" Malone asked her.

"No, I think he lives alone."

"Good. The simpler the better. Looks like he's home. Let's go. You lead."

We followed her up the walk and across the small porch to the door. She knocked and within moments it opened to reveal a heavyset, totally bald man still wearing dress pants and white shirt open at the neck, no tie. Apparently he hadn't been home very long. His eyes, shaded by heavy brows, opened wide as he registered Alison on his doorstep.

"What...?" Then he saw Malone and me. "...is this?"

"Gray. I think you recognize these two from my show. Clint McCall and Devon Malone. They need to talk to you. Please let us come in."

I could see the wheels turning madly as he considered the implications and possible consequences. Then, much to my surprise, he simply stepped back and gestured that we should indeed enter.

"I'm sorry about today, Alison, but I don't write the checks." He was leading us into a small but comfortable looking living room as he spoke. "It was Macintosh's call. What do you hope to achieve by involving your pet P.I.s?" He must have been interested in the answer, since he indicated we should take seats. He didn't offer any refreshments, on the other hand, and sat down opposite the three of us perched on his couch.

I just plunged right in. "Did Macintosh tell you why he wanted you to suspend Alison and her show?"

Wallerby's mouth quirked. "Insubordination."

"No other explanation?" Malone inquired.

"Nope, but I didn't buy it."

"Why not?" Still Malone.

Now he grinned outright. "Alison here would have been fired in the first week if that had been the real reason. She's not the retiring, obedient type, you may have noticed."

"In that case," I interjected, "can you think of any reason Macintosh would want to let her go all of a sudden?"

Wallerby shook his head. "Not a one. Her show is popular, good ratings, good sponsors." He looked at Alison. "You'll be missed."

"So you think I'm not coming back."

"From what I picked up in Macintosh's office, I'd say not." He held up a hand. "But let's just take a moment for you all to tell me the purpose of these questions. Why are you here? What do you really want? If you wanted to talk me into rehiring Alison, you already know that's not on the agenda. So what gives?"

"We're looking into a cold case," I said, "very cold, a young girl found in a downtown alley twenty years ago—physically injured, sexually assaulted, and still with no memory of what happened. We asked Alison to check the news archives for any coverage. When she began checking, Macintosh called her in and told her to leave it alone. That made us curious, so we showed up in person to ask him why he might do that. He refused to see us and two hours later you essentially fired Alison at his instructions. Does any of that ring any bells for you, make any sense?"

He sat back and frowned. "No, that doesn't make any sense at all. Why would he care about some twenty-year-old news coverage? It had to be something else. The timing must have been coincidence."

"I don't think so," I said, "because somebody, or more than one somebody, cares a lot about us opening up that old case—enough to take a shot at us."

That piqued his interest and he sat forward again. "Is that what that was about? That shooting downtown today? How could that possibly be connected to Warren Macintosh?"

"I don't know, but let me give you the rest of the background." I proceeded to briefly describe the dead ends we'd encountered with DHS, the police records, and the original detective on the case.

He sat back, pursed his lips, and gave all that a full minute of thought. "You're right," he finally said. "Somebody with a lot of clout wants it left alone. Warren knows a lot of powerful people and has power of his own as a station owner. He likes to see himself as a mover and shaker...." More pursing, more thought.

"So?" Malone finally asked.

"It could be nothing. It probably is, but as news director I'm in and out of his office fairly often." He looked at Alison. "When did he call you in and tell you to back off?"

"Yesterday."

"What time?"

"I don't know exactly. Mid-morning. Why?"

"Here's the thing. I was sitting outside his office around eight-thirty yesterday morning, waiting to be summoned inside, when he got a call from Ray Devine. His secretary said it was 'Mr. Devine' calling, but I'm sure it was Ray because they're good buddies. I had to wait another ten minutes while he took it. Pissed me off."

"And the significance of this is?" I asked.

"Ray Devine is a Portland City Commissioner, a member of the City Council."

"Yes, I recognize the name. I still don't see the significance."

"Each commissioner has responsibility to oversee certain city bureaus. Guess who has the police bureau?"

"Ray Devine," my partner guessed.

"Got it in one. Now, if I understand city government, and I think I do, there are only three people who could exert the kind of pressure that this police captain must have gotten: the mayor, the police chief, and Ray Devine. As far as I know, only one of them was on the horn with Warren Macintosh before the pressure landed on you, Alison."

"That is interesting," I offered, "but Devine can't tell Macintosh what to do."

"That we know of," Malone said. "It's worth looking at."

"It is," I agreed, and stood. "We should probably get going. We appreciate your help, Mr. Wallerby."

Malone and Alison also stood.

"One last question," Malone said to Wallerby. "Why are you so willing to spill about your boss? It seems...unusual to me."

He chuckled. "You mean it seems disloyal. The fact is, he's a son of a bitch and I don't like him very much. If he ends up getting some grief out of what you're working on, that's fine with me. He's certainly caused enough."

"In that case, one *more* question: Would you be willing to keep your eyes and ears open? Let us know about any other interesting contacts you learn about? Maybe do some digging of your own?"

Wallerby smiled but shook his head. "I don't like my boss, but I do like my job. One totally unplanned conversation in my living room is okay, but after this I don't know you guys and there's nothing more I can do to help Alison." He was urging us toward the front door at this point. "I will wish you luck, though. If Ray Devine is in this, you want to watch your backs."

CHAPTER TWENTY-EIGHT

The agency phone was ringing as I unlocked the door the next morning. I hurried across to the desk and picked it up. "McCall-Malone Detective Agency."

"Clint! It's Daisy. Are you guys all right?"

"We're fine. Why?"

"We just saw a report on the morning news about the shooting in downtown yesterday. They said you guys were the apparent targets, you and some TV person."

Great. We were still getting coverage. "We may have been," I said, "but they missed. Nothing to worry about."

"Sylvia thinks it's her fault."

"We don't know if it's related to her case or not. You can reassure her that, even if it is, it's not her fault. Why am I not talking to her about this, by the way? Are you guys okay? You've had her there with you nearly a week now."

"Other than feeling guilty, she's fine. She didn't want to bother you and she's in her room now, probably writing away, and I'm enjoying the company. I just wanted to check in. I know this is the umpty-eleventh time somebody has taken a shot at you guys, but I always worry when I hear about it."

"I understand. When she comes up for air, tell her I said it isn't her fault."

"Will do."

"Nothing else is going on, I assume. No strangers hanging around, no threats...?"

"Not a thing."

"Okay. Talk to you soon."

"That was Daisy," I told Malone as I hung up. "She says Sylvia Ralston's blaming herself for our drive-by."

"Huh. I'd be inclined to blame the fucker with the gun." She turned from booting up her PC. "So, do we have Eleanor do a deep dive on a Portland City Commissioner or not? We never did come to a firm conclusion last night."

"I don't know. I'm still not sure it's worth the hours. He's been a public figure for a long time. There's going to be massive amounts of information available, half of it probably crap. And I would bet that none of it connects him to a little girl found in an alley twenty years ago."

"Yeah, but you know how this works. We dig a little dirt. That leads to some more dirt. Maybe eventually we get to some relevant dirt."

"Still. That's a lot of hours. I don't know if she has the time. I don't know if I want to spend the money with so little likelihood of success."

My partner sat back and glared. "Okay, so far we're doing a good job of repeating last night's discussion without reaching a conclusion." She paused, then held up a finger. "Here's a thought...that you won't like. We're talking about digging up dirt, right?"

"Yeah."

"Who do we know that's an expert on being dirty? And I don't mean Reuben. Think bigger than that."

It didn't take me long. "Oh shit. Gunther again?" Reuben Keys was a flamboyant local pimp who sometimes provided information or even backup. Carl Gunther, on the other hand, was Portland's long-time crime boss and a big admirer of my wife. Too big, in my view, on both counts.

"I know you're not a fan, but we're even right now and if anybody would have dirt on city officials, it would be Carl. He might help us out again."

"If you ask really nicely," I said.

"Snark does not become you, nor does jealousy."

"Well, la-di-fucking-da."

"Okay, it was just an idea. We can see what Eleanor..."

"We go see him together this time," I interrupted.

Her grin was sly. "Of course. I wouldn't have it any other way. What do you think? We make an appointment or just show up?"

"Let's show up."

"All righty then." She glanced at her watch. "It's after nine. He should be in. Let's do it."

Less than fifteen minutes later, we were in the elevator of Gunther's downtown office building. We didn't speak as it rose to his floor; we'd always assumed he had the elevator cars bugged.

The offices of Gunther Global Import/Export were on the twenty-second floor and we stepped into a spotlessly clean carpeted hallway that extended some distance in both directions. We turned right and walked past framed works of modern art hung periodically on the glowing off-white walls of the wide corridor. We made no more noise walking on the thick carpet than the elevator had made getting us here. The air was fresh as the outdoors.

We arrived at the proper door and entered a simple but tastefully decorated reception area. There was one other door, leading into Gunther's office. A medium-size leather couch sat against the wall to our left and directly before us was a highly polished wooden desk with Mrs. Agnes Pinkerton seated behind it. Although she looked like Central Casting's idea of everybody's favorite grandmother, we knew from previous experience that Mrs. Pinkerton kept a handgun in her desk and knew how to use it. I had a momentary fantasy of introducing her to Agatha Pepper, then dismissed the thought as a nightmare.

"Mr. and Mrs. McCall," she said with a slight grin. "To what do we owe the pleasure?"

"It's Mr. McCall and Ms. Malone when we're working," grumped my partner, knowing full well that Mrs. Pinkerton already knew that. "We're here to see Carl, if he's available."

"Let me see," she said, and reached for her handset. Before she could pick it up, however, a deep voice emanated from the small speaker on her desk. "I'm available, Agnes. Send them in."

Okay, so his reception area was also bugged.

Mrs. Pinkerton simply gestured toward his closed door and went back to her keyboard.

Carl Gunther, Sr., was sitting behind his big desk expensively dressed in a gray pinstripe suit with dark blue tie. In his mid-fifties, about my age, he had a full head of dark brown hair and craggy features. He was a big man, physically as well as criminally, a little over six feet tall with a broad chest and thick legs.

He nodded as we entered and said hello to Malone.

"How are you doing, Carl?" I asked as we sat down, just to ensure he knew I was in the room.

"I'm fine, McCall." He focused back on my wife. "To what do I owe the pleasure of this visit?"

"Looking for some information," she answered him, "that you might be privy to."

One eyebrow went up. "Me, and not others? Having to do with the less savory side of our city then, I would guess."

I decided to just jump right in. "What do you know about Ray Devine?"

That earned both eyebrows up. "He's a city commissioner. Why are you asking about Devine?"

"Possible connection to a case we're working on."

"You're investigating city government?"

"No, it's a very cold case having to do with a kid found in an alley twenty years ago."

He didn't change expression, didn't even blink. "I can't tell you anything really interesting about Ray Devine. He's clean, as far as I know. We don't have any dealings other than showing up at the same municipal events now and then. I know him to say hello. That's it."

Malone snorted. "Oh, come on, Carl. You keep a lot better tabs than that on all the power players in this town. What is it you don't want to tell us?"

Still placid, he just looked at her for a moment. "Not a thing, Devon." Then he checked his watch. "But, as much as I enjoy seeing you, I have another meeting. One that is actually scheduled."

She narrowed her eyes at him. "Really?"

"Really."

"Well, okey-doke," I interjected, just so they'd again be reminded I was in the room. "I guess we'll be on our way, then." And we left without another word.

"That was bullshit," Malone announced as we descended in

the elevator. She gave the elevator ceiling the finger. "And I don't care if he knows that I know it."

"Okay," I said, and we left it at that until we were on the sidewalk, where she continued her thought.

"You can't tell me that Gary Wallerby knows more about Ray Devine than Carl does. And there's a reason he's not sharing."

"Any thoughts about what the reason is?" I inquired as we headed back to the office.

She was silent for maybe a quarter-block. "He reacted when you said it was about a kid found in an alley."

"I didn't see a reaction. I would have said he was expressionless, showed no interest at all."

"That was the reaction. That's not like Carl. He would normally have been all over it, wanting to know what the hell a city commissioner had to do with a kid found in an alley. Instead he gave you the dead eye and denied knowing anything about Devine."

"Okay. You know him better than I do."

"You're sounding a little green."

I ignored any intimation that I was jealous. "If you're right that he knows something about what happened to Sylvia Ralston, he could be behind our dead ends—and the drive-by. I wouldn't put it past him." I glanced over as we made our way through the other pedestrians. "Would you?"

"Probably not," she finally said, "but meanwhile I have another idea."

"What?"

"If Carl won't tell us what he knows about Ray Devine, maybe Ray Devine will tell us what he knows about Carl."

CHAPTER TWENTY-NINE

"I do have a feeling this is going to be interesting," I said to my partner as we approached the Portland City Hall. It was just a couple of blocks farther from the office than the Justice Center. We walked, keeping an eye out for tails, drive-bys, and other threats.

What was already interesting was that we'd gotten an immediate appointment to see Portland City Commissioner Ray Devine. We were back in the office from our visit with Gunther by ten. We talked for a few more minutes about the plan, such as it was, and then we called Devine's office. It was now just before eleven.

Either Commissioner Devine was extremely responsive to his constituents or...there was some other explanation. We didn't know what that would be, but we were hoping to find out.

I have spent a lot of time in the nearby Justice Center, but very little in City Hall. It's a four-story Italian Renaissance-style building that occupied an entire city block between Fourth and Fifth, Madison and Jefferson. We used the main entrance on Fourth, then made our way through the rotunda and up to the reception area for the Commissioners' offices.

Apparently the Commissioners shared one receptionist, an attractive redhead who looked to be in her twenties and the throes of perkiness. She very happily let Commissioner Devine know we were there and a moment later he appeared in the doorway to an office on our right, a big welcoming smile on his face.

I recognized him from an image search we'd done earlier. He was a little taller than me, with neatly trimmed sandy hair topping a slightly horsy face. I put him in his mid-forties. Dressed in pale green polo shirt with a lightweight gray knitted vest and blue jeans, he could have been your friendly neighborhood pharmacist rather than a city official. Except for the eyes. That big smile did not reach his eyes, which even at this distance were cold and hard and broadcast power player.

"Mr. McCall! Ms. Malone!" He met us halfway with hearty handshakes. "Come into my office. Can Thea get you anything? Coffee? A soft drink?"

"No, we're fine," I said as he escorted us into a small but nicely equipped office with a full trophy wall to our left. There were framed photos of our host with a wide variety of important-looking people, a few of whom I recognized as local TV personalities. I didn't see Alison Roberts among them.

We took the two well-padded visitor chairs while Devine settled in the big leather chair behind his desk. He leaned forward, elbows on the desk with his hands steepled, and looked at us expectantly. "So. What can I do for two of Portland's premiere private detectives?"

So he'd either done a quick background check or already knew who we were. The latter wouldn't be surprising. Thanks to Alison, we were practically TV personalities ourselves.

Anyway, no pussyfooting around was required. "Actually it's in that capacity that we're here," I said. "We thought you might be able to help us with a case we're working on."

He sat back with another one of those smiles. "Ah. That's exciting. What's the case and how can I help you?"

"Well, the case is a very cold one. A young girl who was found in a downtown alley twenty years ago with no memory of who she was or what happened to her. Her name is Sylvia Ralston. I don't suppose you remember the case or recognize her name."

He shook his head, his expression blank. "No. Sorry. Why did you think I would know anything about it?"

"We didn't," Malone responded. "But we have reason to believe that Carl Gunther knows something about it and we thought you might have some relevant information about him. He is a prominent Portland figure, in his way."

Devine was very good, but I would have sworn that there was a little twitch at the mention of Gunther. We got the steepled hands again and this time his look was appropriately thoughtful. "I certainly know who he is, but we're not personally acquainted. Are you interviewing all of the Commissioners about this?"

"Possibly," I ad-libbed, "but we thought we'd start with you because you oversee the Police Bureau and would be more likely to have information about a man reputed to be the city's crime boss."

At that he very slightly and subtly relaxed as the hands spread. "More of a liaison than an overseer, really. I'm afraid my involvement with the police is primarily focused on budgets, not investigations. I can't help you—and I seriously doubt that any of the other commissioners could, either."

He looked at my partner. "I understand you used to be with the Bureau before joining your husband in the detective agency."

"He wasn't my husband at the time, but yes. You've done your research."

The smile. "It helps to know who I'm talking to." Hands flat on the desktop now: end of meeting. Almost. "This case, the young girl in the alley, are you making any progress?"

Malone, deadpan: "The investigation is ongoing."

He started to rise and we came up with him. "Thank you for your time, Commissioner," I said.

"No trouble," he replied.

I turned halfway away and then back. "One last question. In your role as...liaison with the Police Bureau, would you have any idea why they would not want to cooperate in our investigation? Why an officer trying to help us would be told by his superior to back off?"

He looked as innocent as an adult possibly could as he spread his hands again.

"No idea. I'm sorry."

"Not even any thoughts?" Malone asked.

"Well, I guess my thought would be that somebody doesn't want you looking into it. Somebody powerful. Possibly dangerous." The smile and the eyes.

With that, we said our goodbyes and left.

"He knew an awful lot about us given that he only had an hour between our call and the meeting," my partner observed as we again crossed the rotunda. "Either he has Eleanor-level tech skills or the research was already done."

CHAPTER THIRTY

We were back in the office after our standard hamburger-and-fries lunch at the Home Run. No interesting messages awaited us, so I was going through the snail mail and paying a few bills while Malone tapped away on her keyboard.

She was so focused for so long that I got curious. "What are you doing over there?" I finally asked.

She didn't look away from the screen. "Research."

"On?"

"Ray Devine. I know we agreed that we didn't need Eleanor to do a deep dive on him, but there wasn't even time for a superficial search because we got that appointment so fast. It pisses me off that he knew more about us than we did about him."

"Are we rethinking the Eleanor deep dive now that we've met him?"

"We should talk about that, but right now I'm just doing a standard Google search. He's a public figure. There's plenty of public stuff."

"And?"

She finally refocused on me and swiveled away from the keyboard. "Everything says he's a good guy. Good husband, good father, good public servant. Clean cut, honest as the day is long, probably goes to church every Sunday. Twice."

"So you think it's bullshit."

"Don't you? You saw his eyes. I wouldn't want to wake up in the morning and see those."

"Ah. You like my eyes."

She snorted. "Your eyes are fine. Get them back on the prize. I did find something on social media that was kind of interesting. And a little weird."

"What?"

She crooked a finger. "Come take a look."

I came around and looked over her shoulder at the screen, which was displaying a photo of some youngish guys, maybe mid-30s, four white and one black, gathered around what looked like a restaurant table and smiling at the camera. One of them looked familiar; it was a younger Ray Devine. I scanned the names underneath and recognized another one: Warren Macintosh.

I squinted in a little closer. "That's Facebook, right, but...." Still closer. "That's not Devine's page. Who is Brendon Donish?"

"Not sure yet. I just checked this page out because Donish had a few posts on Devine's page and it looked like they were friends. Then I searched for Devine here and this photo popped up with some other more innocuous stuff."

"Well, you're right: It is interesting that Warren Macintosh is in this photo with Devine. What's supposed to be weird?"

"Look at the title Donish has given it."

Above the photo was THE SIX, with a smiley face. "So?"

"There are only five guys in the photo."

"Huh. Maybe some kind of private joke among friends. Or maybe the sixth person took the photo."

"Maybe." She looked up and locked eyes with me. "But I think we should check out all these guys and probably talk to them—including Macintosh, whether he wants to or not. See what clicks."

I went back around to my side of the desk, mulling it over as I went. "Fine with me," I agreed after I got settled again. "I trust your instincts." I took a moment to watch the traffic on Stark. "Do you really think there's any possibility that a Portland City Commissioner had something to do with Sylvia Ralston ending up in that alley?"

I looked over at her as she shrugged.

"Don't know," she said, following my gaze out the window. "He wasn't a city official twenty years ago. He would have been, what, mid-twenties, and we don't know what he was doing—though that's another thing we should find out."

She cocked an eye over at me. "So what do you think about us spending the money to have Eleanor dig deep?"

"I think that if there's anything to Ray Devine besides his good guy image, it's very deep. We've got these guys to talk to now. Let's do our thing before we ask Eleanor to do her thing."

My partner nodded. "Sounds good."

Then I noticed her gaze out the window sharpen. "What?"

"Take a look at the second story windows across the street. The way the light is right now, they have a clear reflection of our entryway."

"Ah. So they do." And the reflection showed two big, tough-looking guys lounging against the wall of our building, one on either side of the entrance to our stairway. "I suddenly feel like taking a walk."

Malone was already retrieving her Glock from her drawer. I reached over to open mine. "Let's try not to generate any viral videos or attract a police presence this time, okay?"

"Spoil sport," she replied as we headed for the door.

We didn't even have to discuss the plan. We traipsed down the stairs side by side and, instead of simply stepping out onto the sidewalk, Malone swung out to the right and I to the left. I didn't know about her, but I found myself eye to breastbone with a very large and rather smelly individual wearing a leather jacket and clearly packing heat. Which he had not had a chance to draw.

I looked up at his very surprised expression. I heard a grunt behind me, but it didn't sound like my partner so I ignored it. "What can we do for you guys?" I asked loudly enough to include both of them.

There was a brief pause as I watched my guy get his shit together. "We got a message for you," he said.

Another grunt from behind me, followed by a slightly strangled voice saying "Yeah." Still not Malone, so I didn't worry about it.

"What's the message and who's it from?" I asked politely.

"The message is to back off on the kid in the alley if you want her to stay alive. Don't matter who it's from."

Another grunt behind me. Another "yeah."

"That's it?"

"That's it. Let's go, Justin." That latter was addressed over my head.

He stepped past me toward Third and I watched him hook the other guy's arm, which was about the size of my thigh, to pull him along. Justin was even bigger than my guy, indeterminate age, head totally shaved. Apparently not very talkative.

Short of generating those videos and attracting those police, we didn't have much choice but to watch them walk away.

"What the fuck was that?" my partner asked as they turned the corner and disappeared.

"I think they were supposed to be a little more threatening than we allowed. Why did Justin keep grunting?"

"Because I had my Glock buried in his belly button."

"I thought we didn't want to attract attention."

"Nobody saw it. Not even Justin. I thought it was worth the risk. I like having my gun out when I'm confronting an asshole the size of my fucking Jeep."

"Good call," I said, and we went back up to the office.

CHAPTER THIRTY-ONE

Malone slammed down the office handset. "We've been tailed, we've been surveilled, we've been shot at, we've been warned, we've been stymied at every turn...and now we're not getting any damned cooperation from these guys. Again, I didn't make it past the receptionist. This is beginning to piss me off."

It had taken us very little time to identify the other men in the photo since they all were active on social media. One of them, of course, was Brendon Donish who turned out to be a successful local developer. Then there was banker Scott Abernathy and attorney Vernon Kennett, both also local and apparently very successful.

But, as my partner had said, not cooperative at all. I called Donish while she tried Abernathy and Kennett. She encountered two receptionists who already had instructions not to make an appointment with us. I had to leave a voicemail for Donish, but wasn't optimistic about a positive response. We already knew Warren Macintosh's position on meeting with us. Stymied again—but in a very interesting way.

"Clearly," I said to Malone, "these guys already know who we are. Bankers and attorneys don't usually refuse to meet with the random caller who might be a new customer or client. We're going to get the same from the developer."

"I agree." She tapped knuckles on the desktop. "And all this is weird six ways from Sunday. We've got five men, all local success stories, who've known each other for at least ten years and back then apparently were calling themselves The Six." She tapped again. "First we had a tail that turned into a high-speed pursuit, then we were ambushed, and then we were warned off—which is not the proper order of things." A third tap. "What the hell do we have here? A really bad, but very amateur, bad guy?"

"Maybe a really bad city commissioner?"

She sat back and shrugged. "Maybe. But all we know is that he's the Commission's liaison with the Police Bureau, he called Warren Macintosh about something, and his eyes don't smile when he does."

"Which connects him to two of our dead ends. I think we can put the eyes on the back burner for now."

"Well, we certainly want to be alert for further connections when we talk to our photo subjects."

"But they won't talk to us."

"They won't make appointments with us. They don't *want* to talk to us. So we ambush them and make them talk to us."

"You want to shoot them?"

She snorted. "No, like ambush journalism. You know, we show up when they least expect it and start asking questions."

I gave it a moment and shrugged back at her. "Okay. That sounds like fun."

She refocused on her monitor and started tapping away again. I went back to paying bills.

CHAPTER THIRTY-TWO

"That could be him." I was watching an unusually tall and gangly figure make his way across the parking lot of the City Athletic Club, a couple of blocks east of Grand on Holgate. It was seven-thirty the next morning, Saturday, and Malone and I were staked out with coffee and pastries provided by Veronica.

In line with my partner's plan, banker Scott Abernathy's Facebook page indicated he usually started his weekend very early in the morning at this club, playing racquetball. So we'd been sitting here for the past half-hour. We had a good idea of what he looked like from that same page, though it was hard to be sure at this distance when the person was wearing a jacket, scarf, and knit hat pulled down over his ears.

However, he was clearly male, check. Tall and thin, check. Here early, check. And carrying what looked like racquetball equipment looped over one shoulder. Check.

We bailed out of the Subaru and cut across the lot to intercept him.

He pulled up when he saw us approaching and looked from side to side as if wondering where he might run. Then he raised his hands. "I don't carry any money!"

At which point we stopped, still about ten feet in front of him. "We're not muggers," I assured him. "We just want to talk. You are Scott Abernathy, right?"

He slowly lowered his hands and squinted from one of us to the other. "Yes. Who are you? What do you want?"

My partner pulled out her ID and stepped closer to him, holding it up. "We're private investigators. I'm Devon Malone and this is Clint McCall. We just have a few questions."

His shoulders stiffened and he took a step back. "You two!"

"We two," I agreed as I pulled up even with Malone.

"I thought my secretary informed you that I am not interested in answering any of your questions. I have nothing to do with any investigations."

We'd finally reached something like normal social distance from him. "See, that's what made us even more interested," I said conversationally. "Most people, innocent people, hear that two private detectives want to talk to them and they are very curious about why, even excited, many of them, to talk to a couple of PIs. You know, like on TV. You almost never get people categorically refusing to talk to you unless they have something to hide. What could you possibly have to hide, Mr. Abernathy?"

"Especially," chimed in my partner, "since you couldn't know who we are or what we're working on...could you?"

He was holding up his hands again, this time in front of his chest as if to fend us off. "I have no idea who you are or what you're working on. And I am not most people!" At which point he barged ahead, forcing us to step to either side.

I decided to take a shot. "What can you tell us about The Six?" I asked as he brushed by.

He stumbled and almost fell on his face, then accelerated toward the club entrance. He was practically running by the time he got there.

Malone and I looked at each other. "That was quite a reaction," she said. "Good job, to ask the question before he got away."

"Not that his response really tells us anything."

"It tells me that the five guys in that photo were into something, at least back when it was taken, that they don't want anyone looking at now. Whether it has anything to do with our case or not remains to be seen." She looked around the nearly empty lot. "Meanwhile, we're standing in the open making ourselves a target. Time to move on."

I glanced at my watch as we hurried back to the Subaru. Quarter to eight. Next on our agenda was staking out the Channel 11 parking lot. According to Alison, Warren Macintosh usually met with the weekend news staff first thing Saturday before taking the rest of the weekend off.

We got there in ten minutes and this time we only had to sit for another five before a gray Chevy sedan, not more than a year or two old, pulled into the lot and parked. Macintosh was not nearly as bundled up as Abernathy had been and we recognized him from the photo on the station's web page as soon as he exited the car.

We intercepted him as he crossed toward the entrance. He was nearly as wide as he was tall and moving slowly. You couldn't have found a more exact opposite to our first ambush of the day.

He must have been thinking hard about something, because he looked totally startled when he finally realized that we were blocking his path. He was wearing baggy jeans, a flannel shirt, and an oversized canvas jacket. Apparently the Saturday morning meetings were somewhat informal.

His already florid face reddened even more as he pulled up. "What? Who are you guys? We aren't hiring and we don't do retractions."

I held up a hand, palm out. "We're not interested in a job or a retraction, but we do have some questions about a case we're working on. You could be very helpful if...."

"A case. You're...you're McCall and Malone! I already said I didn't want to meet with you!"

"Which made us very curious," responded my partner. "Which is why we're now meeting in a parking lot. Why would the manager of a TV station, one who comes in on a Saturday morning to meet with the news staff, not want to know what we wanted? It could be a story."

He stepped back as if she'd punched him in the chest. "I'm...I'm very busy. And how do you know all that? You need to leave me alone!"

Okay, so he wasn't feeling any more cooperative than Abernathy had been. This was getting downright intriguing. I took a shot at making it even more so.

"We know all kinds of things," I said. "For instance, we know that Ray Devine called to warn you about our visit to the station. What we don't know is why. Would you care to comment?"

I thought we were going to have to call paramedics, his face lost its color so fast. "How did you...?" He grunted. "Fuck! I'm going to fire that bitch!"

I had no idea what he was talking about, but Malone caught on more quickly. "It wasn't your secretary who told us, Mr. Macintosh. She said nothing except what you told her to say."

"Then who? How...?"

"We're private detectives. We find shit out. It's our job. That's why you should cooperate with us."

"No!" He'd had enough. He surged forward, straight at Malone. Rather than taking him down, she stepped aside and he lumbered between us heading for the door. Shades of Scott Abernathy. Unlike the banker, however, he stopped at the door and looked back at us. "You two are playing with fire," he called out. He raised his right fist at us while opening the door with his left hand. "I'm telling you! Fucking fire!"

And he was gone.

I looked at my partner and she looked at me. "I guess we can skip the where-there's-smoke part," she said.

CHAPTER THIRTY-THREE

Next on our Saturday agenda was our social media source, real estate developer Brendan Donish, and we found ourselves heading for Lake Oswego once again. He lived in the toniest portion of the posh community so we wouldn't be very near our friends Agatha or Daisy; even farther from Rowena and Beck Canham.

"Maybe we should set up a branch office here," Malone observed as we took the freeway exit. "See if Daisy is interested in manning it."

I was still coming up with an appropriately snarky reply when I heard my phone's ringtone. I pulled over and answered it. "Clint McCall."

"Where are you?" hissed a voice that I could barely hear.

"Who is this?"

"Sylvia Ralston. Where are you?"

"We just took the exit into Lake Oswego. Is there a problem? We can be at Daisy's house in less than five minutes."

"I'm not at Daisy's house. We're at Agatha Pepper's house."

That couldn't be right. "Can you speak up a bit? I can barely hear you. Tell me where you are again and what's going on."

She didn't raise her voice, but did take the time to speak more distinctly. "I'm at Agatha Pepper's house. I'm in the bathroom next to the kitchen. There's a guy with a gun. Agatha shoved me in here and told me to call you. You're really close by?"

What the hell was Sylvia Ralston doing at Agatha's house? No time to figure that out right now. I put the phone on speaker, handed it to Malone—who was looking thoroughly mystified and concerned—and pulled out, accelerating in the direction of Agatha's. "Have you called the police?"

"No. She told me to call you." That was weird. Again, I would have wondered if I heard her correctly, but oddly she was a little easier to make out over the speaker, even above the car engine.

"She said to tell you she was handling it," Sylvia went on.

Oh, that was good news. "Sylvia, the people who are out to stop us from asking questions are very dangerous. If one of them has somehow tracked you down, we need the police." I made significant eye contact with my partner as I said that and she pulled out her phone.

"This isn't about me," came the response. "I'm right next to the kitchen and I can hear what they're saying. It's some guy named Butch who's after the young girl here named Beck, if that makes any sense."

Oh crap. "You say he's armed?"

"Yeah, he has a gun—and so does Agatha. It's a standoff. Daisy's out there, too, and the girl and some other guy."

Oh double and triple crap. I motioned at Malone, but she was already punching off her phone. Adding cops to the mix didn't sound like a good idea. They wouldn't know to take Agatha Pepper into account. We were by this time nearly there, anyway.

"We'll be just another couple of minutes," I said. "Do you know if the front door is unlocked?"

"I would imagine so," Sylvia whispered back. "This Butch guy just walked right in."

"Okay. Hang up and hold tight."

Malone held onto my phone as I turned onto Agatha's block. "I must have missed something," she said. "That was Sylvia Ralston, right? Did she say that Agatha is faced off with Butch Faron in her kitchen and Sylvia is somehow there?"

"Yep." I braked to a stop in front of Agatha's house.

"How the hell?"

"Don't ask me." I was bailing out of the car and drawing my Smith and Wesson. My partner, Glock in hand, joined me in hurrying toward the house.

Sylvia had supposed that the front door was unlocked and, needless to say, we didn't knock. I eased the door open and we went in, Malone low and to the left, me high and to the right.

Nobody in sight, but we could make out Agatha's voice farther back in the house.

We heard nothing more as we made our way quietly to the kitchen doorway and I peeked in around the doorframe. One look and I pulled back, holstering my gun. I gestured Malone back far enough that I could safely whisper. "We walk in there with guns drawn and it's going to be like putting a flame to a fuse. We've got to talk them down."

She gave me a dubious look, but holstered her weapon. We stepped together back to the doorway and through.

We were presented with quite a tableau. Agatha Pepper stood on the right side of the room with Rodney, Daisy, and Beck arrayed behind her, frozen in place, and a mean-looking young tough on the other side. They were both in classic shooter's stance, with guns trained on one another. Hers, I noted, was about twice the size of his. The final touch was Morty crouched on the kitchen table a bit in front of his mistress, apparently prepared to take a bullet if necessary. No idea how the tubby little critter had gotten up there. Probably Sylvia was still in the bathroom.

It was, I thought, indeed a good thing that we didn't have armed police officers taking this in. Somebody would have been dead for sure.

"Shoot-out at the OK Kitchen," Malone muttered.

Agatha gave us the side eye and a little smile, but didn't say anything. The rest stayed focused on her and the young man I assumed was Butch Faron.

He was about my height but heavier, mostly muscle I guessed, and probably in his mid-thirties. A round head to go with his bulging shoulders, with hair buzz cut so close that I couldn't tell what color it was. No facial hair. Just a really fierce expression.

He was wearing your classic ratty blue jeans and leather jacket. She was wearing her classic motley, bright yellow muumuu with red polka dots this time. I couldn't imagine where one would buy such a thing. Maybe she had them specially made.

Butch, meanwhile, was paying no attention to us at all. He didn't know who or what we were, had no reason to think we were armed, and certainly didn't want to move his gun and give Agatha a free shot.

All of which, I was happy to take advantage of. He was about ten feet from us, on my left, and I began drifting slowly in his direction. It didn't take long for him to notice, since I was the only thing moving in the whole kitchen aside from some slight trembling on Morty's part.

"Stop right there, old man." His voice was oddly high pitched for his stature, maybe because of the tense situation. I ignored the ageism and continued moving very slowly.

"What's going on?" I inquired politely.

He answered me, not so politely. "This old bitch has kidnapped my girlfriend's daughter and I'm here to take her home. I don't want any trouble from you while I'm doing it."

"I'm not kidnapped, Butch," came Beck's voice from my right. "I'm here because I'm tired of you groping me and my mom not giving a shit. And it looks like you've got plenty of trouble already."

I was sure that if I looked at the kid I'd see she was smirking, or at least trying to. I kept my attention on Butch and edged a little closer while he glared at Beck. Agatha still hadn't said a word and her weapon had not wavered. If only the TV executives could see her now.

At this point I was maybe a little less than five feet away and almost out of his peripheral vision. It was time to end this farce. I drew my Smith and Wesson, took one big step forward, and pressed the barrel against the moron's temple. "Surprise," I said, softly.

"Shit!"

Suddenly his arms were trembling even more than Morty's tubby little body—which, I saw in my own peripheral vision, was now about halfway across the kitchen table. He was ready to do his part in the takedown.

"Just lower the gun and put it on the table." I darted a

glance to my right. "You too, Agatha. There are a lot of people who could get hurt here."

Faron gritted his teeth and growled, but began lowering his gun—then paused as he stared down at Morty, who had arrived at our end of the table. "That little shit is going to bite me."

"Good!" Agatha shouted as she set her own weapon down.

My ever-resourceful wife stepped past me, picked up Morty with a soft grunt of effort, and carried him toward his mistress. Butch Faron carefully finished setting his gun on the table and raised his hands.

A door directly in my line of vision opened slowly and Sylvia Ralston poked her head out. "Can I call the police now?"

"Now would be good," I responded.

The police arrived not five minutes later and Butch Faron was soon in handcuffs—not for the first time, I was sure. Malone and I showed our ID and gave our statements, then hung around until the cops finished and took Faron away.

In the course of listening to the other statements, I learned that Agatha had visited Daisy and then invited her and her guest home to meet Rodney and Beck. Thus they were all together when Butch Faron showed up.

It was only after the police had satisfied themselves and taken Butch away that I asked Agatha *why* the hell she had visited Daisy in the first place.

"I'm nosy. That's why." She gave us a big grin. "It's part of my essence."

We were all sitting around her large living room by then, Malone and I on one couch and Daisy and Sylvia on another with Agatha and Morty ensconced in the biggest armchair, making the third point of a triangle. Beck was in another armchair a bit off to the side and Rodney, as usual, was lurking behind Agatha. I wondered if he had any life of his own. I also wondered why, as his eyes darted around the room, they landed so often on Daisy and Sylvia. Maybe just because they were strangers.

I cocked an eye over at my fellow black belt. "How did you and Sylvia end up here?"

Daisy shrugged, looking a bit bewildered about it herself. Probably because she hadn't expected to find herself witnessing an armed stand-off between a young thug and a retired librarian. "Agatha invited us."

"I was curious," Agatha explained a little more seriously. "I love learning more about what my favorite detectives are doing. How could I resist after I heard that one of your crew and a client were nearby? Then," she offered a shrug of her own, "when Sylvia told me her story, I was intrigued and wanted to help."

"What did you think you could do to help?" asked Malone.

"I wanted Sylvia and Beck to meet. They're both dealing with serious issues and I thought perhaps they would find some solace in one another."

"How's that working out so far?"

"Well, we did have that little interruption."

A few minutes later, as Ms. Pepper escorted us to her front door, she was a little more forthcoming. "I was curious to meet your team member and your client," she shared, "but after I'd had a chance to talk to Sylvia, it struck me that she could be a good role model for Beck and that Beck, in turn, could give her something to think about besides her own problems."

"I thought Sylvia was happy to be hidden away working on her book."

"She was," agreed Agatha. "She is, and it's not like I want her to spend all her time with Beck, but you have to have something to do besides writing or you don't have anything to write about."

"You realize," I said, "that she might be in danger and might endanger the people around her. Somebody seems pretty intent that she not find out what really happened to her."

"Piffle. We can take care of ourselves. I have my guns and I'm even teaching Rodney how to shoot."

"Are you keeping Beck here now?" asked Malone.

"If she's willing. I think she's a fine young woman, though her fashion sense seems to be lacking."

"What about her mother?"

"I'm going to try to get her some help now that her previous support system has been arrested in my kitchen. Who knows? Maybe everybody can have a happily ever after."

"Well, Agatha," I said, "if anybody could pull that off, it would be you. Good luck."

"Thanks," she whispered as she waved out the door. "I'll probably need it."

We were halfway to the car when Malone muttered out the side of her mouth, "She said guns. Plural."

"That she did."

"And Rodney."

"Yeah."

We were both shuddering a little as we got into the Subaru.

CHAPTER THIRTY-FOUR

"Did you notice Rodney making eyes at Sylvia Ralston?" my wife and partner inquired as she finished off one of the pieces of the KFC we'd brought home. A thigh, it was.

"I noticed him paying particular attention to Ralston and Daisy."

"It was Sylvia. I think he's smitten."

"Oh, wow. Good luck to him."

"Yeah." She tackled a breast.

Having run out of time to pursue Ray Devine's acquaintances, we were spending a quiet evening at home and looking forward to an equally quiet Sunday. Stella and Maxine had had their evening kibble and were snoozing by two different heating vents while we finished our dinner.

I picked up the last leg. "I was surprised to see Daisy and Sylvia there. You never know what Ms. Pepper is going to do next."

"True enough, but I wasn't so surprised. You did mention Daisy to Agatha twice, almost as if you wanted her to be interested in them."

I had to think about that as I chewed. "Hmm. I didn't consciously intend to provoke her interest, but you're probably right that that's what did it."

"Lots of good material for Sylvia's next book."

"No kidding."

We'd already agreed that we wouldn't talk about the Ralston case again until tomorrow, when we'd hopefully have all day to kick it around while doing chores and otherwise relaxing. There had been no tails that we could see, no new threats to us or Sylvia. Time to let it perk.

We went to bed early and to sleep late, which should have meant a very good night's rest for yours truly.

Thus, I was surprised to find myself suddenly wide awake at

quarter to three in the morning. The room was dark, lit only by the glow of the bedside clock. I could feel and hear Devon snoring softly next to me.

Then I realized that I could also hear a very faint growl coming from the foot of the bed. I raised my head a bit and could just make out Maxine standing and staring at the bedroom door. She was indeed growling, a little louder now.

The thing about Maxine is that she thinks she's a dog. She gets excited when she sees cars driving by and she growls when strangers come up on the porch.

Only we were currently nowhere near the living room, where she'd know if someone was on the porch.

So what was she growling at?

I held my breath and tried to hear something, anything, beyond the snoring and growling. Perhaps a faint click, or maybe not. Then I took a deep breath. No smoke. At least the house wasn't set on fire again. Still, it had to be something....

I gently nudged Malone and turned my head to whisper when her snoring stopped with a snort. "Don't speak. There may be someone in the house." I waited a moment. Meanwhile, I was pretty sure I did hear something move in the direction of the kitchen. Maxine jumped off the bed, probably to go check it out. "Nod if you're awake."

She nodded.

"Guns," I whispered again, "then on three."

We each kept our weapon next to the bed. I reached over and got mine while, I was sure, she was doing the same. Then I put my left hand on her hip and dropped first one finger, then two, then three.

We simultaneously and carefully threw back the covers and got to our feet, making as little noise as possible. I moved to the doorway with my partner at my shoulder.

We don't have a nightlight in the kitchen at the end of the hallway and I didn't see any light moving around, either. But there was the tiniest screech as someone bumped a kitchen chair. Then I heard a mutter. And an answering grunt. More than one someone.

How were they moving around without any light? The curtains were closed and it was pitch black in the kitchen except for the glowing numerals on the microwave and that wasn't going to show anyone the way. Night-vision equipment? Not your friendly neighborhood burglars, if so.

It struck me then that I was standing next to a light switch for the hallway and night-vision goggles could be a good thing. If suddenly there's bright light, you're blind until you can get the goggles off. We had two seventy-five watt bulbs in the hallway. That would do.

I turned my head and put my mouth right against Malone's ear. "At least two. Duck back in the bedroom. We wait for them to head this way, then I flick the switch and we step out."

I turned away so she could access my ear. "Night vision?" You can't say the woman isn't quick.

Another turn. "Or at least a good surprise. Let's move."

There was no need for her to respond to that. We eased back around the doorframe, just far enough that I could still reach the switch. Malone was on my left, ready to step past me into the hallway. She'd go for the far wall and leave me this side. No need to plan that.

I did hope that Maxine wasn't going to try to confront them before we did. You can carry canine roleplaying too far.

It was only about ten seconds later that I heard a faint combination of soft footsteps and material brushing against the wall. At least one of them had entered the hallway and was coming our way. They had to have night-vision goggles—and good ones.

I didn't need to count down this time. My partner would know to go when the light came on. I flicked the switch and stepped into the hallway.

I had to squint for a second, make my own adjustment to the sudden bright light, but it was nothing compared to what the two men at the end of hall were experiencing. They were both desperately reaching up to push their goggles up when I yelled, "Drop the guns! There are two of us armed and we can see! You don't have a prayer."

Ah, the best laid plans. That was when the third guy, still in the kitchen, fired.

He didn't hit either one of us, probably because he had to shoot with his two compatriots partially blocking his view, but it got me back into the bedroom and Malone prone in the hallway. She fired back and somebody yelled, "Fuck!"

I peered around the doorframe in time to see two large bodies disappearing into the depths of the kitchen heading for the backdoor. They were not trying to be quiet now. It sounded like they were destroying the kitchen table and chairs on the way.

We began moving fairly fast down the hallway. We heard the backdoor crash open and we sped up. It took a couple of seconds to cross the kitchen because the furniture was all over the place. We didn't stumble over anyone, so they were all three mobile even if Malone had hit one of them. We paused on either side of the backdoor frame, then swung out, guns ready...and saw nobody in the back yard, nobody breaching or scaling the fence.

"Shit," I said. "They're running around the front."

We turned and took off for the front door, but I already knew there was no point. If they had equipment that good, they also had an effective getaway set up. And indeed we heard the squeal of tires before we had made it across the living room. All I saw when I got the front door open was taillights turning the corner onto Hawthorne.

Then I heard sirens in the distance. No surprise. You have to expect your neighbors to call in gunfire coming from your house, even if they should be used to it by now.

CHAPTER THIRTY-FIVE

It was nearly seven-thirty Sunday morning before the last uniformed officer left. They'd taken our statements, inspected the damage to the interior of the house including a busted kitchen chair and bullet holes in the hallway. There was, it turned out, no sign of blood, so Malone either didn't hit the guy who cried out or he hadn't bled much before they got away.

They canvassed the neighbors to see if anyone had gotten a better look at the perps or the vehicle. No one had. So all any of us knew was that three armed persons, almost certainly male, had entered through the backdoor and exchanged gunfire with us before they fled.

Meanwhile, I had spent almost an hour looking for Stella before I found her on a shelf in the closet of our guest bedroom. It was about five feet off the floor and I couldn't imagine how she'd gotten up there. I guess she found gunshots to be highly motivating.

Her bigger and braver sister, of course, had simply taken shelter under the bed and came out right away when we returned to the bedroom to get dressed.

Mike Whitehall had shown up around seven, having heard references to our address on his scanner after waking up. He remained behind and suggested we all go around the corner to the Pen and Pastry for breakfast and a strategy session.

It was windy and chilly as the three of us made our way past the old movie theater on the corner and approached the coffee shop owned by our good friend Veronica Fortune. There was dampness in the air even though it wasn't quite raining. Needless to say, we were all on high alert, eyes on our surroundings and the passing vehicles.

Warm air redolent with the odors of fresh pastry and strong coffee greeted us as we entered. The Pen and Pastry is larger than the average coffee shop, twenty-plus tables that each sit four patrons but can be moved together for bigger groups. The café is a very successful business equally because of the excellent pastry kitchen and Veronica Fortune herself.

She was there, as she nearly always is, at forty-nine still extremely attractive, her long red hair falling loose over a pale blue caftan. She wore dangly earrings as well as multiple necklaces and bracelets. Not what you would call a low-key woman, our friend.

And she wasn't the only attraction for the single males I could see grouped around various tables: her wait staff is composed exclusively of other ex-prostitutes. What safer way to enjoy a tasty meal and indulge a few minor fantasies at the same time? And no doubt some of the female customers were here because of Veronica's success in finding a new career and her willingness to help these other women do the same.

Sonny Sampson, however, was not among the women I could see. Probably sleeping in on a Sunday morning, which had been our original plan.

Luckily, a party of four was just leaving so we managed to snag a table toward the back.

Veronica herself came over to say hello and take our orders. She obviously had not heard of any trouble at our house and we didn't burden her with the news.

"I've got the word out to local hospitals and clinics in case Devon did hit one of those guys," Mike shared as soon as Veronica headed back toward the kitchen. "It's a long shot, but you can never underestimate the stupidity of villains." He took a good long sip of coffee while looking from one of us to the other. "So," as he put his cup down, "what in the name of all that's holy have you two gotten yourselves into? Any new thoughts now that you have shooters visiting your kitchen?"

"Not a one," I replied. "Somebody out there really doesn't want us finding out what happened to Sylvia Ralston twenty years ago, but we don't know who or why."

"Yet," added my partner as she set down her own cup.

"I find it hard to believe that Ray Devine has anything that bad to hide," Mike said. "He's been around forever, active in the community and the church, married, kids, your classic all-American Portland City Commissioner...."

"That may be the public record," I observed as our orders were delivered—by a regular waitress, this time. "But that's not what we're hearing from some of his old buddies: Watch your back. You're playing with fire...."

"Old buddies?"

Malone picked up the thread. "We found a photo on social media. Long story. It was taken maybe twenty years ago and showed Ray Devine with four other young men—all of them currently important players here in Portland: Brendan Donish, Warren Macintosh, Scott Abernathy, and Vernon Kennett."

Mike pulled a sour face. "Ugh. Kennett. We don't love him at the Justice Center. I recognize all those names except Macintosh. Who's that?"

"He owns and manages Channel 11, Alison Roberts' station. He's the one who pulled her off doing background for us—and then fired her."

"Fired her!"

"Well, technically she's on hiatus but she's pretty sure that's just until the lawyers come up with an excuse to formally terminate her."

"Shit."

"Yeah."

"So, anyway," I took it up again, "so far we've tried to talk to each of these men. Devine was all friendly and helpful on the surface, but the others have run for their lives. They do *not* want to answer any questions, even before we can tell them what the questions are about."

"We did have some luck," Malone added, "with the news director of Channel 11, Gray Wallerby, who's no big fan of Macintosh and told us that Devine had called him before our visit. Probably gave him the heads up what we were after." She snorted. "Probably gave all of them the heads up."

"Still," Mike said thoughtfully after swallowing the last of his pastry, "Ray Devine's been a public figure with a spotless reputation for a long time. What could he have to do with Sylvia Ralston?"

"No idea," I said. "Which is something I find myself saying way too often lately. It's pissing me off." I took a moment to finish my current cup of coffee. "Stand back and look at all this, though, Mike. We've been stymied at every turn. Records disappear. People are warned off, even fired. As soon as we begin to investigate, stuff starts to happen and keeps escalating. We're threatened, surveilled, tailed. We're shot at. Our home is invaded by armed men." He was nodding along with my litany and then I held up a finger. "But we're still unscathed. All that and not a scratch. What does that make you think?"

He considered my question as he drank more coffee. "A panicked amateur," he said finally.

"Exactly. Somebody with some power and connections, but no experience at using that power and those connections for these kinds of purposes."

"That could be Macintosh or Kennett or any of those guys in that photo, though. Anything else about this photo that's interesting? Where it was taken? What they're doing?"

"They're all just posing together," my partner answered, "big smiles on their faces, looking like friends having a good time. One interesting thing."

"What?"

"Donish—it was his Facebook page-labeled the photo The Six with a smiley face, like that was an in-joke for the rest of them. We've gotten no explanation for that."

"The Six. And there are five guys in the photo. That is interesting. Certainly makes you wonder if there was a sixth. If so, we could be talking about him, if it's a him, rather than Ray Devine."

I swallowed the last of my own pastry. "I refuse to say 'no idea' again."

"Oh, hello." Malone tapped me on the arm and directed my attention to the entrance. Alison Roberts was standing just inside, surveying the crowd. She saw us about the same time that I saw her and headed swiftly in our direction.

"Maybe *she* has an idea," said Mike.

CHAPTER THIRTY-SIX

"Glad I found you," Alison said breathlessly as she arrived at our table and gestured at the empty chair. "Okay if I sit?"

"Sure," I said.

She was dressed for the chilly wet weather with heavy slacks and ski jacket with a hood that she'd already pushed back.

"How did you find us?" I asked as she sat down. "And why were you looking for us at this time of a Sunday morning?"

She unzipped her jacket and shrugged it off to reveal a pale gray pullover. "I heard your address on the scanner as I was getting up this morning, so I came to see what was happening. You didn't answer the door and both cars were in the driveway, so I figured maybe you'd be over here. And here you are." She gave us all a big grin.

"Does everybody have a scanner nowadays?" asked Malone.

Mike was the one to offer a little snort at that. "I'm beginning to think so."

By that time a waitress had arrived at the table. After she'd departed with our friend's order, Alison turned more serious. "Are you guys okay? It must be serious if you've got a homicide detective here."

"I'm here in the capacity of friend," Mike said, "although there was a home invasion and some shots were fired."

"Jeez. And damn, I wish I still had my show. You're sure you're okay?"

She drank coffee and ate pastry as we ran through a blow-by-blow, or rather shot-by-shot, story of our night, along with a very quick reprise of finding the photo on Donish's Facebook and the interviews we'd done.

"So," I concluded, "do you have any thoughts on what your possibly former boss was doing in that photo or what kind of relationship he still has with those other four men?"

"Well," she replied, looking a little smug, "it just so happens I've been researching Warren Macintosh."

"Good for you," offered my partner.

"The man is trying to fire me for nothing more than checking out an old story. That right there tells me he's worth looking at."

"What kind of research?" I asked.

"I've still got access to all the resources at the paper." Now she looked really smug. "My *hiatus* began very abruptly and I guess they forgot to cancel my password."

"What have you found?"

"Besides Ray Devine, a couple of those names ring bells. I can tell you that Macintosh has invested in several of Donish's development deals and that Vernon Kennett has been his attorney for as far back as I looked. I don't recall seeing Abernathy's name, but what do you bet Warren uses his bank?"

"Anybody else's name come up a lot?" asked Malone.

Alison frowned. "Well, sure. Lots of newspaper people and so on. What are you after?"

"Just a shot in the dark. Donish's photo of the five men was entitled The Six. We were just speculating about what that might mean when you showed up."

"Like there's a missing person? I don't know who it would be."

"Well, keep an eye out for someone else who was part of their circle twenty years ago. It might be nothing, probably is—but then again it could be a key."

"I'll let you know if I come up with anything. How's your client, the cozy writer, doing with all this?"

"She's fine," I said. "We've got her in what we hope is a safe place. Meanwhile, she's got no recollections or connections that seem to help explain any of it. And she only got the one written threat. Since then the focus seems to be on Devon and me."

"Huh."

With that we traded conundrums for a few more minutes as we all finished our coffee and then Alison excused herself.

"I know," Mike said as the rest of us also stood up to leave, "that you guys have a good fire detection system at your house now. Finally." His mouth quirked with a grin. "Maybe you should consider a full security setup: alarms on all the doors and windows, a motion detector in the back yard, a few cams...."

"That would probably be a good idea," said Malone. "Though we do already have Maxine," she added dryly.

"Who?"

"Never mind. We'll look into a security system."

We said goodbye to Mike on the sidewalk and headed back around the corner to our house, both our heads on a swivel the whole way.

We were nearly to the front door when Malone put her hand on my arm. She squeezed when I started to go for my gun. "No, that's not it," she said. "I don't see anybody. But I don't want to sit around on my ass for the rest of Sunday, either. Let's check on the cats and then go look for Brendan Donish."

"Sounds like a plan," I said as I unlocked the door. "With any luck, we'll at least make it to his house this time."

CHAPTER THIRTY-SEVEN

So it was back to Lake Oswego yet again—and this time we made it without any detours. Brendon Donish's home was a two-story Colonial-style, light gray with white trim, probably originally built by somebody who moved here from the East Coast.

We parked at the curb right in front of the house and followed the walkway through a well-tended yard and up some steps to the portico. I knocked but didn't get a response. It was late morning. Maybe they were church-goers or out to an early brunch. Malone found a doorbell off to the right and pushed it.

We were about to turn away when I heard a lock snick. The door opened to reveal a tall, sharp-featured woman with thick shoulder-length black hair. Maybe mid-thirties, she was casually dressed in jeans, light blue long-sleeved blouse, and what looked like mukluks—gray, ankle-high slippers. "Yes?"

"Mrs. Donish?" I inquired.

"If you want us to attend your church, we already have one, thank you." She started to close the door, but Malone's very loud snort stopped her. It was Sunday morning, after all, but I was quite certain neither my partner nor I had ever been mistaken for missionaries before.

I found my voice. "My name is Clint McCall and this is my partner Devon Malone." I reached for my ID. "We are private investigators and we'd like to talk to your husband if that would be possible."

Her dismissive expression perked up substantially at that and she took a step back. "Private detectives? Really?" Then a slight frown. "Brendan's not in trouble, is he?"

"Not at all," I assured her. "We're hoping he has some information that will help us with a case we're working on."

A smile and another step back. "Well, come in. My husband's in the living room. We just finished breakfast. I'm sure he'll be fascinated to talk to some real live private eyes. We love those shows on TV, you know."

Oh good. From pet detectives to TV detectives. We followed her from the foyer down a short hallway to a substantial room with the obligatory huge flat screen and viewing area directly ahead, a well-stocked bar to our right, and a conversation grouping around a coffee table to our left. The color scheme was gray and blue to match our hostess. The man sprawled in a recliner watching a football game appeared to be seriously mismatched with our hostess. He didn't look around as we entered the room.

"Bren? There are some private detectives here to see you."

She might as well have hit him with a cattle prod. I could see his body stiffen and then the effort to relax again. He must have had the remote in his hand already because the TV shut off before he finally moved. It was several seconds, time enough to get himself together, and then he smoothly came to his feet and turned to us with a smile that didn't come within a mile of his eyes.

As noted, Brendan Donish was not what I would have expected given his wife. He was at least six inches shorter with a cushiony body, soft features, and poorly trimmed graying hair. His attire was even more casual than hers: gray sweatpants and shirt, bare feet.

"What can I do for you two?"

No inquiry about who we were, but we already knew that he knew. I pretended that we didn't.

"My name is Clint McCall and this is my partner Devon Malone. We're investigating a twenty-year-old cold case, an abused child abandoned in a downtown alley with no memory of who she was or what had happened to her. Your name came up in the course of our inquiries."

I watched what had been a somewhat florid complexion grow more pale, practically word by word. So whoever told him about us didn't tell him what we were after. Interesting.

He frowned, probably trying to make himself look as innocent and bewildered as he could. "My name? How could my name have come up in connection with something like that?"

His wife spoke up at that point. "Bren, we're being rude." She focused on us. "Why don't you two have a seat? Can I get you anything? Coffee? Tea? Water? I'm Delores, by the way." A little smile. "Yes, Delores Donish. I've learned to live with it."

She indicated the conversation grouping and Malone and I moved to the couch, where we sat as Brendan Donish reluctantly followed.

"We don't need any refreshments," my partner said. "We just have a few questions and then we'll be on our way."

Donish grimaced slightly as he took one of the two armchairs opposite us while his wife took the other. "I still don't see how you got my name," he said.

"It's a little complicated," I responded.

"You look like someone from a TV series," Mrs. Donish suddenly said. I realized she was speaking to my partner. Apparently I did not look like someone from a TV series. "How long have you been a private detective?"

Malone shifted on her seat. "Just a few years. Before that I was a police detective with the Portland Bureau. Why?"

The woman shrugged and glanced at her husband. "I wanted to be so many things when I was a little girl. Private detective never occurred to me."

"So what did you end up doing?"

Delores Donish sat back and spread her arms to take in the room, the house, maybe the universe. "You're looking at it."

"Ah."

We all simply sat for a moment, trying to figure out what to do with that exchange. I gave up and refocused on Mr. Donish.

He obviously hadn't lost the thread of our conversation. "What's complicated?"

"In the course of investigating the circumstances around the child in the alley, we keep running into dead ends. That's to be expected, of course, when you start looking into a twenty-year-old case—but these seem to be intentional dead ends. Missing records. People who would normally be able to provide us with information being warned off, even fired if they try to help us."

"What does that have to do with me?"

"Do you know City Commissioner Ray Devine?"

He paled a little more and opened his mouth but nothing came out of it.

His wife bounced a little forward on her chair. "Of course we know Ray! He's a dear old friend. He and Bren practically grew up together."

A hand palm out to his wife. "Let me handle this, Dilly."

I had to suppress a smile. Dilly Donish was far worse.

"As my wife says," he went on, "we know Commissioner Devine. He is a long-time friend. I still don't understand your line of questioning. I'm sure we have nothing to offer that can help you."

"That's quite possible," I agreed, "but Devine's name came up and in the course of doing a little research on him my partner found a photo on your Facebook page that you entitled 'The Six.' We're talking to all the people in that photo just in case any of them can provide relevant information."

He sat back and squinted at me. "You're talking to me and all those other men about a twenty-year-old case because I posted an old photo of us together? That's awfully thin. What's really going on here?"

Malone spoke up. "The honest answer, Mr. Donish, is that we don't know. We're mystified about a number of things concerning what should have been a straightforward set of inquiries. Somebody doesn't want us to know something for some reason. That's how much in the dark we are. So we're following every thread, no matter how thin." She sat forward. "One thing I'm curious about."

"Yes?"

"Who took the photo?"

Delores Donish held up her hand and giggled. "I did. That was soon after we started dating and Bren had bought me this little camera...." Both her voice and her fond expression faded as her husband glared at us.

"Why in the world do you care who took the photo?"

My partner glared right back. "There are five men in the photo and yet you called it The Six. We thought perhaps the sixth person was the photographer. But that person wasn't your wife, your future wife, was it? So, tell me: Why did you call it that?"

He took a moment for that one. "It's just an old inside joke."

"Can you explain further?"

He was regaining some color and looking grim. "No, I cannot. It was a joke. Between friends. Nothing more."

She gave him the look. "Then I wonder why Scott Abernathy literally ran away from us when we asked him about it."

Sitting forward now, beginning to flush, heading toward downright hostile. "I have no idea. You would have to ask him—and I think you should leave now. I have nothing further to say."

"Bren...."

"I've got this, Dilly."

"Do you know who the sixth person was, Mrs. Donish?" I asked.

She looked genuinely bewildered at this point. "No, I have no idea. There were five of them in the photo. I didn't even know Bren had posted it, much less what he called it."

"We have nothing further to say," announced her husband.

I exchanged a look with Malone and then we rose together. Mrs. Donish also stood. "I'll show you out."

At the front door, she lay a hand on Malone's arm, just for a split second. "I don't know what's gotten into my husband. Bren is not like that. I'll talk to him."

My partner handed her a card. "My number's on here. If you think there's something we should know, give me a call."

Delores Donish looked at the card held delicately between two fingers, then up at Malone. "If I think I should, I will."

We said our goodbyes and left her standing in the doorway, watching our backs.

"I'm betting that she will think she should," my wife and partner muttered as we approached the car.

"You think she'd be willing to betray her husband?" I asked as I put the car in drive and pulled away.

"I think she's a good woman who's a big fan of female detectives. If she does learn something, my bet is she'd see it as helping, rather than betraying, him. But I could be wrong. Maybe she won't learn anything. Maybe she won't call."

"We could certainly use some kind of break."

"That we could." A block later: "Do we want to check in with Sylvia or Agatha while we're in Lake Oswego? I'm getting tired of the commute."

I thought that over. "Well, we've got nothing new to tell our client and I don't even want to know what's going on at Agatha's house, so I vote we head back home. Enjoy our Sunday evening."

"Roger that."

CHAPTER THIRTY-EIGHT

"There's still one to go, you know."

I looked over at my partner. We'd just gotten in to the office the next morning and already established that there were no emails or voicemails of compelling interest. Which is to say, none relevant to Sylvia Ralston's case.

"Vernon Kennett," I agreed. "I'd suggest we not ambush a big-time attorney in some parking lot. No telling what he might sue us for—and that approach hasn't worked for us with any of the others, anyway."

She turned to her keyboard. "I haven't checked his social media. Maybe there will be another way to get to him." She hit two or three keys and then stopped to turn to me again. "And, you know, we don't want to forget that Sylvia's adoptive father could still tie into this somehow. We've got those years of unexplained payments hanging out there. Wouldn't it be a bummer if we were going down the wrong rabbit hole all along?"

I shook my head. "I don't think that's possible at this point. Whatever it is we're not supposed to find, whether it has to do with Mr. Ralston or one of the guys in that photo or a yet-unidentified Mr. X, clearly there is someone here and now, in Portland, doing his or her best to foil our investigation. We don't have to figure out why if we can identify who. That should give us the why."

She snorted. "Foil. I like that. We should keep an eye out for a man with an old-fashioned pointy mustache."

I huffed right back at her. "Yeah, you do that. Meanwhile, you might as well check Macintosh's and Abernathy's social media while you're at it. We still need to find good opportunities to chat with them. I'll get Eleanor on a parallel search, if she's free. No more parking lots."

"Agreed. No more parking lots." She went back to typing.

Eleanor did have some time, but even with all three of us on the quest, Malone and I had no new ideas, no good ones anyway, as we finally called a break and headed across the street for lunch at the Home Run.

"We know Kennett belongs to a men's club, but ambushing him there wouldn't be any more effective than in a parking lot," I said as we crossed the street. "Misrepresenting ourselves to get an appointment wouldn't buy us any cooperation," I went on. Malone didn't even bother to reply as we reached the entrance and made our way inside to the blare and glare of a noon-time sports bar.

We found a free table toward the back, ordered our standard burgers and fries, and spent a minute or two inspecting the various TV screens in sight. Mostly American football. One European football. One tennis doubles match.

"There's got to be a way to break this open," my partner finally said.

"We'll find it."

"Hopefully before one of us gets killed."

"That, too."

Our food arrived and we ate in further silence. I found that our miserable lack of progress and new ideas robbed me of my appetite. I managed to finish the burger but left half the fries on my plate, an occasion almost unprecedented.

Not to worry. My lovely wife and partner, who wouldn't lose her appetite if the earth was going to be destroyed by a rogue asteroid five minutes from now, finished them for me.

We were settled back at our desks and I was just beginning to wonder once again what the hell we were going to do next when the agency line rang. I picked it up. "McCall-Malone Detective Agency, Clint McCall speaking."

"Hey, Clint." It was Daisy.

"Hey, kiddo. Everything all right?"

"I guess you could say that."

"Which means?" I caught Malone's inquiring eye and mouthed Daisy's name, then hit the speaker button.

"We're seeing a *lot* of Agatha and her crew now that she's discovered us." Malone and I both smiled at that. No surprise.

"It's keeping my guest author from her writing—or at least it was."

"You mean she's off in her room and leaving you stuck with them?" I chuckled. "Though I'm assuming they aren't in the room with you right now."

"They aren't. And she isn't in her room, either. Apparently she's decided to stop complaining about the interruptions and go with the flow. They're dancing."

My partner leaned forward at that. "Dancing?"

"Yep. There's like a little party in the living room and they're dancing to country music."

I realized then that I could hear "Wichita Lineman" faintly in the background and I had to ask: "Who's dancing with who?"

"Agatha's dancing with Beck, Sylvia with Rodney, and Morty is dancing around my cat Xerxes who is not impressed." She lowered her voice slightly. "I think Sylvia and Rodney might become an item."

That drew a major snort from my partner. "I told Clint that Rodney was smitten," she said to the speaker, "but it's hard to believe that Sylvia's smitten back. She's talented, intelligent, successful. He's...not."

"Opposites attract?" suggested Daisy.

"Hah."

I found it hard to believe, too, but my concern was with our client's safety rather than her love life. "No new threats?" I asked Daisy.

"Not a thing. How's the investigation going? When do you think it will be safe for Sylvia to go home?"

"You getting tired of having her around?"

"Not really, but all things considered I'd kind of like my house back."

Now the Dixie Chicks were singing about Earl in the background. "I understand, but the truth is that our investigation is going nowhere so far and not even fast. She needs to stay put for a while."

A sigh. "Okay. Keep me updated. I'd better go try to save Morty from Xerxes. Talk to you later."

"Sylvia and Rodney?" Malone asked the room at large after I hung up. "Didn't see that coming."

"At least we know nothing's happening at Agatha's house." I was about to add that we needed to make some progress so that poor Daisy could have her house back when the agency line rang again. I answered and a very smooth, if unfamiliar, male voice said, "This is Vernon Kennett. I'd like to stop by your office and have a chat. Perhaps this afternoon?"

I had to take a second. "That would be fine," I replied as the adrenaline surged. I glanced at the time. One-thirty. "How about two o'clock? Do you know where our office is?"

"Two o'clock will be good. You're above the used bookstore, right?"

"That's us."

"Two, then."

I hung up and met Malone's inquiring gaze. "I think we finally just made some progress."

CHAPTER THIRTY-NINE

"Mr. McCall, Ms. Malone. I'm Vernon Kennett."

The man had aged well in the ten years since the photo, looking very much like a mature Eddie Murphy as he paused in our doorway to take in our classic PI ambience. The bespoke gray suit, high-end loafers, well-trimmed mustache, close-cropped black hair with just a hint of gray, and the deep, smooth-as-silk voice all added up to high-priced lawyer with panache.

I stood and gestured invitingly at our guest chairs. "Come in, Mr. Kennett. We're looking forward to talking with you."

"Glad to hear it." He settled into the chair on my side but was looking at Malone. "I hope I didn't offend you. Do you prefer 'Mrs. McCall' now?"

He'd done some research.

"No, I kept my maiden name."

"Ah." Ever so subtly, his tone added, "one of those."

He transferred his attention to me, but I chose to remain silent. I knew my partner.

"You asked for the meeting, Mr. Kennett," she said, taking the control he didn't want to give. "What can we do for you?"

His left eyebrow twitched just a bit as he turned back to her. "You've been talking—or attempting to talk—to my clients, efforts that begin to verge on harassment in some instances, and I'm wondering if there's a way we could satisfactorily redirect or even end your investigation insofar as you seem to think it might involve them."

I was just thinking to myself that that was an obfuscatory mouthful when Malone zeroed in on what I agreed was the most important part: "Clients? Plural? Who, exactly, are you representing?"

A slight tilt of the head. "All of them, myself included."

She tilted hers right back. "All six, or all five?"

That froze him in place for a moment. Good for you, Mrs. McCall, I thought to myself.

"Five," he finally said.

I jumped in. "And you want us to leave all of them alone, yourself included."

He took a breath, maybe a little rattled by us coming at him from both sides, but trying his best not to show it and doing a pretty good job. "I understand that you are working on behalf of a woman who was found in a Portland alley twenty years ago, trying to determine her history prior to that and an explanation for her presence in the alley. Traumatic amnesia, I believe. I can assure you that none of my clients know anything that could be of help."

"Then," I asked, "why didn't they all just meet with us as Ray Devine did, as you are, and say that? Brendan Donish threw us out of his house. Macintosh and Abernathy got away from us as quickly as they could when we tried to talk to them, refusing to answer any questions at all. That doesn't sound like people who are entirely innocent...of relevant information."

"Some prominent people do not want to be bothered by private investigators. They have enough to deal with already."

Malone leaned in to him a bit. "We'd still like to talk to Warren Macintosh and Scott Abernathy."

He sat back from her a bit. "I'm afraid that won't be possible. They have nothing to contribute and they're both very busy men."

She scooted slightly forward on her chair. I was enjoying her much more than Vernon Kennett apparently was. "Then tell us this: Who is the sixth person, the one *not* in Brendon Donish's Facebook photo?"

He pursed his lips and firmed up his shoulders. No female was going to push him around. "I'm afraid I can't reveal his name."

Aha. We finally had confirmation that there was such a person.

"What is the meaning of the photo? Clearly it has some serious significance."

He took a deep breath. "Not really."

Malone locked eyes with him and I swear she did not blink.

After maybe ten seconds, he took another audible breath and sat back, making a point of relaxing his body. "Let me tell you a story."

I glanced at my partner and gestured that he should proceed.

"About twenty-five years ago, six teenage boys, good friends since early childhood, made a pact to have each other's backs and support one another in reaching their maximum potential. They were all smart boys, each with his own set of talents, and they wanted one another to succeed in life. It was a serious pact and it has held up all this time, with each of us reaching a level of success we might not have reached without the support of the others."

"And yet," I said, "there were only five in the photo of The Six."

"There was a falling out. By the time that photo was taken, one young man was no longer part of the group, part of the pact."

"What was his name?"

"I'm not prepared to give you that information."

"Why not?"

"It simply isn't relevant. He hasn't been an associate of ours for a very long time. You asked about the significance of the photo and I have given you an explanation."

"So why not tell us who he is?" asked Malone.

"I repeat: because it isn't relevant. There is simply no need for you to know."

"And if we don't agree? If we find out by other means? What's the harm in that?"

He threw up his hands. "I can't stop you from pursuing irrelevant information. I can, if necessary, stop you from harassing my clients. Keep coming back to them and there will be consequences."

I held up my own hand. "If they have nothing to do with our client's case, you have nothing to worry about."

He nodded and stood. "Then I believe our business is concluded. Good day."

And, with that, he left.

I looked at my partner and she looked at me. "What the hell was that?" I asked.

"*That*," she replied, "was pretty fucking solid proof that we need to keep harassing these guys—all six of them."

CHAPTER FORTY

"It could be the mystery man who's sending the threats and the shooters and the thugs." Malone filled Maxine's dish with kibble. "The mysterious number six, rather than Devine or any of the others that we know about. Who's to say how powerful and connected Mystery Man is. Maybe it's the mayor. Or the head of the Chamber of Commerce. Or, hell, the Police Chief. That would explain Mike getting push-back, for sure."

From my seat at the kitchen table, I watched Maxine dive in while Stella, with reasonable patience, awaited the filling of her own bowl. "Is that what we're officially calling him now? Mystery Man?"

My wife put the cat food back in the cabinet. "Well, we finally know for sure that there is such a person. We have to call him something until we get a name." She closed the cabinet door and glared at me. "And we will get a fucking name."

I held up both hands. "I agree. We will definitely get a name." I waited until she sat down across from me. "I don't think the Chief has control over much besides Mike, though. How do we explain all these dead ends?"

She snorted. "The police chief with backing from a city commissioner, a big-time lawyer, a media mogul, a wealthy developer, and a major banker would have no trouble creating all those obstacles—and threats."

"Yeah, but Mystery Man has been on the outs for years. He wouldn't have their backing."

"So says the guy who might be his attorney."

"Point taken." It struck me that we'd been home for more than half-an-hour and Devon had said nothing about dinner. "You hungry? Should we nuke something or go around the corner to the Pen and Pastry?"

She stood up and headed for the refrigerator. "I don't want to go out again. I want to bat this around until we have some clarity and a plan for tomorrow." She opened the fridge and checked the freezer. "How about a couple of chicken fried chicken meals?"

"Sounds yummy. Redundant, but yummy."

She removed them from the freezer and headed for the microwave. Maxine and Stella, meanwhile, butted heads over their water dish.

Malone popped the two frozen dinners into the microwave, closed the door, and started the timer. She leaned against the counter to give me a considering eye. "So we think one of these six men had something to do with what happened to Sylvia."

"That's one possibility," I agreed, "maybe even the most likely one, but it's also possible that one of them is protecting a person who was involved, or is being paid or otherwise leveraged to derail the investigation for some other reason. It's possible that inquiries into Sylvia's past could reveal information having nothing directly to do with what happened to her. Maybe about those payments to her father, for instance."

The microwave dinged and she turned to retrieve our speedy but minimally nourishing dinners. "That's too damned many possibilities. No wonder we're still running in circles— while being shot at, home invaded, and God knows what else before we figure anything out."

We ate and talked, played with the cats and even watched some TV. As had been the case too often lately, we finally had to try to go to sleep without any new insights or ideas.

Which meant that our landline ringing at three in the morning was even less welcome than usual. There was an extension on my side of the bed and I eventually managed to pick it up, noting the time and already feeling a knife-edge of adrenaline cutting through my grogginess.

"Hello?"

"Clint, it's Mike Whitehall."

I sat up, wide awake. "Who's dead?"

"The lawyer, Vernon Kennett. From his calendar, it looks like you and Devon were his last meeting. We need to talk."

CHAPTER FORTY-ONE

He meant right then, at the crime scene, so we were up and dressed within minutes and headed for Kennett's office near the corner of 11th and Main—not that far from our own office.

We couldn't miss it: three patrol cars with lights rotating, a CSI van, the medical examiner, and several other official-looking vehicles obstructed 11th. Even at 3:20 a.m., the nearest parking spot we could find was a block away on Main.

Kennett's block was tree-lined, with multi-storied multi-use buildings on both sides, and probably would have projected a peaceful ambience without all the death groupies in attendance. His was the second building on the right side as we came around the corner from Main.

We identified ourselves to a uniform manning the entrance and he told us to proceed to the fifth floor where we would be met by Lieutenant Whitehall.

There was another uniform stationed by the elevator and still another by the doors on the fifth floor. He indicated we should hold there until Whitehall appeared. We were standing in a spacious, well-appointed corridor with just three or four doors on each side, meaning that the office suites were probably very large. The real hive of activity was at the far end to our left, where the corridor ended at double doors, wide open now, with a busy, posh-looking reception area visible beyond.

Mike Whitehall strode through the crowd of uniforms and forensic specialists and down the hallway to us.

"Thanks for coming," he said as he shook first my hand and then Malone's. "I wanted you to see the scene in case it brings to mind any connections to your meeting earlier today—and, of course, I want to know all about that meeting." He stopped us for a second, nearly at the double doors. "You did have the meeting earlier today, right?"

"We did," I answered. "He came to our office. We haven't been here before."

He motioned us ahead, through the doors and into the reception area. "Good. No fingerprints."

My partner, as is her wont, snorted. "Are we on the suspect list, Mike?"

"Yours was the last meeting on his calendar and you were already looking at him in connection with your case, so let's say persons of interest."

"That's fine."

Meanwhile, I was eyeing the security camera focused on the wide doorway that was now behind us. "I assume you've checked the security footage."

"We would if there were any. The system was shut down at eleven-thirty last night, probably either by Kennett or his killer."

"And the TOD?"

"About a half-hour later."

"Who found the body between midnight and three in the morning?"

"Cleaning crew. None of them saw anyone else in the building."

"So," Malone said as she surveyed the reception area, "either he shut down the system because he didn't want his visitor identified or an intruder shut it down somehow before getting in here to kill him."

"I'm betting on the former, myself," Mike responded. "We've already determined that Kennett owns the building and therefore would have access to the security system—which is very high quality. Our guys say it would take CIA-level expertise to even have a shot at hacking it."

"Huh." I took a breath. "Let's go look at that crime scene."

It was a classic high-end attorney's office: big desk a little off-center to our left and facing us, bookshelves heavy with legal tomes, comfortable leather-covered furniture, floor to ceiling window looking out over the street. The ambience, however, was somewhat ruined by the body sprawled forward across the desk.

He was no longer the handsome gentleman we'd met just hours before. It looked like he'd been seated but either had started to rise or had been blown out of the chair and across the desk by the impact of the bullet. The latter was possible. Even though there wasn't a lot of room between his chair and the credenza behind him, he'd been shot in the back of the head—and it must have been a big gun, at least a .45. His head was turned toward us and he had very little face left.

"Blech," my partner muttered.

We all stood in silence for a minute, surveying the scene. "It doesn't look like anything is disturbed," Malone said thoughtfully, "aside from the victim himself, of course. No fight. No robbery. Nobody looking for something."

"And he was shot in the back of the head while sitting at his desk," I added, "which means that he let the killer walk behind him...to look over his shoulder? Maybe pour them a drink?" There were a couple of bottles of good whiskey and several empty glasses on the credenza. "It had to be somebody he trusted, somebody he needed to meet in the middle of the night with no record of the meeting."

"I agree," Mike said. "Any thoughts on who that might have been?"

"He's had a successful practice for many years," Malone noted. "He's got hundreds of clients. Could be any of them, or someone else in his life."

"But he's killed just hours after he met with the two of you, who are interested in several of those clients."

I shrugged a little. "Yeah, well, I'd say coincidences happen...."

"If," Mike finished for me, "you believed in coincidences." He paused a beat. "Like I said, I'm going to want to hear *all* about that meeting—and anything you can add to what you've already told me concerning Sylvia Ralston."

CHAPTER FORTY-TWO

Considering that our Tuesday had started at three a.m., it was no big surprise that we made it into the office right at eight, our usual time.

We'd gotten no more sleep after a long conversation with Mike over coffee in a bistro near Kennett's office building. He now knew everything we did about Sylvia Ralston, including all of our speculations that we could bring to mind. Which, unfortunately, resulted in him being as mystified as we were. New eyes led to no new conclusions.

The end result was that he would proceed with his own investigation, starting cold from Kennett's crime scene, while we carried on with ours. Our focus was still on Ray Devine, Brendon Donish, and the other two remaining men from the photo.

Mike needed more reason than our speculations to immediately question such prominent citizens about a grisly murder, but he assured us that he would keep an eye out for any possible connections.

Malone and I had returned home to get more properly dressed, feed the cats, and have breakfast. We agreed that we were going to take another shot at Devine, Donish, Abernathy, and Macintosh before Mike got to them, if he did. They might have some interesting reactions to the murder of their lifelong friend and attorney.

In the office we spent an hour responding to a couple of inquiries and pinned down a possible new client who, fortunately, was not in a big rush. Speaking of clients, we decided that before doing anything else we should have a sit-down with our current client. We hadn't really talked with her about the case on Saturday, what with the focus on the kitchen confrontation between Agatha Pepper and Butch Faron, and now there was a possibly related killing. She deserved to be at least as up-to-date as the Portland Police Bureau.

I called Daisy's house right at nine to see if Sylvia was awake and willing to meet with us. She was, so we headed for Lake Oswego yet again.

The drive was without incident and we soon found ourselves sitting in the same chairs in the same spacious living room that we'd occupied the previous Wednesday, only this time Daisy stayed with us at Sylvia's request, seated beside her on the couch. They were both dressed casually in sweatpants and tops, both barefoot.

I hadn't really thought about it when we were dealing with Butch Faron, but it appeared that staying with Daisy had been good for our client. She no longer looked quite the rail-thin waif that she had when she first appeared in our office. She'd put on some weight, her color was better, and overall she seemed to be feeling more confident. I hated that we'd likely undercut that confidence more than a little with this meeting.

"How's your writing coming?" I asked by way of easing into it.

She flushed a little and grinned. "Great. I'm well into the next book. The space that Daisy has given me to use is just perfect and of course it's really nice to have someone to visit with when I take breaks."

"More than one someone lately," Daisy observed with a grin of her own.

"Oh yeah?" From my partner's slightly dubious expression, I knew she expected the same answer I did.

"We've suddenly begun to see a lot of Ms. Pepper's nephew," our hostess confirmed. She glanced at her watch. "In fact, I wouldn't be surprised if he showed up any time now."

Sylvia, meanwhile, was flushing even more than before. "I do usually take a break around nine-thirty." She breathed deeply and seemed to gather herself. "But you're not here to talk about my books or my social life. Do you have news?"

I took my own breath. "We do, but it isn't good. There's been a death, a murder, possibly connected with the case."

Just like that, the flush went to pale and both women sat forward, Daisy laying a hand on Sylvia's arm. "What?" our client gasped. "Who was murdered? How? Why?"

I held up both hands, palms out, realizing that maybe I could have done a little more easing in before I dropped the murder bomb.

"An attorney named Vernon Kennett was shot and killed in his office last night. It may have nothing to do with you at all, but I have to ask: Does the name ring any bells?"

She did give it a moment's thought. "No. No, I've never heard of him. Why do you think his murder could have anything to do with me?" She was already calming and getting a little color back. She patted Daisy's hand that still rested on her arm as if to indicate she was okay. And maybe she was. Maybe she'd found a new core of strength here at Daisy's house.

In response to Sylvia's question, Malone laid out the sequence of events and discoveries that had led us to Vernon Kennett, or rather him to us. I had to admit, it sounded convoluted even to me.

When Malone finished and sat back, both young women were kind of squinting at us.

"So...," Daisy finally drawled, "you really have no idea whether any of the men in that photo have anything to do with Sylvia. And one of them is a city commissioner?"

"Yep," I agreed. "That's about the size of it. We have a lot of mysterious dead ends and someone seems to be behind it. It could be one of them. It could be someone else. Whoever it is probably *does* have something to do with Sylvia."

"Or my father," our client noted.

I nodded. "Or your father. We've nothing new on those mysterious payments, either."

Daisy held up a finger. "I wonder if it could be more than one person."

"Well," responded Malone, "we're talking about five or six old friends, so sure."

"No, I mean two unrelated people, operating independently."

"That's interesting. Why?"

"Because it's such an odd combination of organized and chaotic. On the one hand, it looks like somebody has had a plan in place for twenty years to deal with inquiries about what happened to Sylvia. This highly organized person obviously has a lot of power, know-how, contacts, resources.... But, on the other hand, you have this weird sequence of tail, threats, shooter, drone, threatening thugs, home invaders, a drone outside our office window for God's sakes, and finally a proper visit from a reputable attorney who immediately ends up dead. That's about as disorganized as you can get."

"Good points," I said. "We've talked about that disparity, though we've not considered that it could be two completely unrelated people."

"Or," Sylvia chimed in thoughtfully, "one highly organized person who got triggered, had some sort of psychological break, and became disorganized."

"Ah, yes," agreed my partner, "that's possible, too. More likely, in my opinion."

"But still.... Is it all to cover up the story behind what happened to me? Who the hell was I, if that's the case?"

I almost chuckled. "And we're back to what you hired us for. It's our case, whether it's *the* case or not."

"And maybe the biggest irony of all this," added Malone, "is that if we hadn't hit all these dead ends, had all these threats, etc., we might not have come up with much more than those mysterious payments anyway. We'd have looked at the foster care records, the police report, whatever news coverage our reporter friend could have come up with...and what would all that have told us that you can't remember? Not much, I'm thinking. And you know what else I'm thinking? The fact that we had no real trouble coming up with the info about the payments tells me that they are probably not what you need to worry about."

Our client frowned. "I'd still like to know what they were for. A cover-up? A benefactor?"

"We'll find out if we can," I said. "We're not going to let any of this go, not after everything that's happened."

"Thank you."

There wasn't much more to say, so Malone and I took our leave. Rodney Pepper was hurrying up the walk as we came down it. His hair was combed and he was wearing a polo shirt rather than a t-shirt, generally looking older than his years and more mature than was likely. "What are you two doing here? Is Sylvie all right?"

Sylvie?

"She's fine," I said. "We were just updating her on the case, talking things over."

"Oh gee. You guys probably used up all of her break. She'll want to go back to her book now."

"I have a hunch she'll need a little more break time."

"Good. That's good." He trotted away toward the front door.

I looked at Malone. Malone looked at me. There was nothing to say. We both shrugged and headed for the car.

CHAPTER FORTY-THREE

"Do you think we should add Sonny Sampson to the mix at Daisy's house?" Malone asked as we mounted the stairs to the second floor of our building. "We know we're dealing with a killer now."

"I don't think so," I said as we walked the short distance down the hallway to our door. "There's been no further direct threat to Sylvia."

"Maybe Sonny could protect her from Rodney."

I laughed as I unlocked our door. "I'm afraid that's out of our hands."

Malone stowed her Glock in its drawer and sat down. "Yeah, I guess you're right. In that case, the next item is to plan how to re-approach the remaining four of The Six. Or five. Whatever the hell."

I stowed my own gun in the drawer and sat down, noting that there were no new voicemails. "Do we really think it will do any good? Only Devine was really willing to meet with us before. Donish wouldn't have if his wife hadn't had a girl crush on you. Abernathy and Macintosh fled like scared rabbits."

She shrugged. "You never know what impact the murder of a friend may have. They could be frightened into talking or vice versa. We can at least see what Ray Devine and Brendon Donish have to say now. Certainly the pot has been stirred a good deal more since we talked to them last."

"True enough." I picked up the phone and dialed City Hall. I was soon transferred to the ever-perky Thea, who put me on hold while she checked Commissioner Devine's schedule.

She returned sounding substantially less enthusiastic about life. "I'm afraid the Commissioner is tied up for the rest of the week. It's a very busy time right now."

Aha. Now he didn't want to talk to us. "Oh? What's going

on? I haven't seen anything in the papers about unusual activity at City Hall."

She sounded definitely taken aback. "It's...it's several special projects that Commissioner Devine is working on. He's just...very busy. You could try calling back next week."

So much for that. I thanked her and hung up. "Young Thea," I said to my partner, "is not a good liar. Devine has 'special projects' that are keeping him too busy to talk to us this week. Maybe next week."

Malone frowned. "Or, maybe not."

"That would be my guess. So: do we think it's because Kennett's murder has frightened him or because he murdered Kennett?"

The frown turned into a grimace. "I don't know. The killer commissioner scenario is a little hard to swallow, but he doesn't strike me as a guy who frightens easily."

"We should rethink Eleanor doing that deep dive on the Ray Devine of twenty years ago. I believe it would be worth the money."

"I agree. Why don't you go see if she's got the time while I find out how Warren Macintosh is feeling about us now? Maybe I can get Alison her show back."

I gave her a look from our doorway. "I'm sure she would be very grateful."

I heard Malone's snort as I closed the door behind me.

Eleanor was in her office, but in the midst of a client tax crisis and unwilling to commit to when she could do the new research for us. Maybe tomorrow, she said as she shooed me back into the hallway. I muttered something about it being important, but since I was muttering at a closed door it probably didn't do any good.

I reentered our office to find my partner slamming the handset back into its cradle.

"No luck?" I inquired as I crossed to the desk. "Which one was that?"

"Abernathy, who actually said something interesting before politely telling me to go fuck myself."

"You got past his receptionist?"

"I did, but only because he wanted to tell me that he valued his life and never wanted to hear from us again."

I sat down at that. "Ha. So he thinks that Kennett was killed because he talked to us."

"Or he knows that he was."

"Yeah. Yeah." I gestured to the phone. "You're on a roll. Give Donish a call and see what he has to say."

She put this one on speaker and punched in the number. After a couple of rings, Delores Donish answered. "Donish residence."

"Mrs. Donish? This is Devon Malone. Is your husband there?"

"No, he's at a building site. I don't expect him home until this evening. Maybe late. And I don't think he wants to talk to you anyway."

"I'm sorry to hear that. It would really be helpful if we could sit down with him again."

She made an odd little clucking noise. "I seriously doubt that. Did you hear about our friend Vernon Kennett being killed?"

"Yes, we know about that."

"It has Bren very upset and he seems to think it's your fault, yours and Mr. McCall's. I can't imagine that he'd be willing to help you with anything."

"Nevertheless...."

"What if I offered you some information? Would that be good enough? Would you leave us alone?"

Malone exchanged a look with me. "That would depend on the information."

"How about the identity of that sixth person you were asking about?"

I'm sure my eyes went as wide as my partner's did, but I kept quiet. She was doing fine.

"That would be good. So you knew all along?"

"No, I had no idea when you guys were here. I did take the photo, but I didn't know Bren had posted it and called it The

Six. Your questions made me curious, though, and his reluctance to tell me more about it made me even more curious, so yesterday evening I fed him his favorite meal, which happens to involve a lot of wine, and asked him again. Bren is easy when he drinks too much."

"So what did he tell you?" I was curious to see if he told her the same story that Kennett had told us.

"He said there were originally six friends. That was what the title meant."

So far so good. "Did he happen to tell you who that sixth friend was? That's what we really need to know."

"Yes, he did. It was somebody named Carl Gunther."

CHAPTER FORTY-FOUR

"I am going to kick that son of a bitch right in the gonads. When I'm done with him, he'll never walk again!"

Malone had jumped up and started to pace back and forth the second the call ended. I had rarely seen her so angry. Maybe never.

"That fucker looked us right in the eye and claimed to barely know Ray Devine. Now it turns out they've known each other for decades!"

I kept my seat but held up both hands to try to slow her down. "They knew each other when they were young, but remember that Kennett said there'd been a falling out before that photo was taken. If they haven't been friends for more than twenty years, maybe Gunther didn't see the point in mentioning it. Devine didn't admit to it, either. Maybe they've really had nothing to do with each other all this time."

She waved that off and kept pacing. "Bullshit. I told you Carl reacted when we told him about Sylvia being found in that alley. He *knew* what we were talking about. I would swear to it." She planted herself back in her chair and glared at me. "And now we find out he was part of...something with Devine and these four other guys maybe back around that same time." She pounded a fist on the desk. "What the fuck were they doing back then?"

"I'm guessing that Gunther would have the answer to that. Maybe we should go ask him."

"I'm guessing Carl knows a whole shitload he could tell us and chose not to." She took a deep breath and seemed to calm a little. "Before we go running off to his office again, ask yourself this: Who do we know that might be able to stymie record searches and certainly would be able to come up with all the shooters and home invaders and other thugs that he wanted?"

That gave me pause. "You think Gunther is behind all this? He's your biggest fan, next to me of course."

"That could be why I'm still uninjured. It could all be just to warn us off."

"He knows better."

She slapped the desktop this time. "Well, then, what the hell do you think is going on?"

"If you were right about his no-reaction reaction, he knows or at least has an idea about what happened to Sylvia Ralston. If Delores Donish got the truth from her drunk husband, we know that Gunther was into something with Devine and the rest at some point *before* Sylvia was found in that alley. We have no idea how it all ties together, if it does."

She was on her feet again and retrieving her Glock. "Then I'm going to ask him."

I was on my feet. "No. We're going to go ask him."

It was faster to walk than to tackle the late-morning downtown traffic. At eleven-forty-five exactly, we were standing before Mrs. Pinkerton's desk and I was hoping Gunther hadn't taken an early lunch.

No such luck. "He's not here," Mrs. Pinkerton announced in an unusually clipped manner, "and I don't know when he'll be back."

"I thought you were the keeper of his schedule," Malone said. "You always know where he is and when he'll be back. You sure he's not in there hiding from us?"

That jerked the elderly receptionist to attention. "Hiding from you? Carl Gunther doesn't hide from anybody." She dropped her right hand to the drawer where we knew she kept her gun. "Get out of here. Now."

I put a hand on Malone's arm. "Wait a minute," I said to Mrs. Pinkerton. "This is not like you. And not like Gunther to be off your radar. Something has you worried. Maybe we can help. Spill."

She pursed her lips, took a moment, and looked at Malone rather than me. "He likes you, you know. He doesn't like many people."

I too looked at my partner, who was currently squinting in apparent bewilderment at Mrs. Pinkerton. "I'm not following you, Agnes," she finally said.

The right hand came up from lurking near the gun drawer, joined the left hand in front of her, and she began twisting them together. "Carl got a call right after we arrived this morning and he left. He didn't tell me where he was going. For the first time in fifteen years he didn't tell me where he was going. He hasn't called and he's not answering his cell. All I know is that his car is parked in the six-thousand block of northeast Ainsworth."

That was so unexpected that I laughed. "How the hell do you know that?"

She reached over and held up what must have been her own cell phone. "I have an app that can track his GPS, just in case he ever gets in trouble."

"And you think," Malone said, "that he's in trouble."

"Well, he's not here when he's supposed to be, I can't reach him, and that's a first. Plus, whoever called him was using a burner. I already checked that."

"I guess," I said to my partner, "we'd better go see what's in the six-thousand block of northeast Ainsworth." I looked at Mrs. Pinkerton. "You want to come along?"

"I'll hold the fort—and call you if his car moves."

"Okay, what kind of car are we looking for?"

"A gray 2018 Bentley Continental."

"Wow," I said. "Okay. Not too many of those around town. We'll be in touch."

We got out of the building as quickly as possible, given the leisurely, twenty-two-floor elevator ride, and headed back to our parking lot across from the office, walking at a pace just short of a trot.

We were within a block of our goal when my cell phone signaled an incoming call. I expected to see Gunther's office number on the display, but it was Mike Whitehall.

I put it to my ear as I kept up with Malone. "Hey, Mike, any leads on Kennett?"

"No, but I do have another dead body."

CHAPTER FORTY-FIVE

I grabbed my partner's arm and stopped us both abruptly in the middle of the sidewalk. Whatever my expression was, it caused a young woman pushing a stroller to give us a wide berth as she went by.

"Who is it?" I asked. I held my breath, half-expecting to hear Carl Gunther's name.

"Brendon Donish."

"Shit." I held the phone and punched on the speaker. "It's Mike," I told Malone. "Brendon Donish is dead."

"Where are you guys?" Mike asked. "I hear traffic."

"On foot, about a block from the office. We're heading for the lot because we need to be someplace."

"Yes, you do. You need to be here at his house. Again, you were among the last people to talk to my victim and besides that I could use some help dealing with his hysterical wife who seems to think it's her fault he's dead—and somehow you guys seem to be involved in that, too."

"He was killed at his house?" Delores Donish had said he wasn't home when we called.

"At one of his work sites. He took a bullet in the forehead. No witnesses. About an hour ago." Just about the same time that his wife called us.

Malone was frowning mightily by this point.

"Look, Mike," I said, "we've got a fairly urgent matter going on here. How about one of us comes to you and the other takes care of what we need to do here?"

"Sorry. A second murder trumps fairly urgent. I want you both. Now."

There was no point in trying to persuade a Portland police lieutenant that a city crime boss should take precedence over his homicide investigation. I said we'd be there as soon as possible and we continued on to the parking lot.

It took nearly half-an-hour to reach the Donish home. It was just before noon and as we walked from the car up to the house my partner alternated between muttering about lunch and about that hypothetical branch office in Lake Oswego.

Mike met us at the front door. "I've got an officer sitting with the wife in the kitchen," he said without preamble. "I'm hoping you can help me get a coherent story out of her. She keeps saying it's her fault, which seems to have something to do with the two of you, but I can't understand it. Come on."

"Nothing on the shooter?" I asked him as we hurried through the house.

"Nada," he replied. "Donish was apparently the first one on site. His body was discovered by the crew when they arrived. We're still checking for security cameras in the area, but nothing so far."

In the spacious and inappropriately cheery-looking kitchen we found a woman who was nothing like the put-together wife we'd met on our first visit. She was semi-slumped on a chair at the table, a uniformed female officer standing next to her with one hand on her shoulder. She was dead pale, wearing a blue robe over a nightgown, and her thick black hair looked like she'd had an unpleasant encounter with an electrical outlet. Her hands were clasped tightly together on the tabletop.

"Thanks, Grady," Mike said to the officer. "You can go back to the scene and help with the canvass now."

"Yes, sir," she said, and left the three of us standing awkwardly in front of the new widow.

Malone moved first, rounding the table to sit beside Delores Donish and cover the woman's hands with one of her own. She leaned in a little. "We're very sorry for your loss, Mrs. Donish."

Mike and I quietly seated ourselves across from the two women as Delores Donish took some deep, ragged breaths. "I'm afraid it's my fault," she said softly, practically a whisper.

"You said that before, Mrs. Donish," Mike responded. "Why do you think it could be your fault?"

She took a breath, eyes down and hands twisting under

Malone's. Then she looked up at us. "I woke up during the night and Bren wasn't in bed. I heard him on the phone. I couldn't imagine.... He was so tipsy when we went to bed and it was the middle of the night. What was he doing on the phone?"

"Who was he talking to?" I asked.

"I don't know. He was sobbing. I never heard him cry like that before. It sounded like he was apologizing for something, like he was scared. I couldn't imagine."

"Didn't you ask him about it when he came back to bed?" That was Malone.

"Yes! He just told me to go back to sleep, that we'd talk about it in the morning. But then he put me off again this morning, seemed angry with me, with himself, I don't know. We were supposed to talk about it when he got home, but now...." She carefully pulled her hands out from under Malone's, looked at her, then me. "I'm afraid it's because of what he told me, what I called you about. He was apologizing, afraid, about *something*. Maybe that was it."

Mike opened his mouth, but my partner cut him off. "That doesn't seem very likely, Mrs. Donish. He just told you last night and it sounds like he was killed at about the same time you called. No one could have known that you told us."

By this point our homicide lieutenant looked like his head was going to explode. "What are we talking about here? What did your husband tell you? What did you tell them?"

"There was this photo that I took years ago of my husband and some friends, before we were married...."

Mike was glaring at me. "The photo that you guys were telling me about, Devine and Donish and the rest?"

I nodded as Delores Donish went on. "Mr. McCall and Miss Malone wanted to know why Bren called it The Six when he posted it on Facebook and he wouldn't tell them. But later I got him to tell me, so this morning I called Mr. McCall and Miss Malone to tell them what he said. At the time, I didn't even think to connect it with his weird, drunken phone call in the middle of the night, but now...."

Mike zeroed in on me again. "So what was the answer and could it have gotten Brendon Donish killed?"

I bit the bullet. "The sixth person was Carl Gunther."

"Jesus Christ." All homicide lieutenant now, Mike caught my eye and stood up. "We'll need a formal statement, Mrs. Donish. Meanwhile, is there someone we can call to be with you?"

"I have a sister. I'll call my sister. She lives in Gresham. She'll come."

In the living room, near the front door and as far from Delores Donish as possible, Mike stopped and glowered at the two of us. "You knew that Carl Gunther was in this?"

"We don't know that he is," I said. "All we know is that he was originally part of the group in the photo—and we didn't know that until Mrs. Donish called us this morning."

"Well, I'm sure as hell going to want to talk to him and I don't want either of you calling him or going near his office until after I have. Understood?"

I wasn't about to share that Gunther might be missing and in trouble himself, but I had no problem agreeing with Mike's request.

CHAPTER FORTY-SIX

Thirty minutes later, after an extremely quick stop at a drive-through burger place because Malone threatened divorce as the alternative, I was speeding north on Cully, about to jog left onto 60th.

My partner, between hefty bites of her burger, had called Mrs. Pinkerton to confirm that Gunther's car had not moved. The closer we got to the intersection of 60th and Ainsworth, the more that appeared to be very bad news. The area was remarkably rural-looking, considering that it was inside the Portland city limits.

The undeveloped land right around the intersection we were approaching meant we could easily see that there was only one car parked near the corner on Ainsworth, a gray Bentley Continental. Oddly, it was parked right next to what looked like an abandoned motor boat on the side of the road.

I slowed, pulled around the corner, and stopped about thirty feet short of the car on the opposite side of the road—"road" being a more accurate description than "street" at this point. There was no sign of life around the car and I couldn't see at this distance and angle whether there was anyone inside it.

"This is not looking good," Malone said.

We drew our weapons. "Time to go see how bad it is," I said. We opened our doors simultaneously and eased out onto the rough roadway. We both did a slow 360-degree survey. "I don't see any problem. Do you?"

"No. Let's check out the car."

We approached the vehicle slowly, doing our best to keep an eye out in every direction as we went. There appeared to be no threat and I couldn't see anyone in the Bentley even as we came closer.

I was just thinking this was going to be a bust and a bigger mystery when I heard my partner gasp. One more step and I was also close enough to see that someone was slumped across the front seat of the big car.

Two more big steps and Malone jerked open the door. I could see it was Gunther and I could see blood, a lot of blood, on and around his head which was against the passenger-side door. She had her phone out before I could reach in to grasp the nearest wrist. She was already talking to 911 when I pulled back with the news that he had a weak pulse.

After listening for a moment, she headed around the front of the car to the passenger side, motioning me to follow. She tried the door on that side and found it unlocked, pulling it open, still listening to the phone. "She says to check the wound and see if it's bleeding a lot." She stepped back, still listening.

Well. Okay. It looked like I was nominated, like it or not. I shucked my jacket and tossed it on top of the car as I stepped up to the task; I wasn't going to use that to staunch a bloody head wound. I'd pull off my polo shirt if it could be of use.

Even before I checked Gunther's head, I saw that there was a handgun on the floorboard in front of the passenger seat. Probably his. I wondered if he'd gotten a shot of his own off, but that was for later.

The head wound was definitely treatable, a deep gouge down the left side of his head rather than an entry point, and, luckily for my polo shirt, it was beginning to coagulate. Apparently he'd been lying here for at least an hour or so. I checked his pulse again and it seemed a little stronger. He had to have one hell of a concussion, but with any luck he would live. How well, remained to be seen.

Malone held the phone away from her ear, looking over my shoulder. "You think he's going to make it?"

"I'd say he's got a good chance. The bullet didn't penetrate his skull, the bleeding has almost stopped, and he has a good pulse."

"That's a lot of blood that he lost."

"Yes, it is." I could already hear sirens in the distance.

"I shouldn't have insisted we stop for food. We might...."

"That made no difference," I interrupted. "The blood

spatter on the seat here is already coagulating and so is his head wound, for that matter. This was done before you ever took a bite of your burger."

"Still, if he bleeds out...."

"He won't, not now."

Just then we could see the ambulance and two patrol cars about three blocks away, coming fast. "They're here," she told the operator, and hung up. I kept applying pressure with the polo shirt, grateful that I'd chosen to wear a t-shirt under it this morning.

After a moment of silence: "Who could lure Carl Gunther out to an area like this," she asked, "with no backup, and then catch him off guard?"

I didn't have to think long about that one. "Maybe an old friend?"

CHAPTER FORTY-SEVEN

Malone called Mrs. Pinkerton while the paramedics were very carefully extricating Gunther from the Continental, letting her know what we'd found and that her boss was still alive. She was going to meet us at the hospital, my partner reported after she hung up.

And said hardly another word as we followed the ambulance away from the scene, soon losing sight of it because they were going full-out lights and siren. I didn't try to provoke an exchange as I fought through mid-afternoon traffic to the Providence Medical Center downtown as quickly as I could. Malone was blaming herself and there was nothing more I could say. She was a smart woman; she could confirm the timeline for herself when she settled down—though admittedly that would come easier if it looked like Gunther was going to recover.

When we finally got to the trauma unit's waiting room, Mrs. Pinkerton was already there, fierce-faced, puffy-eyed, and somewhat disheveled, pacing up and down while paying no attention to the looks she was getting from the other anxious, frightened people sitting around the room. She didn't note our arrival, either, until Malone stepped over and brought her to a stop with an arm around her shoulders.

"Any news?" I heard her ask as I joined them.

Mrs. Pinkerton glared at the nearest nurse's station, where a nurse glared back. "They took him away, but they're not going to tell me anything. I'm not *family*." The last word came out almost like an obscenity. "He doesn't have any *family*," she said loudly enough for the glaring nurse—and everyone else—to hear. "*I'm* his goddamned family."

Malone squeezed tighter. "Why don't we sit down? Before they call security."

There weren't many open seats available, but we did find two together and the person Mrs. Pinkerton would have been sitting next to immediately abandoned his, so that problem was solved.

I took his seat, so that we were on either side of the elderly lady who was looking more like a fire-eating dragon than a grandmother at the moment. She was taking deep breaths, none actually flammable, and beginning to calm a little.

"You didn't see anyone?" she finally asked me. "No idea who did this?"

"We didn't see anyone, but we have some possibilities for who did it."

She looked off toward the double doors where I assumed they'd taken him. "He has so many enemies."

"True," said my partner, "and it could have been any of them, but the timing says it may be related to a case we're working on. That gives us a place to start. We'll find out who did this if we can, Mrs. Pinkerton."

She looked down at her hands, lying loosely in her lap. "You might as well call me Agnes."

"Agnes. Sure."

We were interrupted at that point by the abrupt entrance of Lieutenant Mike Whitehall, looking just about as red-faced and pissed off as Agnes Pinkerton had. He stopped just inside the entrance, scanned the room, zeroed in on us, and came striding over.

He pulled up in front of us and glared down with his hands fisted on his hips. "You knew. This was your urgent matter. You knew Gunther had been shot and you walked away without a word."

I kept my seat, as did Malone, but I held up a hand. "Whoa. We had no idea he'd been shot. We had an idea where he might be and that he might be in trouble. You were in the middle of a new murder investigation and had your own problems to worry about."

"Yeah, and I should still be in the middle of that, but you know what? Since your recent home invasion I have standing orders with dispatch that any time your name or Devon's comes over the radio, I'm notified. Those names in connection with a shooting victim named Gunther caught my attention. So here I am. What the hell is going on?" He seemed to finally realize that we had a flushed and agitated elderly woman sitting between us. "And who is this lady?"

She looked up at him. "I'm Mrs. Agnes Pinkerton, Mr. Gunther's secretary and assistant."

Mike's eyebrows rose. "Ah. Mrs. Pinkerton. I've heard of you. Do you have a weapon on you?"

"You want to see my concealed carry permit?"

"No. I'm sure you have one. Just checking." He looked over toward the nurse's station. "Any word on Gunther's condition? I understand it was a head wound."

"A deep graze," I said. "Lots of blood, probably a severe concussion, but he's alive as far as we know. We haven't heard anything since we got here."

"None of us are family," Mrs. Pinkerton said, "not officially. But you're official. You can find out what's happening."

Another look to the nurse's station. "I'll be back." He took a step and then paused to look down at us. "Then I'm going to need statements from both of you."

Malone squeezed Agnes Pinkerton's arm again. "He'll make it," she said to the older woman, who was slowly shaking her head.

"I still don't understand why he was out there alone." She looked up, first at my partner and then at me. "What is there? I'm not familiar with that area of the city."

"Not much," I replied. "It's practically rural. Right at the intersection, there are no buildings of any kind. Open land a couple of blocks in every direction."

"Huh. It had to be somebody he trusted. Carl doesn't make that kind of mistake. I don't understand."

Over her head, I saw Mike heading back in our direction. At least he didn't look totally grim.

"The prognosis is mixed," he announced as soon as he reached us. "The blood loss apparently wasn't as bad as it looked and he's in no immediate danger of dying, but he's still unconscious and likely to remain that way for a while." He focused on Mrs. Pinkerton. "Maybe a long while."

"I see," she said.

"Will you be okay if I grab these two for a few minutes?"

"I'm all right. I just wish I could see him."

The corner of Mike's mouth twitched up. "You can, after they get him settled in a room. I told them you were his aunt. I'm not sure they believed me, but I'm a cop so they're going with it."

That brought a tiny smile to her face. "Thank you. Very much." She started to rise. "You can talk to Clint and Devon right here. I'll wait over by the nurse's station for word that I can go in."

She tottered off in that direction as Mike claimed her seat between the two of us.

Before he could even ask, I launched into an explanation of how we ended up finding Gunther, starting with our last visit to his office.

Mike mulled for a minute after I finished. "Okay, so you didn't know for sure where he was or what was going on? You still could have given me a heads up that you were on your way to look for him."

"You're right," I said. "I'm sorry."

"Apology accepted. Moving on, do you have any idea why he was out there by himself in no-man's land? And the even more interesting question, to me: Why the hell did somebody go to all that trouble and not make sure he was dead?"

"Did you check if his weapon had been fired?" Malone asked.

"It had not. But he did obviously have it out, so he either suspected something or saw it coming. But, again, whoever shot him had an easy kill and they didn't take it. Why?"

"Amateur hour," my partner responded. "That's my theory. I don't know if it was one of his old buddies from that photo or not, but it certainly wasn't a pro. My guess is that they saw they'd shot him in the head and all that blood and they assumed he was dead. Maybe they panicked or couldn't bring themselves to confirm it."

He sighed a little. "Yeah, well, I suppose that would fit. Who's left now? A banker, a TV station owner, and a city commissioner?"

"Yes," I said, "and I'm betting it is one of them. All we have to do is figure out which one."

CHAPTER FORTY-EIGHT

It was up to us. As far as Mike's investigation was concerned, Scott Abernathy, Warren Macintosh, and Ray Devine were just three among many of Vernon Kennett's clients. He knew, because of our investigation, that they were also old friends of the three victims, but he had zero evidence and no motive linking any of them to the shootings. He couldn't go confronting three such prominent citizens without more, especially not the one with influence over police funding and policy.

But we could.

First, however, we checked in with Daisy and Sylvia. Malone called and put them on speaker as I drove us back to the office through late afternoon traffic.

"Another shooting?" Sylvia's voice quivered a little. "And this time it was some kind of boss gangster? What in God's name could he have to do with me? This is just totally nuts!"

"Have either of you seen anything suspicious?" I asked. "Felt any kind of threat?"

After a moment, Daisy responded. "Other than the gun-wielding boyfriend over at Ms. Pepper's, no. Nobody lurking or driving by in a sinister vehicle. Are you even sure that this shooting, or the two dead guys for that matter, are related to Sylvia? I mean, why would they be shooting at everybody else and not her? Sorry." That last was obviously an aside to Sylvia.

"It would be one hell of a coincidence if none of this related to Sylvia's case," Malone said as I concentrated on getting through the last blocks of downtown traffic. "We don't have the answers yet, but we will. Meantime, you guys stay put, be careful, and let us know if you feel threatened at all. We can add another detective to the mix if you feel the need."

"I appreciate that," Sylvia responded, "but...I'm wondering...."

"What?"

"Maybe I don't need to find out what happened to me, who I was before the childhood I remember. It was a good childhood...and if people are getting killed because of me...."

"It's not because of you. You can't keep blaming yourself." Malone's reply was brusque. "It's because of whoever's behind the killings—and all the rest of this. Who may also be the person that left you in that alley, the person with all the answers." She took a breath. "We work for you and you can fire us, but I think the ship has sailed. There's no way to notify whoever's behind this that the case is being abandoned. We'd be better off to keep going and, like I said, we could probably get Sonny Sampson over there."

Big sigh over the phone. "I understand. I guess you're right about going ahead. I can't say that I don't feel threatened, not with all these people getting shot, but there's nothing happening here so I guess we're okay for now. Rodney is here, helping us keep an eye out."

Oh, jeez. "Does that mean Agatha is alone at her place?"

"No." Rodney's voice answered. "Beck and her mother are both there now. Aunt Agatha's new project."

"Ah," my partner responded, and very softly, under her breath, added "crap."

There wasn't much to say beyond that. We wished them well and assured them we'd stay in touch as I parked in my spot across from the agency.

A couple of minutes later we topped the stairs to see Eleanor Ivory just turning away from our office door back toward her own. "Eleanor!" I called. "You looking for us?"

She swung around. "Yes! I had a cancellation, so I was able to start that deep dive on Commissioner Devine that you wanted." She grinned as we approached. "I already found some good stuff."

I felt an adrenaline rush as I unlocked the office door. Maybe at last we'd have some answers, or at least a more focused direction.

It took just a few moments to rid ourselves of jackets and weapons and get settled at the desk with Eleanor in the visitor chair nearest me. She was wearing a tailored skirt and a simple wool sweater with her hair pulled back in a ponytail. And that grin.

I gestured for her to proceed. "Okay. What do you got?"

"A sealed juvie record. Records, I should say. And they're good."

Malone practically jumped out of her chair. "You hacked sealed juvenile records?"

The grin faltered a little. "Well, yeah. I almost missed them, they were buried so deep. There wasn't anything else, so I went for it. And, let me tell you, it wasn't easy to get in and out without leaving any trace."

My partner was laser-focused. "You're *sure* you didn't leave any trace. Absolutely positive?"

The grin was gone entirely now. "Yes, I'm sure. What's the problem? I've done plenty of hacking for you guys."

Malone sat back. "I guess it's the old cop in me. Juvenile records are supposed to stay sealed, especially if they belong to a sitting city commissioner." She took a deep breath. "But...what's done is done." Another breath. "What was in them?"

"There were several minor convictions, a couple of vandalism convictions, a petty theft. No big deal." She held up a finger for a moment. "But the odd thing is, there was another sealed record, completely separate. An investigation that was inconclusive, was not adjudicated."

"What was it?" I asked.

"When he was fourteen, Devine was accused of the sexual assault of a ten-year-old girl. She's not identified in the report and it didn't go anywhere, dismissed when she refused to testify. Years later, the report was sealed, just like a regular juvenile record." The grin was back big-time. "The irony is, that I would never have found it if it hadn't been with the other sealed records."

I looked at Malone. "Amateur hour again."

CHAPTER FORTY-NINE

"So," my partner said after we'd thanked Eleanor and she'd left to return to her office, "we know almost to a certainty that it's Devine. We still have zero proof but, personally, I'm certain. You?"

"It makes sense," I agreed. "The fourteen-year-old who sexually assaulted the ten-year-old becomes the 20-year-old assaulting the 11-year-old. And his lifelong good buddies either help him cover it up or at least know about it."

"And twenty years later he's a highly respected city commissioner desperately trying to derail our investigation, desperate enough to start killing his friends who might rat him out. Or having them killed. We've got a long way to go before we can take this guy down. Talk about a circumstantial case."

"Still, it's good to have someplace to focus."

She picked up the phone. "I'm going to call the hospital, see if I can get Agnes to the phone and find out if Carl is conscious yet. I really want to hear what that son of a bitch has to say for himself. He sat right there in his office and played dumb about a child rapist and abuser." She paused amidst the punching of numbers. "That doesn't sound like him, you know?"

"I think you have too much confidence in Carl's character, or maybe just in his fondness for you," I replied. "City crime boss, remember? For more than a decade? You don't get and keep that job by being a soft touch or particularly honest. But it would be a big help to have the commissioner overseeing the Police Bureau owing you a huge favor."

She frowned and went back to punching.

I could tell from her end of the conversation that she'd managed to persuade them to page Mrs. Pinkerton to the phone and from her frown that Gunther was still unconscious, or at least not available to be interviewed.

"Still in a coma," Malone confirmed as she hung up.

I'd been thinking hard in the meantime. "Okay, I've got some ideas—but, first off, do you think we should clue Whitehall in on this information right now or wait until we have something in the way of evidence?"

She grimaced, shrugged. "Clue him in that we hacked sealed juvie records? You've known him a lot more years than I have, but I would vote no."

"Then we wait. I can't see him sitting back with this new information and doing nothing, whatever he might think about the hacking, but it would be really tricky and dangerous for him to go poking around in Devine's business after already setting off alarms. We'll bring him on board as soon as possible, but not today."

"That's fine with me."

"Okay, then I think the next step is to give Reuben a call."

"I thought we weren't going to use him as backup while we have Sonny."

"Not backup. Our connection to the local lowlifes. Devine has been hiring guys who are not exactly top-notch pros, even when they have top-notch equipment. My guess is that they're all local, by way of people who know people who know people. So I want to ask Reuben if he's heard any rumors of somebody paying high dollar for low talent. That kind of thing gets around."

"Not a bad idea."

I checked the time. Ten minutes after four. Reuben Keys would be out on the street keeping an eye on his stable of streetwalkers, maybe making a drug deal or two on the side.

He answered his cell phone on the first ring. "Keys." Even with that one word, his voice sounded a little ragged.

"It's Clint. You got a minute to talk?"

"Hang on. I gotta finish something first." He was definitely breathing heavily.

"Okay." Then I listened to what was clearly someone thrashing around and moaning. What the hell?

After about a minute of that, everything went quiet and Reuben came back on the phone. "Okay, what's up?"

"What's up with you? Are you in trouble there?"

"Nah. A guy tried to get rough with one of my girls. I was just taking care of that."

"Jesus, you didn't kill him, did you?" While I was listening to it on the phone?

"Nah. But he's not going to be wanting to pick up any women for a while—maybe quite a while before his equipment works again."

"Oh, ow."

"Yeah. Now, what you want?"

"Have you heard anything about somebody who doesn't know the game but with real money hiring low-level talent lately? Muscle? Shooters? Anything like that?"

"I mighta heard something, yeah."

"Any names?"

"No, but I can do some checking around."

"Any chance one of the names will be the person doing the hiring?"

"I can probably come up with one or two of the morons that got hired. Then we'll see what they know."

"Good. Find out what you can, as soon as you can, and give me a call."

"Will do. I gotta go. I need to wake this fucker up so he can take himself to the hospital."

I hung up and saw that Malone was already on her feet, holstering her Glock. "I've got Abernathy's address and he should be home by the time we get there. Banker's hours."

CHAPTER FIFTY

To my partner's great relief, Scott Abernathy did not live in Lake Oswego. He lived in the Southwest Hills neighborhood of Portland, an upscale residential area known for Washington Park, the Japanese Garden, and the Zoo.

We found his imposing gray house on a little lane off one of the meandering main streets. It was three stories with a two-car garage that was almost as big as our home. The house was somewhat eccentric, with the main entrance apparently on the second level, at the top of steps leading from the paved parking area in front of the garage. More than likely there was a way into the house on the first level from there.

Anyway, we were not in the garage, so we had to trudge up the outdoor stairs and use the ornate door knocker. We could not see a doorbell to push.

The door opened after my second rat-a-tat-tat to reveal a remarkably beautiful young woman who looked like she was dressed to go clubbing: perfect make-up and hair, a sparkly red crop top, cargo pants, and boots. Her sky blue eyes were wide with curiosity. "Yes?"

We both held up our IDs and I introduced us as usual. She leaned a little forward and inspected our IDs, as her face shifted from curious to puzzled.

"Are you from the security company?" she finally asked.

That was an interesting leap. "We're private detectives," I told her again. "We would like to speak to..." I paused for a second. Her father (who married very young)? Her husband (who married someone very young)? "...Scott Abernathy."

Still puzzled. "Why would the security agency send private detectives?"

I was rapidly coming to the conclusion that this woman's looks far exceeded her intellect. Probably a trophy wife.

Meanwhile, my partner took up the burden of getting through to her.

"We are not from a security agency...Mrs. Abernathy, is it? We're here on another matter and need to talk to Scott."

Processing...processing.... "Well, my husband didn't say anything about detectives, but do come in. You can wait here in the foyer while I see if he's available."

We entered. She closed the door behind us and swayed off into another room. Okay, so she was the wife, she was much younger than her husband, and there was no indication that she was French other than pronouncing foyer as *foyyay*.

The foyer, by the way, however you pronounce it, was both expansive and expensive, with a large oval shag rug covering inlaid tile, several antique side tables, and a fancy crystal chandelier. A wide stairway wound up toward the next floor and a double door to our left opened into what looked like a library, the room into which Mrs. Abernathy had swayed.

A moment later, we heard a man's voice, a sharp "What?" Then an exchange that I couldn't make out. Then a few moments of silence, followed by the appearance of a very flustered Scott Abernathy in the double doorway.

He was tall and thin, as I remembered from our first meeting, clean shaven with close-cropped brown hair, a few gray strands already showing, dressed for a casual evening at home: loose-fitting wool pants, polo shirt with the tail out, slippers. His expression was interesting, as if he couldn't decide whether to be angry, frightened, or glad to see us.

He stopped for a moment, practically quivering with apparent indecision, and then steadied. He stepped back and gestured for us to follow him into the other room. He had yet to say a word to us.

I exchanged a glance and a shrug with my partner. We followed along. It was a library, with floor-to-ceiling bookshelves on three walls and a fireplace on the fourth, along with another single doorway—through which his wife had apparently gone, since she wasn't in the room.

Abernathy gestured at a comfortable-looking couch and said his first word to us. "Sit."

We sat.

He did not, as I half-expected, take a seat behind the large, highly polished desk, but rather in an armchair directly opposite the couch.

I leaned a little forward. "Mr. Abernathy...."

He held up a hand. "I assume that you each are carrying a gun?"

I'm afraid my mouth dropped open at that one and I exchanged another look with Malone.

"Don't private detectives carry guns, or is that just on TV?"

"Yes, we're armed," I finally said. "We aren't going to shoot you."

"I'm not worried about you shooting me. I'm just glad to have someone here who has a gun and knows how to use it. I've called a security company and they are supposed to have people here any time now. Could you stay until they arrive? We don't have any guns in the house. Not even a B-B gun." The hand came up again. "I'm not going to answer any of your questions, though."

"Ookay, so we're just supposed to sit here and shoot anyone who threatens you until your own people show up, is that right?"

He had the good grace to look a little embarrassed. "Well, ask your questions. Maybe I can answer some of them."

My partner jumped right in. "What are you afraid of?"

He looked at her like she had an extra head. "Two of my oldest friends have been murdered in the last twenty-four hours. I could be next."

"And another one shot," I noted.

He sat back. "Oh shit. Warren's been shot?"

Interesting. "No. Carl Gunther."

He looked confused. "Carl? Why...? How...?" He made an effort to gather himself. "Why do you think Carl Gunther has anything to do with me?"

"Vernon Kennett told us about The Six," Malone answered him. "We know Gunther was originally part of the group."

"That was a very long time ago." A beat. "What else did Vernon tell you?"

I didn't bother to correct his assumption that Kennett had revealed Gunther's name. "He told us about the pact that the six of you made as teenagers and how successful it had been—at least for the five of you." Not that Carl Gunther hadn't done equally well, in a somewhat different arena. "But," I went on, "I'd like to focus for a moment on something specific."

"What's that?"

"If you don't count Carl Gunther among your friends, that leaves Warren Macintosh and Ray Devine. Why didn't you ask us which one was shot? Why did you assume it was Macintosh?"

His eyes darted from side to side as he tried to come up with an answer. "I, uh, I assumed that if a city official had been shot I'd have heard the news by now."

"So," Malone picked it up, "the shooting of a TV station owner, another prominent citizen, wouldn't have been news?"

Mouth twitching was added to the eye darting. This was kind of fun. "I...I don't know. I suppose so. Warren's name just occurred to me first. I...I like him better."

Malone snorted as I did my best not to laugh out loud. "You like him better?"

"Tell us more about that pact," I interjected. Jerk him around a bit, come back to Devine versus Macintosh in a minute. "And what happened with Carl Gunther?"

"We were kids," he responded immediately, clearly relieved to have a different line of questioning. "We were full of ourselves, ambitious, smart. It was like blood brothers, but without the blood. We pledged to have each other's backs. We'd do everything we could to support each in our life goals."

"Which were?"

"Well, you know, standard stuff: money, respect, power, position. It turned out to be a good pact, until now anyway. We did stand by each other and we all achieved a lot."

"Except for Carl Gunther," my partner pointed out again. "What was the story there?"

He took a moment, a breath. "Five of us were from the same upper-class neighborhood, not really rich but smart and very ambitious. We kind of hero-worshiped this older kid from a nearby, more middle-class neighborhood, a kid who already seemed to have power and know where he was going."

"Gunther."

"Yes."

"So he was the leader."

"For a while, but...he wanted to go in a different direction than we did. We thought lying and cheating were fine, but stealing and overt criminality not so much."

"That's a remarkably frank admission," I said.

"I'm trying to be honest with you."

"So," Malone said thoughtfully, "you guys split off and lied and cheated your way to riches and respectability while Carl lied and cheated his way to crime boss."

"I don't think I'd put it quite that way, but...."

"But somebody," I interjected, "is doing more than lying and cheating now. Somebody is killing. So let me repeat the question I asked earlier: Why did you assume Macintosh was the victim and not Ray Devine?"

I could see his body stiffening, his lips firming up. He was already starting to shake his head when we were interrupted by his wife, who had made her way back around to the double doors we'd entered.

"Honey, the security people are here."

We all turned to look. She was one of four people in the doorway, dwarfed by the three large men standing around her.

Abernathy must have jumped to his feet because he was already striding past us toward his wife. "Thank you, Ashley. Gentlemen, I'm Scott Abernathy, your new employer, and your first task is to escort this man and woman..." He had stopped and was gesturing grandly at the two of us. "...out of my house."

CHAPTER FIFTY-ONE

"Did you catch that Abernathy's wife was named Ashley?" Malone glanced over at me as she typed away on her keyboard.

We'd just settled in the office the next morning, a Wednesday, after going to bed early and sleeping late. Yesterday had been a very long day.

"I did. What are you doing?"

"Actually, I was checking to see if marrying an alliteration was part of the pact—if there's a Karen Kennett, a Dorothy Devine, maybe a Melanie Macintosh. I know there's not a Gloria Gunther. Just Mrs. Pinkerton."

I supposed that was one way to kill time until Warren Macintosh would be in his office, where we'd decided we'd try to see him again. "And the results of your research?"

"Macintosh isn't married. Devine is married to a Nancy and the wife Kennett left behind is Madeline Murphy, who achieved alliteration by keeping her maiden name. So three out of six."

"Well, good. I'm glad you got that out of your system—and I wonder if we'll hear from Mrs. Pinkerton today. Come to think of it, now that we're on a first name basis, has it struck you that Agnes Pinkerton kind of sounds like Agatha Pepper?"

My partner snorted. "We really must make absolutely sure those two never get together."

"Agreed. Anyway, Agnes said she'd call if Carl woke up and could talk."

"Good. I'm looking forward to having a chat with Carl."

"I'm sure." I checked the time. Just coming up on nine. "Meanwhile, Macintosh should be in his office pretty soon if he isn't already. We might as well go see what he has to say now, if anything. He has to be running scared, too, but he's a very different personality from Scott Abernathy."

"I want to ask him directly about Ray Devine," Malone said as we both stood and retrieved our weapons from their drawers.

"To my mind, Abernathy confirmed what we had already concluded by assuming it was Macintosh and not Devine who'd been shot. But we still don't have any proof."

"If Gunther does wake up, we might have a pretty good witness—at least for our purposes if not for a trial."

"You think Devine did that himself?"

"Maybe. The shootings, like everything else in this case, are all over the place. It looked like Kennett was shot by someone he knew. That could certainly be Devine. But then Donish is taken out with a perfectly placed head shot from a distance. That sounds like a pro. And then there's Gunther, who must have thought he was meeting someone he knew and could trust...but was that who showed up? I wonder what Devine was doing at that time. Maybe we can find out."

"After we see Macintosh," my partner agreed as I locked the office door behind us.

Ten minutes later we approached the same dark-skinned receptionist we'd encountered the first time we visited Channel 11. The fact that her welcoming smile dropped away the second she raised her head told me that she remembered us, too.

"Can I help you?"

"Is Mr. Macintosh in?" I asked.

She grimaced a little. "You'd have to check with his secretary about that." Which was exactly what she'd said the first time. She didn't look optimistic that the check would be successful. "His office...."

"We remember," Malone interrupted her. "Second floor, in the back. Don't open any doors that have red lights lit."

"That's right," she agreed, and waved us on. As we passed her desk, I heard the "good luck" that she added under her breath. I would love to have known what she'd been told about us.

We made our way up the stairs and down the long, plain hallway to the anything-but-plain lair of owner and manager Warren Macintosh. Just as we'd found the same receptionist downstairs, we found the same beautiful blonde behind this desk.

She took one look at us and pressed a button on her phone set. "They're here," she said.

I exchanged a look with my partner. Apparently this was going to go a little differently than it had the first time.

She was listening to the response as we arrived at her desk. After a moment, she nodded and looked up at us. "Mr. Macintosh will see you now."

We didn't have to ask where to go because, as she spoke, a door to the rear of the reception area was opening and he appeared in the doorway, nearly filling it. Unlike his casual attire in the parking lot, he was now wearing a well-fitted blue suit and tie. Given how tall and heavy he was, it must have been bespoke.

His face was every bit as florid as during our first encounter. He might have been willing to see us now, but he wasn't happy about it. "This way," he said in a clipped and angry monotone.

We followed him into his office. It was even more plush and fancy than his reception area. He lowered himself into an oversized chair behind his oversized desk, his lower lip trembling slightly even as his eyes flashed with fury. The wall behind him was covered with framed photos of him looming over various local and national personalities.

We took two of the three visitor chairs even though he had not actually invited us to sit. He glared at us. We looked at him.

"I told you that you were playing with fire," he said. "You didn't listen and now my friends are dying."

"Who do you think is killing them?" asked my partner, jumping right into the deep end.

He jerked back as if she'd slapped him. "I have no idea, but I know it's because they talked to you."

"You're talking to us," she responded reasonably enough.

"I only want to persuade you to drop your investigation. It's a police matter now. You have to butt out."

"That's all Vernon Kennett wanted."

Another slap. "What?"

"Kennett came to our office and asked us to drop the investigation. And then he was killed."

"That...that can't be all...."

Malone was to the edge of her chair and Macintosh was pushing back from his desk. I was enjoying myself.

"What else do you think he might have said, Mr. Macintosh? You know who's killing your friends, don't you?"

"I...no, no, of course not. I have no idea who's doing it."

I decided to join the fun. "How about Ray Devine? You think he might be involved?"

His chair hit the wall behind him. "Are you crazy? You think a Portland City Commissioner, a man well-respected and without blemish, is going around killing people?"

I scooted for the edge of my chair. "Let me ask this, then: What about Carl Gunther? Is he still one of your friends? He was shot, too, you know, but he's still alive."

"He's.... How did... Is that...?"

My partner shifted back into her chair and relaxed, which I thought was a lovely move at this point. "Take a breath, Warren," she said. "You sound like you're about to have a seizure."

I shifted back as well. "And after you've calmed down, tell us about Carl if you don't want to talk about Ray."

The big office echoed with silence for almost a full minute as Macintosh got his breathing under control, relaxed his shoulders, and slowly pulled himself and his chair back up to the desk. His lip still trembled and his eyes still glared, but he had it under control.

"I can't tell you anything about Carl Gunther. I haven't spoken to him in years and we do not exactly go to the same meetings." A deep, full breath. "There's nothing I can tell you about any of this, nothing, except that you should leave it alone."

CHAPTER FIFTY-TWO

"I'm guessing that Macintosh wishes he'd never invited us into his office," Malone said as I drove us back downtown.

"I'm sure it didn't go the way he wanted."

"I can't figure these guys out. Do they really think that asking us to drop the investigation is going to work, even combined with very vague threats? *You're playing with fire.* Bullshit."

"And he was surprised that Kennett had done the same thing. Apparently they don't talk to one another. Aren't you supposed to consult with your clients before you go off to confront the people investigating them?"

A little snort from my partner. "I don't know. Maybe not if you've known each other since you were teenagers."

"Did you notice Macintosh started to say something more about Kennett and then stopped himself? It sounded to me like he was going to insist Kennett must have said something besides warning us off."

"Well, he did. He told us the story of the teenagers making the pact."

"And for that he got killed?"

"Don't ask me. It does sound unlikely."

"Then," I went on, "there's Donish. He didn't tell us anything. He told his *wife* about Gunther—and that got him killed? If so, somebody out there has got a very low threshold."

"Maybe simply talking to us gets you killed."

I snorted this time. "Tough for Abernathy and Macintosh, then—but they must not think so; they both invited us in. And then there's Carl. He didn't admit to any knowledge at all and somebody tried to kill him."

Malone was silent until I pulled into our parking spot and turned off the engine. I looked over at her before opening my door.

"We don't have a case," she said to my unspoken inquiry about her thoughts. "We've got a fucking conundrum."

I let my own silence stand as agreement while we made our way from the parking lot across the street and up to our office.

We'd barely stashed our weapons and sat down when the main agency line rang. I recognized the number. "It's Reuben," I said, and hit the speaker button. "This is Clint."

"Yo. Just you and Malone?"

"Just us. What do you know?"

"I know that somebody with lots of cash has been wasting it on white dudes who couldn't think their way out of an unlocked room."

"Any names for the rich guy or the white dudes?"

"Nope. He's smart enough and they're worthless enough that nobody has names."

"Shit."

"But...."

Aha. "But?"

"I guess the money guy figured out finally that he was hiring crap and went for a pro. I don't know how he found him, but word is that a shooter named Harvey Quire was hired to take out a local real estate guy. Don't have the target's name."

"We do," Malone spoke up. "Where is this Harvey Quire now?"

"Beats me. Probably Argentina. Not in Portland, anyway. Like I said, he's a pro."

"Okay. All that's interesting, but not very helpful, Reuben. Nothing about somebody hired to kill a local attorney named Vernon Kennett?"

"No."

"Or shoot Carl Gunther?"

"Are you kidding? Gunther was really shot? I thought that was a bullshit rumor."

"You thought what was a rumor? That he'd been shot?" I jumped in.

"Nah. I heard that the guy with cash tried to get somebody to go after Gunther—but there were no takers, not even Quire.

I couldn't believe anybody'd be dumb enough to even suggest it. Gunther is solid on top in this town—or he was, anyway. Somebody went for him after all? Is he dead?"

"He was shot, but not killed. He's in the hospital."

"I'll be damned."

"Anything else, Reuben? You sure you don't have any other names? No hint who the money man is?"

"Sorry. It's somebody with power but not a lot of connections, at least not the kind of connections he was looking for. Not somebody trying to replace Gunther, for sure, not unless they're reaching way above their pay grade."

"No, I don't think they want to replace Gunther. Well, thanks for the information." Such as it was. I ended the call.

"Shit," said my partner after I punched off the speaker. "Just like we were thinking. He must have done Kennett and Gunther himself."

"You're still certain it's Ray Devine."

"Absolutely. It had to be somebody that Kennett and Carl knew, somebody they either trusted or at least didn't fear. Old high school friend, city commissioner...you're not going to expect to be shot."

"Even if you helped him cover up child sex abuse and whatever else put Sylvia Ralston in that alley twenty years ago? Even if it's all coming undone now?"

She sighed. "We don't know enough yet. We don't know what happened before she ended up there. We don't even know for sure that Kennett and the others knew about it all this time. We don't know why Carl was cut off, or cut himself off, all those years ago."

"That's one of the most interesting questions, it seems to me. Even if they had some conflict back then, these guys were all committed to becoming rich and powerful. It seems like it would be handy to have the city's crime boss on your side. Why didn't they try to make up with him?"

Malone shrugged. "Maybe they did try. We haven't heard from Mrs. Pinkerton, so I assume Carl is still not in any shape to tell us." She suddenly grinned. "Which means the only thing left to do is go see if City Commissioner Ray Devine is in his office and willing to speak to us this time."

CHAPTER FIFTY-THREE

Ten minutes later we arrived at City Hall. Thea, the commissioners' redheaded receptionist, was at her desk and apparently not so thrilled to see us again.

"Good morning. You're the two detectives, right? Mr. McCall and Miss...Malone, right?"

"Is Commissioner Devine available?" I asked in response to her somewhat subdued greeting. We both knew that she'd recently said he was busy for the whole week, but she did pick up her handset and punch a button.

"I don't think so. Let me check. Commissioner? Those two detectives are here to see you again." Pause. Surprise. "Yes. Okay. Will do."

She hung up and gestured to our right with a big smile. "Commissioner Devine will be happy to talk to you."

We headed for his office, the door of which was closed. He wasn't going to pop out to greet us as he had the first time. "This is going to be interesting," muttered my partner as I knocked politely on the door.

"Come on in!" No hint of tension in that voice.

We entered to find him standing behind his desk, wearing a light gray suit and matching tie, much more business-like than the polo shirt and jeans of our first visit. The big smile and the cold eyes were the same, though, as was the offer of coffee or a soft drink.

"We're fine, Commissioner," I said as we took the indicated visitor chairs and he settled in his leather chair. "We're glad you're not so busy."

He sat back and steepled his hands. "What can I do for you two today?"

So far, in fact, we were practically repeating the script of the first visit. Time to change it up, I was thinking...but, as I could have predicted, my partner beat me to it.

"We were wondering why you failed to mention last time that Carl Gunther is an old friend of yours. You claimed, in fact, that you weren't even acquainted with him."

His smile barely wavered but the intensity of his look at Malone would have burned a hole in a lesser person.

"I guess I felt that my private life, who I'm friends with and who I'm not, was none of your business. I still feel that way. I'm happy to discuss public policy with you, even do what I can to aid in your investigations, but my personal life is mine."

"Unfortunately," I said, "it appears that your personal life is very much part of our investigation. Surely you're aware that two of your close friends have been murdered in the last twenty-four hours and Carl Gunther shot."

He gave me a long, considering look, obviously taking the time to decide how to respond. "You're talking about Vernon Kennett and Brendon Donish. Why do you think they're such close friends of mine?"

Malone sat forward. "I don't know how active you are on social media, Commissioner, but Brendon Donish has a Facebook page and, not long after we visited you the first time, I found a photo that he'd posted and captioned The Six. It was of you, him, Kennett, Warren Macintosh, and Scott Abernathy. There was no indication of who the sixth person was, but we've since discovered that it was Carl Gunther. And, before he died, Vernon Kennett told us the story of how you'd all pledged as teenagers to support one another on your respective roads to success. In fact, he may have died *because* he told us that."

I had to hand it to Devine. His neutral expression didn't twitch during that entire exposition. Finally, he smiled. "Well, then. Very good. You know everything there is to know."

"I don't think so," I responded.

"I don't know what else there would be to tell." He spread his hands in a gesture of innocence. He might have looked innocent if it weren't for those eyes. "We have supported one another through the years and we've all been very successful as a result. Even Carl, though he didn't have our support for very long—for reasons that I imagine you understand." He leaned forward, sincerity oozing. "I must say, though, I can't imagine why you think Warren was killed because he shared our inspiring story with you."

Then my partner went for it. "Tell me, Commissioner, would your support of one another include collusion to cover up a crime?"

His face flushed, he pulled back a little, and slapped his palms down on his desk. "That is an outrageous suggestion. You're talking about some of the most prominent and powerful citizens of Portland. These are good men who wouldn't think of such a thing."

"And you include yourself in that."

He stood. "You're damned right I include myself in that, Miss Malone, and I believe that's all I have to say on the subject. Or any subject. I'd like the two of you to leave."

We'd pushed as far as we could. We stood and left, nodding to the effervescent Thea on the way out.

I cocked an eye over at my partner as we exited City Hall. "Guilty?"

"As fucking sin."

"We didn't get a chance to ask him if he's worried about being the next victim."

"We didn't get a chance to ask him a lot of things I'd like to ask, but I'm pretty sure he isn't concerned at all about being a victim."

CHAPTER FIFTY-FOUR

"It was a performance."

I looked up to see my partner staring at me across the partner's desk. "What?"

"I've been trying to figure out why Ray Devine was willing to meet with us this time. It was a show. He was performing for us, just having a good old time."

"So why did he blow us off the time before?"

She shrugged. "He didn't have all his ducks in a row yet. He hadn't killed the people he needed to kill. I don't know."

I offered a shrug of my own. It was as good an explanation as any. "We still don't have any evidence that he's done any of it or even has any connection to any of it other than the longstanding friendships. His sealed juvie record is compelling, but not probative."

"Maybe we should have another talk with Mike."

"Not yet. He's got two murders to investigate and he's a good cop. He might be able to independently connect Devine to them, though it's going to be tough. This Harry Quire person is long gone already and it would not be unusual for Devine's prints to be in Kennett's office; he was an old friend as well as a client. Mike will do his best. He knows we think Devine might be a factor, but he has to start from the crimes, not from the suspect. Especially not when the suspect is the city commissioner overseeing the Police Bureau. If we get anything more solid, we'll share it with him right away."

A sigh this time instead of a shrug. "I guess you're right." Then she perked up and started tapping away on her keyboard. "I'm going to print out a copy of Donish's photo of The Six."

"For?"

"For Sylvia Ralston. When we met with her and Daisy yesterday, we told her about the photo but now that we're more certain about Devine she needs to see it. Maybe it will jog her memory."

"We should be careful how we do it," I cautioned as I heard the printer spring to life. "We're playing with traumatic amnesia here and that's not exactly our field. We don't want to accidentally cause a psychotic break or something."

Malone retrieved the copy and stood for a moment as if weighing it in her hand while she looked thoughtfully at me. "That sounds pretty unlikely," she finally said, "but I agree we should take care. How about we just casually ask her to look at a photo? No indication that it might be scary. She feels secure at Daisy's and she trusts us. She's lived with her concerns for two decades and she's a smart, strong woman. I say she can handle it."

I had to smile. "Well, you do know what it's like to be a smart, strong woman. Okay, let's give it a go."

And back to Lake Oswego we went once again.

Daisy opened the door for us with a rueful smile. "Good to see you guys. Join the party."

"Who's here?" I asked as we stepped into her foyer. "I don't hear any music this time."

"Rodney and his aunt." She leaned in to whisper, "No dancing. More like courting."

We all traipsed back to the sumptuous living room, where we found Rodney and Sylvia sitting close together on a couch with Agatha Pepper beaming at them from a nearby armchair. She transferred the beam to us as we entered.

"Look who's here! Do you have any good news?"

I shook my head as Daisy took another armchair while Malone and I settled on a second couch in the same grouping. "We're making progress, I think, but we don't have any real answers yet." I cocked an eye at our client. "How are you holding up today, Sylvia?"

A little shrug. A little smile at her companion. "Still confused, but maybe a bit better than yesterday."

"Are you two...?" Malone left her question hanging in the air.

Sylvia moved a hand over to rest gently on one of Rodney's. "Rodney has been very supportive."

"Hmm," offered my partner as a response. It crossed my mind that if they kept smiling at each other like that I might have to leave the room.

Malone took care of the problem by casually pulling out the photo of The Six and leaning forward to offer it to Sylvia. "I just wanted to check something. Do you recognize anybody in this shot?" She was doing a great job of seeming to be entirely relaxed about it.

I watched our client closely as she examined the photo. She seemed mystified at first, scanning the faces. Then there was a tiny shiver, barely discernible, and she handed the photo back to Malone. "No, I don't recognize any of them. Who are they?"

"It's just a photo we happened upon in the investigation and wondered if it had any significance." My partner focused more intently. "You did seem to have a slight reaction there. You sure you didn't recognize any of them?"

"No, I didn't. But...maybe there was something creepy...." Rodney laid a hand gently on her arm.

Malone really leaned in now. "I want you to think hard: when you first ran your eyes across the faces, was there one that your eyes jumped back to? Think about it."

Reluctantly, Sylvia held out her hand. "Let me see it again."

She looked down at the photo for what seemed like a long time, then pointed and gave another little shiver. "Yes, I guess that one." She turned it so that we could see who she was pointing to. "Who is it?"

"A man named Ray Devine," I answered. "He's a Portland City Commissioner."

She looked at me, taking a moment to process, and then relaxed slightly. "That explains it. I've probably seen him on TV or in the papers."

"Probably so," I agreed. I certainly wasn't going to tell her it was also possible he had been the one to abuse and abandon her twenty years ago.

She nodded in further agreement, but still seemed a little

jumpy. Abruptly she stood up. "I...I need to go to the bathroom. I'll be back." She fled the room. Rodney frowned and then followed her out.

Daisy and Agatha looked bemused while Malone and I exchanged a worried glance. Hopefully we had not provoked some kind of crisis after all.

"That was a little odd," our elderly friend observed. "Do you think there was something about that photograph...?"

"How is Beck?" I jumped in because we certainly didn't want to tell Agatha about the photo or our most recent conclusions. She'd probably go downtown and try holding Devine at gunpoint until he confessed.

Ms. Pepper welcomed my interruption with a big grin. "She's doing quite well and I'm greatly enjoying her company, especially now that Rodney is spending so much time over here."

"I thought," Malone joined in, "you said that Beck wouldn't be staying with you all the time. Has that changed?"

Agatha nodded. "It has. Her situation at home was just too hopeless, so I persuaded..." She rubbed a couple of fingers together. "...her mother to enter a very nice facility to dry out. If she sticks with that and is willing to participate in an ongoing sobriety program, I'll set her up with a job and she can have her daughter back. Assuming they want to live together at that point."

"That's very generous of you," my partner allowed.

Agatha waved that aside. "You can't give all your spare money to Friends of the Library. Beck is worth saving and some of that worth must have come from her mother, so maybe she's worth saving, too."

I looked off toward the door through which the two young people had left. "I guess our interview with Sylvia is finished. I hope she's not upset."

"She'll be all right. My nephew is good for her."

Agatha Pepper chuckled at our expressions. "I know. I'm saying that my worthless nephew who tried to kill me for my money is good for that talented young woman." She leaned forward as if about to share a secret. "The fact is, he's coming along quite nicely. It turns out he's not so dumb and he has a good heart. He went badly astray, yes, but I think I've got him back on the straight and narrow."

"Really?" Malone sounded more dubious than I felt. I had to remember that my daughter's long-time boyfriend had come into our lives because he intended to kill me. These things happen.

Ms Pepper sat back and clapped her hands on her knees. "I'm a very good aunt," she said.

Who could argue with that?

CHAPTER FIFTY-FIVE

"Given Sylvia's reaction to that photo, I agree with you it's almost certain that Ray Devine was her abuser and is behind everything that's been happening now." I swiveled my chair back and forth a bit.

We were in the office after a very late lunch across the street.

"And," my partner responded, "given the wild variety of everything that's been happening, it's almost certain that the man is batshit crazy—no matter how nice and normal he might appear to the public."

"No kidding."

"I mean, think about it: If it's all Ray Devine, or all any one person for that matter, why aren't they going after Sylvia herself? She's the reason for all this, the driver, and she got one lousy threatening note; that's it. They've even given up on us, apparently, or at least taken a break, after a few failed attempts. If it is Devine, now he's killing his friends rather than his enemies. It makes no sense."

"Batshit crazy isn't supposed to make sense."

Malone gave me the gimlet eye over our mutual desktop. "*If* he's crazy. Certainly he isn't predictable. I know Daisy has a good security set-up for her house, but we could still consider adding Sonny to the mix. No telling when all this could flip again."

"I agree." I gave her my own gimlet eye. "Not least because you outright accused him of collusion with his friends to cover up a crime. And he knows what crime we're investigating." I took a moment to consider while watching the early afternoon traffic on Stark. "I doubt that Daisy would be thrilled at having another guest."

My partner sighed. "Still, it's something to consider. I don't think I know anybody at the Lake Oswego department, but I could give them a call and see if they'd be willing to do some extra drive-bys."

"That's a good idea."

Just then the agency line rang and, speaking of cops, the display said it was Mike Whitehall. I punched up the speakerphone. "Yo, Mike. Making any progress?"

"On Kennett or Donish? No. What did you say to Commissioner Devine?"

Uh oh. "Why?"

"Devine has a meeting later this afternoon with the Chief to talk about harassment by some local PIs. Sounds to me like he might be going after your license."

"Holy crap on a donut!" Malone exploded. "Are you sure?"

"My source is good. What did you say to him?"

"No explicit accusations, but Devon might have hinted— strongly—that we suspected he was behind our client's abuse and abandonment."

"Oh, that's just great."

"Have you come up with anything to connect him to the killings or to Sylvia Ralston?"

"Other than both victims being his friends, nothing. If he has any connection to your client, that's long buried and gone."

Malone leaned in to the speaker. "I don't suppose your source has any influence on the chief."

"Not a bit, but she will probably be able to tell me how the meeting went."

"Okay," I said. "We'll look forward to that." I punched off the speaker.

"Good thing our lawyer is right across the hall," my partner observed drily. "Sounds like we may need him soon."

"What we need even more is some kind of evidence that Devine is our man. Actually, we need a *lot* of evidence to accuse a city commissioner of kidnapping, child abuse, murder for hire, murder, and miscellaneous other crimes. Who haven't we talked to?"

"Carl, of course, not since we found out he was lying the first time, but we've not heard from Mrs. Pinkerton so I guess that's not possible yet. Devine has a wife...."

I snorted at that. "What are the chances she'd talk to us? Or that she knows anything relevant if she did?"

The agency phone rang again. I didn't recognize the calling number, so I picked up the handset and offered the standard greeting. It was Mrs. Pinkerton calling from the hospital. Her message was so hurried and brief that I didn't even have a chance to put it on speaker. She hung up without even waiting for my response.

"Speaking of the devil, Carl is awake," I told Malone as I hung up. "And he wants to talk to us."

"Hot damn," my partner said as she stood up.

It took almost half-an-hour in mid-afternoon traffic to reach the hospital, find a parking space, and make our way inside to find Agnes Pinkerton.

She was in a different waiting room on the third floor, looking much better than when we'd seen her last. Her color was good but she frowned as we approached. "He can only have two visitors at a time and only for five minutes. He's a little groggy and in pain, but he insisted that he needs to talk to you." She reached out and grasped my arm firmly while giving Malone an equally firm look. "Don't upset him."

"Has he said what happened out there?" my partner asked. "Who shot him?"

She shook her head, the frown deepening. "He hasn't told me because he knows I would go after them. Maybe he'll tell you—and then you can tell me."

Malone shrugged. "We'll see. Which room is his?"

Mrs. Pinkerton let me go and pointed down the hall. "Second door on the right. It's a private room. There are no cops on it right now. They haven't been notified yet."

I didn't ask how she managed that. We needed to take full advantage of our five minutes while we could.

CHAPTER FIFTY-SIX

I braced myself as we approached the room, expecting to find a somewhat diminished and woozy crime boss with his head encased in bandages and his bed surrounded by beeping medical equipment.

The bandages and equipment were more or less as expected and Gunther did look distinctly pale, but he was propped in a sitting position and the good-looking nurse leaning in close to his smiling face was something of a surprise.

She jerked upright as I cleared my throat and Malone snorted. "Oh, you have visitors! Are you sure...?"

"I'll be fine, Marion." His voice was a little raspy, but he didn't sound like a man near death for sure. "They're friends and I need to talk to them."

She stepped away from the bed and focused on us, looking all serious and nurse-like now. "Mr. Gunther has only recently come out of a coma resulting from a serious head wound. You have five minutes, no more than that." She looked back at the bed. "I'll be right outside, Carl."

She swept past us and we approached the bed.

"You're looking good for a guy who nearly had his head blown off," Malone observed. "And your own private nurse?"

The smile reappeared. "It's good having the indefatigable Mrs. Pinkerton as my aunt. I'm wondering if there's some way to make it official."

Personally, I was feeling the time pressure. "We have questions."

He took a breath, sighed, looked a little diminished after all. "I know. And I have answers. Some of them."

"Let's start with who shot you and why," my partner said.

"The who is Ray Devine. I can only guess about the why."

"Then we've got him. Just like that."

Gunther shook his head very carefully. "No you don't. My

word against a well-respected City Commissioner? I don't think so. Plus, I can guarantee that Ray has an ironclad alibi."

"From one of the remaining six?" I asked, just to introduce the subject.

"Maybe. They're probably both scared shitless now. Providing an alibi might seem like a good idea."

I glanced at my watch. Half our time was gone already. "Tell us about Sylvia Ralston, Carl."

"I can't tell you as much as you want to know. I didn't know her name and I don't know how Ray ended up with her. Something about a deal gone bad with her family, maybe her father. I was already splitting off and going my own way when all that happened."

"Why?" Malone asked. "Short answer."

"The short answer is because the others wanted to retain the appearance of legality while they lied, cheated, and stole. I didn't see the need for that. They didn't agree. I think I'm going to turn out to be right."

"Did you know what Ray had done to the girl?"

"Not all of it. Not much of it. I knew there was a kid he'd done something to and he supposedly felt guilty about it, if you can believe that. He was doing what he could to help her and that's why the others, who knew more, were willing to keep quiet. All things considered, I assume the kid I heard about at that time was this Ralston woman."

"She was abandoned in an alley, Carl, so beat up and abused that she still can't remember who she was, much less what happened to her."

"I didn't know that at that time and I don't know what Ray was doing to supposedly help her, if he was doing anything. I only know what I picked up from the distance I'd already established."

My partner stepped closer to the bed. "Why didn't you tell us when we asked you in the first place?"

"Like I say, I didn't know your client was the kid I remembered hearing about. I didn't know that after twenty years Ray would go nuts and start trying to kill everybody."

The door opened behind us and the nurse cleared her throat loudly. Our time was up, but Gunther had one more thing to say as we turned to leave: "If you don't get him, I will."

The nurse reentered the room as we headed down the hall toward the elevator.

"We could just sit back and let him do it," Malone observed.

I glanced over at her smirk. "Yeah, right. Let's consider that a last resort."

Somehow we managed to avoid Mrs. Pinkerton on our way to the elevator, which was just as well since I certainly wasn't going to sic her on a City Commissioner. We arrived at the elevator and Malone punched the button. "And the first resort?"

I pulled out my cell phone. "We need to bring Mike up to date. All the way up to date. If he knows everything we do, he might be able to get his investigation focused on Devine. That would be our best bet."

She and the elevator sighed at the same time. "I'd rather we get this son of a bitch ourselves, but...give Mike a call."

CHAPTER FIFTY-SEVEN

All things considered, we thought it would be a better idea to meet with Mike in our office rather than call him.

He'd only just settled in one of the visitor chairs when he exploded to his feet again. "Gunther is awake and talking? How do you know that and I don't?"

I spread my hands and, I admit, grinned a little. "The wonders of Agnes Pinkerton. What can I say?"

He paced for a minute. He took a deep breath. He sat down again. "Well, shit. Let's keep this short because I want to get over to the hospital to get a formal statement from that asshole."

"He'll tell you that Ray Devine shot him," Malone said, "or maybe he will. He doesn't expect you to believe him."

Our friend's face had begun to redden but now noticeably paled. He opened his mouth, closed it again, and finally found his voice. "The city's crime boss claims that a Portland City Commissioner shot him?"

"Yep," I answered, "but he also assured us that Devine would have an ironclad alibi."

"Do *you* believe him?"

"Absolutely," responded my partner and I nodded in agreement.

"Oh, that's great. That's really great. What the fuck am I supposed to do with that?" He reached inside his jacket and pulled out his phone. "Hold on. I'm going to have one of my guys go take Gunther's statement right now. I'll follow up later, but eyes in the department are already on me. It'd be better if I'm not the one who returns bearing this news."

"It will be interesting to hear what Carl tells your officer," said Malone. "He indicated to us that he wanted to take care of the problem himself."

Mike looked at her as if she had two heads. "This just keeps getting better and better," he finally said. "Okay. I'll send two guys, one to take the statement and one to take up a post outside the room to ensure Gunther doesn't go gunning for Devine. Give me a minute." He stood, started to turn away. "Do you know if Gunther has access to his phone?"

"Don't know," I answered. "Didn't see it."

"All righty. Check for phone and confiscate if found. Don't want him ordering a hit from his hospital room." Whitehall was beginning to sound slightly giddy as he stepped into the hall to make his call.

"I would not want to be him right now," I said to my partner.

"Are you having all that much fun being us?"

I had not yet come up with an answer to that when Mike stepped back into the office. He re-took his seat.

"Okay, I've got two people on the way to the hospital."

"I hope he tells your guy the same things he told us," I said.

The corner of Mike's mouth turned up. "I'm having Sergeant Kowalski take his statement."

That obviously meant something. I looked a question at Malone and she also grinned. "Sergeant Cynthia Kowalski. Mid-thirties, blond, very attractive, tough as nails."

"Ah. That could work."

Our friend ran a hand over his close-cropped blond hair and took a breath. "Okay, now I want everything you haven't told me and all your speculation."

So, to the best of our ability, that's how we spent the next twenty minutes while Mike sat mostly silent and taking notes. He did not look any happier when we finished than when we'd started.

"This is a massive clusterfuck," he finally said. "Even if Gunther is as forthcoming with Kowalski as he was with you, which is highly unlikely, he doesn't have any info or evidence about the current crimes except his claim that Devine shot him—and who's going to believe that?"

"There's no way I can take all your conjecture about Devine to the captain who told me to lay off the cold case. You guys have no more actual evidence than Gunther does. But I'll keep pursuing that line as best I can on the quiet. I have a contact in the city attorney's office and a couple of judges who have done me favors in the past. Let me feel them out a bit. If you guys come up with any new avenues or information in the meantime, let me know. And watch your backs."

"Let us know what Gunther says in his statement," Malone asked as Mike stood to go. "If he refuses to put it on the record that it was Devine, the Commissioner should probably also be watching his back."

That stopped Whitehall, half-turned toward the door. He pursed his lips. "And how am I supposed to warn him without giving away that we think he's the shooter?"

My partner shrugged. "If he's the shooter, then he's also the killer, the kidnapper, and the abuser. Against whom we have zero evidence. Maybe not warning him is the way to go."

Mike shook his head. "Clusterfuck," he said again, and left without another word.

CHAPTER FIFTY-EIGHT

I hung up the phone. "Daisy reports that all is well. Sylvia is writing away and there have been no threats besides Rodney courting her."

My partner snorted and went back to looking through the Friday morning mail. It had been a frustratingly quiet two days for us and a similarly frustrating two days for Mike Whitehall. Gunther had refused to name Ray Devine in his official statement to Sergeant Kowalski, though he had asked if she'd like to meet him for a drink when he got out of the hospital. Not surprisingly, she felt that dating the city's crime boss would reduce her prospects for promotion in the Police Bureau.

As of yesterday afternoon, Mike had made no significant progress on the murders of Kennett and Donish, nor had we on our own investigation. I was thinking that maybe we should go talk to Mrs. Devine, after all, since we'd talked to everyone else—who would talk to us—at least twice. It would be one tough interview if we did it. What would we say? We're investigating the possibility that your husband abuses children and murders his friends?

I was about to voice the suggestion, nevertheless, when there was a quick knock on our door and it opened to reveal Alison Roberts, her long black hair in some disarray and her cheeks flushed. She appeared to be out of breath and definitely not dressed to go on camera: ratty jeans, sweatshirt, and tennis shoes.

"Alison," my partner greeted her. "You excited about something or did someone shoot at you again?"

"Excited," our visitor announced as she practically trotted to the visitor chair nearest me and plopped down.

"Okay, what have you got?" I asked as she took a breath and grinned real big.

"I know who the sixth person is!"

"Carl Gunther," Malone and I said together and Alison's grin collapsed into a deep frown.

"Well, crap. Shit. Fuck. Do you have any idea how much work I put into that? And you knew it already? Why didn't you tell me?"

I resisted reaching over to pat her knee. "I'm sorry, kiddo. Just didn't think of it."

She scowled. "It's good to know how important my help is to you guys." Another breath, the scowl morphing into a very slight smile. "You probably already have the rest of what I found out." She folded her hands in her lap and looked from one of us to the other. Apparently we were going to have to ask. Which meant it was up to me, since I knew my partner wouldn't ask before hell froze over.

"So what else did you find out?"

"I found a woman who says that our esteemed city commissioner, Ray Devine, sexually assaulted her when they were both kids."

I exchanged a look across the desktop with Malone. Could it be? The sealed file?

"Who is this woman," asked my partner, "and how did you find her?"

"Her name is Melody Channing and I don't reveal my sources or my methods," Alison replied smugly. "I gather this is *not* something you already have."

"We discovered a sealed juvenile file, or rather Eleanor did, that referred to such an incident...but we didn't have a name or any idea that the person was still around. How old was she when this happened?"

"Ten."

"Then she has to be the person referenced in the file. Is she here in Portland?"

"Gresham. She owns a mixed martial arts studio there."

"Interesting," my partner said and then cocked an eye over at me. "You ever heard of a Melody Channing?"

I shook my head. "Not that I recall. There are a lot of martial arts teachers in the Portland metro area."

"Still, that might give us an in." She transferred her attention back to Alison. "I assume you've talked to this person. Did she tell you why she's never exposed Devine as her attacker? Did you tell her that we'd be wanting to talk to her?"

"I spoke to her on the phone, just to confirm that the info I had was correct, but I didn't really interview her. I didn't know how you'd want to play it. I did tell her it was part of an investigation and that she'd probably be hearing from you two. She wasn't thrilled, I'd say, but she didn't tell me to stuff it." She squinted hard at me. "And then I'll be wanting the whole story from you guys, of course."

"Even though you don't have a job?"

"If this turns out to be as big a scoop as it sounds like, I'll have a job." She dug into a pocket and came up with a slip of paper. "Name, address, home and studio, phone numbers," she said as she laid it on our desk. "Don't forget to call me again. You owe me."

"We will not forget," I said. "This could be just what we needed."

"Good." She rose and headed for the door. "And you're welcome," she tossed over her shoulder.

"Thank you!" we responded together as she stepped into the hall and grinned back at us before closing the door.

I picked up the paper and looked at it. "Call her first?" I asked Malone.

She stood and opened the desk drawer to get her Glock. "Better to show up before she has a chance to say she doesn't want to talk." She glanced at her watch. "It's just after ten. What do you think? Would she likely be at home or at her studio?"

I was up and stowing my own weapon in its holster. "Let's hit the studio first. There could be classes this early and she'd be more in her element, probably feel less threatened."

"Black belt to black belt."

I shrugged. "It could work."

CHAPTER FIFTY-NINE

We arrived at the studio on a side street just off Gresham's main shopping district. A big sign above the front entrance announced Melody Channing Mixed Martial Arts. It was a freestanding, well-maintained wooden structure, single story but filling a good-size lot with another half-lot devoted to parking.

The parking area currently held about a dozen vehicles ranging from a newish Mercedes to a beat-up Ford van, so it appeared that we would definitely find somebody inside.

The heavy, oversized front door opened into a lobby decorated in eclectic martial arts flags and paraphernalia: Taekwondo, Kung Fu, Tai Chi, judo, Muay Thai, Aikido, Krav Maga, and others.... Mixed martial arts, indeed. To our left was a hallway that I guessed led to dressing rooms, restrooms, and maybe the office. To our right was a small lounge area, currently unoccupied.

Straight ahead of us, through a rather ornate archway, was an expansive training area that was very much occupied. I could see at least three separate groups, male and female, a wide range of ages, all wearing blue outfits similar to the white ones we wore in my own dojang. There was a group that appeared to be doing Taekwondo, one that was probably Judo, and one that was doing a Tai Chi routine. The instructions being shouted by the three different teachers, two male and one female, made the place sound like a movie boot camp.

It was quite a show.

"Wow," my partner muttered. "I guess we'll have to wait for a break in the action."

"Maybe not," I said, and pointed out that there was one woman roaming the space from group to group, adjusting a stance here and commenting on a move there. "I'll bet that's Melody Channing—and she's going to notice there are visitors in another minute."

We waited and she did, breaking away from the Tai Chi group to head in our direction with a smile of greeting. I could see as she approached that she was lithe and unusually tall with buzz-cut silver hair and a pale complexion. She was incredibly fit and I'm not using the adjective "incredible" lightly. I have a number of good friends, including Eleanor and Daisy, who are talented and tough black belts. This woman looked like she could take any of them. Maybe all of them at once.

"Welcome," she said as she joined us in the lobby, "I'm Melody Channing." She offered us each a firm handshake, but focused on my partner. "What can I do for you?"

"I'm Devon Malone and this is my partner Clint McCall. I believe Alison Roberts told you we would be getting in touch."

The smile faltered only a little. "Ah. Yes. The private detectives." She glanced at her watch. "Let me tell *my* partner I'm taking a break and then we can go to my office."

She hurried back into the training area and briefly whispered in the ear of the female instructor, another tall and very fit woman, then returned. "This way," she said as she led us into the hallway.

We passed dressing rooms and restrooms, a couple of supply closets, and at the far end we arrived at the office. It was fairly spacious, with two desks, presumably for her and her partner, several padded chairs, a couch, coffee table, and shelves laden with martial arts books and more paraphernalia.

"This is a very nice operation you've got here," I said as she settled behind one of the desks and we took the two nearest chairs.

"Thank you. It's taken a lot of blood, sweat, and money to get where we are."

"I imagine."

"Clint here is a fourth-degree black belt in Taekwondo," Malone noted, "and has his own private dojang in downtown Portland."

That interested Channing, as we'd hoped. "Oh? Private, you say? What is that, members only?"

"Sort of," I replied. "I rent the space along with some other black belts, just for us to work out together."

"Ah. Nice." She sat back, looked from me to Malone, then let out a breath. She sat straighter in her chair, almost rigid. "Ray Devine. You have questions."

"Lots of them," my partner responded, "if you're willing, about what he did and how he got away with it. But why don't you start at the beginning, wherever you think that is, and we'll probably ask a few questions as you go along."

"I haven't talked about this since I was a child. I think about it, still, almost every day, but...."

"Just take your time."

"Okay." Another deep breath. "I grew up just on the edge of the Forest Park neighborhood. My parents were well-to-do, but not nearly as rich as some of our neighbors. Ray was the classic boy next door, four or five years older, good-looking, with parents who were much wealthier and more politically connected than mine."

Another breath. "He seemed to have a crush on me, paid a lot of attention, even though I was so much younger. I was kind of pleased by that, but I was ten years old, for God's sake, and I wasn't exactly in touch with my sexuality. I wasn't into boys. I'm still not, as a matter of fact."

"What happened?"

"There came a day when my father was at his office and my mother was on a long conference call and I was bored. I saw Ray out in his backyard and asked him what he was doing. He said he was playing a game. I thought that was funny since he seemed to be all alone, and I asked him what game."

She paused again, for more than a few breaths this time, her eyes down but her body still very upright. "I know it's difficult," I finally said, "but this could help us finally get some justice for you—and for some others."

Melody Channing looked up at me. "Have there been others? I always wondered about that."

"At least one other, we're pretty sure."

"Okay. Okay. I won't go into all the details. I can't. I just can't...but, long story short, we ended up in a room in his house that had a bed. I don't know if it was his room or not. I don't know if his parents were home. It was a big house; they might have been and I...didn't really make a lot of noise. I didn't scream or anything. I was kind of...flabbergasted is a funny word in this context, but I was. I didn't know what to do with what was happening."

Malone leaned forward a little. "Did he...?"

"Rape me? No, not literally. We ended up both of us naked and he...played with me and I touched him, but...we didn't actually...."

"Was he violent at all?" I asked.

"No, not at all. He was very gentle, but...very intense, I guess I'd say."

"Like he could have gotten violent if you hadn't cooperated."

"I guess."

"He said it would be best if I didn't tell my parents about the game, we put our clothes on, and I went home."

"I gather that you did tell your parents, nevertheless."

"After sleeping on it, or rather failing to sleep that night, yes, I did. I knew it wasn't right, that it wasn't any fricking game, but I wasn't ready for the reaction that they had. They were terribly upset, at least at first, and immediately called the cops—which probably frightened me more than anything Ray had done."

"How," asked my partner, "did all this end up in a sealed report about which no action was taken?"

Channing for the first time seemed to sag a little. "Ah yes, that's the rest of the story. You probably noticed that I said my parents were very upset *at first*."

I exchanged a glance with Malone. "Yeah, we noticed."

"A female plainclothes cop showed up, a detective I guess, and talked to my parents, then me. Then she left, I think to go next door and talk to the Devines...and that was it."

I could tell that my partner barely resisted jumping out of her chair. "That was it?"

"Well, there was a lot of tension in the house for a few days. I heard my parents shouting at each other a few times, which was a rarity in my family, but I never saw another cop and my parents never said another word about what happened to me—so I didn't, either."

I was having a hard time believing this. "They just let it go?"

"Like it never happened."

"Do you know why? Were they threatened? Bought off? Surely they didn't simply decide it was okay."

"I didn't know at the time. I didn't know squat. I guess I thought that maybe I was wrong. Maybe what happened wasn't that bad, that it really was a game. I knew on some level that that wasn't true, that it was a truly horrible thing that had happened to me and that it wasn't right for them to let it go, but...I was ten fricking years old. I wasn't going to call Child Services on my own. I didn't know there was such a thing."

"You never talked to a teacher?" Malone asked. "A counselor? A friend? Anybody?"

"Not a fricking soul. Not until that reporter, Alison whoever, called me. I couldn't believe it had come back after all these years...but maybe I'm glad it did. Especially if you can get that justice you mentioned."

"And you have no specific idea why your parents backed off."

"Well, I do now. I'm pretty sure it wasn't a coincidence that we sold the house just a month later and moved to a much bigger and better place in Lake Oswego."

Malone rolled her eyes slightly and I knew she was thinking, *of course Lake Oswego*. Melody didn't seem to pick up on it, fortunately.

"Do your parents still live there?"

"No, they've both passed on."

"I'm sorry."

"It's been a while and we were pretty thoroughly estranged by then. The older I got, the more I realized how totally they had let me down."

"Yet you never talked to them about it," I confirmed.

"Nope. Like I said: estranged."

"You live here in Gresham now, right?"

"Yes, only about a dozen blocks east of here. I can easily run to and from work. Part of the warm up and warm down."

I had another thought. "After the...incident...and before you moved away, did you have any further contact with Ray Devine? Have you since then?"

I encountered him several times before we moved, yes, and it was very weird."

"How weird? Weirder than your encounter in his room?"

"In a way, yes. He was very nice, very polite, I'd even say very caring when we saw each other. If I didn't know better, I'd swear he was genuinely sorry about what he'd done and wanted me to feel better."

"Huh." I couldn't come up with anything better at the moment.

"I've not seen him since then," she went on, "not in person anyway. I've seen him on TV since he got into city politics. That's weird, too."

"I'm sure."

"You think he's somehow continued *playing games* all this time and gotten away with it?"

Malone frowned. "We don't actually know of anything in the past twenty years. What we're investigating goes back that far."

"Wow. A cold case. Isn't that what they call it? A cold case?"

"Yeah, very cold. We can't tell you any more about it. Client confidentiality."

"Oh, okay. I don't think there's anything more I can tell you, either, except to ask that you keep my name out of it if you possibly can. We don't need that kind of publicity and I sure as hell don't want to have to go over it again. I told the reporter the same thing and she promised my name wouldn't be in anything she wrote."

"We will do our very best, but your story might play a very

important part in finally bringing Devine down, so it could well become public knowledge."

She shuddered slightly. "I understand. Your best is all you can do."

We left her sitting quietly at her desk. Even the lobby was quiet. Apparently the morning training sessions were done.

CHAPTER SIXTY

"We have to tell Mike," Malone said as soon as we were back in the car.

I nodded as I pulled away from the curb. "It'll provide further support for our belief that Ray Devine is our guy—but Mike doesn't need Melody's name. He couldn't do anything with it, anyway."

"Agreed."

We hit the Home Run for a quick burger and fries, then up to the office to call Mike. He was very interested in Melody Channing's story, a bit frustrated that we wouldn't share her name, and very frustrated that he still wouldn't have anything he could use on Devine even if we did.

"He does have an alibi for the Gunther shooting, by the way," he said over the speakerphone. "He was supposedly in a meeting with his banker buddy, Scott Abernathy."

"How convenient," Malone muttered.

"I thought you weren't going to check on that, because you didn't want to raise any flags," I said.

"It occurred to me that most likely any alibi he set up would be on his public schedule, so I requested the schedules of all the commissioners for the last few days. I'm hoping that will not attract any attention. I'm sure I'll hear soon if it did."

"Which reminds me," I said. "Did you hear anything more about that meeting between Devine and Chief Lowell? Do we need to consult our attorney?"

"I'm sorry, I've got nothing. Even my impeccable source was left entirely out of the loop. Your lawyer's right across the hall, right?"

"Yeah."

"If I were you, I'd pop over there and give him a head's up."

I heaved a sigh. "Okay. It's about a hundred bucks per heads up."

"Might be worth it. Anyway, thanks for the call. I've got homicides to solve."

"So what do we do now?" my partner asked after I punched off the phone.

I shrugged. "Before Alison burst in on us this morning, I was thinking about suggesting we talk to Devine's wife. I'm still not sure how we'd approach her, though, and I have to wonder what his reaction would be if we did."

Malone did a little pretend-shudder. "I hate to think. Hopefully he wouldn't kill her."

"Probably not. She wasn't involved in the pact and I seriously doubt that she knows anything about it."

"Which makes it kind of pointless to talk to her unless we want to *really* stir the pot."

"And that would not be a good idea," I agreed. "God knows what he might do if he's provoked any further. We do have a couple of potential clients to call back. We might as well, since we're so totally fucking stymied by this case."

My partner didn't reply, staring out at Stark Street, apparently lost in thought.

"What?" I asked after a few more seconds of silence than I could handle right then.

"It's very odd."

"What?" I asked again.

She turned from the window. "Devine's pattern, or lack of one, that we know about." She held up a hand to stay further questions, pursing her lips a moment, and then continuing. "Here's what we think we know so far. As a young teen, he gets a little girl naked in his room and abuses her but doesn't physically injure her. Was that the first such incident? Was that the precipitating event somehow?

"Then in his early twenties, he leaves Sylvia Ralston in an alley so severely abused and traumatized that she doesn't remember who she is, much less what happened to her." She paused again. "Was there anybody in between, any other victims? Was he escalating or did he jump straight from naked games to violent sexual assault?"

"We don't know. Not yet, anyway."

"Then," she went on as if I hadn't spoken, "there's twenty fucking years of apparent stability and respectability: job, family, political career. No hint of any wrongdoing, sexual or otherwise. Again, are there victims we don't know about or did he really put it away all that time? What sense does that make?"

I didn't bother to reply this time. She was on a roll.

"Now he's out there killing people, hiring hitmen, apparently going totally bonkers just because we started asking questions. And somehow still managing to look, for all intents and purposes, like a stable and respectable city official." She stopped, took a long breath.

"We aren't psychiatrists, Devon. All we can do is go with what we believe we know and try to prove some of it. We need to shut this son of a bitch down before he gets triggered to do even more damage."

"I know." She looked like she was about to say something else when there was a sharp set of raps on our door. It sounded downright hostile. I exchanged a glance with my partner and, instead of calling "Come in!" as I usually would, I went over to the door while she slid open the drawer containing her Glock.

I opened the door and there stood what was obviously a high-ranking Portland police officer: fiftyish, stocky with bushy steel-gray hair, in full dress uniform adorned with numerous service medals. And a name plate: Captain Horace Melman.

Despite Mike's caution, the flags had definitely been raised.

CHAPTER SIXTY-ONE

I looked at him. He glared at me.

"Let me guess," I said. "You're here on behalf of Commissioner Ray Devine."

"I'm here," he said in a truly wonderful basso profundo voice, "on behalf of the city." I swear my ribs vibrated a little in response. No wonder he made captain. Probably all he had to do was announce, "You're under arrest," and people would confess.

I heard the desk drawer slide shut behind me and moved aside with a theatrical welcoming gesture. "Do come in."

He stepped over the threshold and paused to take in the entire office. I noticed that he scanned right past Malone as if she were part of the décor. She noticed it, too.

I returned to my chair and gestured at the two visitor chairs. "Have a seat, Captain. What can we do for you?"

As I expected, he took the chair closest to me and remained entirely focused in my direction. My partner might as well have not been in the room. I could tell already, from her expression, that this was going to be fun.

"I am here on behalf of the city," he said again.

I sat back and tried not to grin as Malone clasped her hands on the desk and leaned a little toward him. "What can we do for the city?" she asked politely but with an undertone of venom that I, at least, could hear.

It was as if she'd gripped his head and was forcing it to turn toward her. I watched his eyes flare as it happened.

"And you are?" he asked coldly when he finally focused on her.

"Devon Malone." Still polite. "One half of the McCall-Malone Detective Agency." She gestured at me. "He's Clint McCall. The other half." Pause. "And you are?"

She had a point. He'd seen me register his name plate, but he hadn't introduced himself.

"Captain Horace Melman of the Portland Police Bureau."

"I'm familiar with it. Now. What do you want, Captain Melman?"

He started to turn back toward me and she dropped her voice several degrees colder than his had been. "I asked the question, Captain. I expect the answer."

The man was ruddy to start with but was rapidly approaching ripe tomato territory. He gritted his teeth as he shifted slightly to face Malone again. "I am here to inform you that your licenses are in jeopardy."

"And why would that be?"

"Harassing a public official. Making false accusations. Encouraging others to make false accusations and harass the official in question. Attempting to corrupt a police officer. Endangering...."

"Whoa!" I interrupted him. "How have we attempted to corrupt a police officer?"

"I have come to believe that you have an undue influence on Homicide Lieutenant Michael Whitehall and have encouraged him to operate outside the proper parameters of his duties. His career could also be in jeopardy as a result."

"Are you kidding?"

"No, Miss Malone, I am not kidding."

"What are we supposed to be endangering, by the way?" I asked. "I interrupted you before you finished that one."

"The public welfare, through the reckless and borderline illegal actions I've already noted."

"Ah. Of course."

"I have another question for you, Captain." Malone again.

He reluctantly turned back to her. "Yes?"

"What are you doing here in our office?"

"I thought I just got through telling you that."

"No, I mean, why did you dress to impress and come here rather than asking us to come to your office at the Justice Center where you would normally be in plainclothes? That would have been standard procedure, wouldn't it?"

"Well...."

"Could it be because you don't want any of your fellow officers to know that you're doing Ray Devine's bidding rather than your job?"

For a moment I thought he was going to lunge at her and my adrenaline surged; then he caught himself, took a deep breath, and slowly rose to his feet.

"I've said what I came to say," he announced. "The consequences to your reputations, your careers, and your friends will be severe if you don't heed my concerns."

My partner tilted her swivel chair back and smiled up at his beet-red countenance. "We'll certainly take that under advisement. Have a nice day."

Captain Horace Melman attempted to glare a hole in her, then turned and marched out of our office without another word.

As soon as the door closed behind him, we both sagged in our chairs. Malone gave me a look. "What the fuck was that lame bullshit?"

"I have no idea. I've never seen anything like that. I wonder if he really thinks he can just walk in here and tell us to back off. Or maybe he just does what Devine tells him to do, without thinking."

"I've gotta say, it's pretty handy to have a high-ranking tool in the bureau if you want to maintain your position while you go around murdering people."

"God, I hate to think what Mike is facing right now."

We had contemplated that for only a few moments when the agency line rang. I picked it up and offered my standard greeting.

"This is Melody Channing," the caller announced to my surprise.

"Miss Channing. Did you think of something else? Do you mind if I put you on speaker so that my partner can hear you?"

"That would be good, since I want to thank her as well."

I punched on the speaker. "I'm here, Miss Channing," said Malone.

I followed up on her last comment. "You said you want to

thank us? What for? We've not made any progress since we talked to you."

"Maybe not, but I have."

"Oh?" I had a feeling I was not going to like this.

"I guess finally talking to someone about it, letting it out, freed me to take action."

"You didn't go after Devine, did you?"

"No, I didn't go after him. But I did call his office and make an appointment. I'm going to confront him."

CHAPTER SIXTY-TWO

"Oh shit," I said as I heard a gasp from Malone. I felt my whole spine go cold.

"What? What's wrong with that?" Melody Channing's tone was plaintive. "Now that I've finally confronted it to myself, why shouldn't he have to deal with it, too?"

I had so many simultaneous considerations that I thought for a moment my brain was going to explode, but then my partner jumped in. "Are you still at your studio, Miss Channing?"

"Yeah, the afternoon session just started. Lisette has that and I'll do the evening session. Why? I don't understand. Is it a problem that I called his office? Is it going to screw up your investigation somehow?"

I'd regained my focus. "I think it would be best if we came back and talked to you a little more. You stay put and we'll get there as soon as we can."

"Okay," she agreed a little hesitantly. "I still don't understand...."

"There are a few more things we need to explain when we get there." No shit. "Let me ask you this: Did you specify any reason for wanting an appointment with Devine?"

"No, I just told his secretary it was personal. Is that a problem?"

"When is the appointment?"

"It's Monday afternoon." She was beginning to sound irritated. "Look, if it's going to cause you guys a problem...."

I cut her off. "We'll explain when we get there. Stay put and stay alert. See you soon." I punched off the phone.

Malone was already on her feet with her Glock holstered. "What did Mike say about a clusterfuck? He has no idea."

"Oh man," I said as I stood and grabbed my Smith and Wesson, "Talk about triggering Devine. If something happens to that woman...."

"It will be our fault. Let's go."

We got down the stairs, across the street to the lot as quickly as we could. Malone's Jeep was closer than my Subaru, so we piled into that.

"At least she didn't talk to Devine himself," my partner noted as she pulled aggressively into the downtown traffic. "He doesn't know she's coming."

"Unless he checks his calendar for upcoming appointments. He's bound to recognize her name and, given everything else going on...."

"With any luck, he won't check until Monday morning."

"We're not having a lot of luck lately."

"Too fucking true," Malone agreed as she blew through a yellow light.

I checked to make sure my seat belt was secure as we barreled toward the freeway. I wanted to ask Malone if she thought we should have told Melody Channing about the likelihood Ray Devine had recently turned to murder, but this was no time to take her attention off her driving. Channing wouldn't have been making any appointments if we had given her more information, but...why would we? She hadn't even talked to anyone about what happened for more than two decades. Who could have guessed she'd turn right around and call Devine's office for an appointment?

I couldn't help feeling that we should have, but I kept it to myself and left my partner to break as many traffic laws as possible without killing us both.

We made it to Gresham studio in under thirty minutes and snagged one of the last available spots in the parking lot. At least Melody Channing was currently surrounded by people with fighting skills. Not that I expected Ray Devine to show up and try to take her out with a spinning sidekick.

She met us in the lobby, looking more mystified than fearful, and led us back to the same office and chairs we'd so recently left behind.

"What is going on?" she asked the moment we were all seated. "You said there's more you need to explain? Look, if I screwed up your investigation because there's something you didn't tell me, I'm sorry, but that's not my fault."

"No," I agreed, "it's our fault for not giving you more information about what we're investigating and what's been happening."

"Long story short," my partner chimed in, "we believe Ray Devine has, just in the last few days, killed one person and attempted to kill another while paying to have a third shot dead—all because we've been looking into his past on behalf of another woman we believe he abused."

Melody Channing paled and sat back as if she'd been hit. "Well, crap."

I kicked myself for not having thought of it sooner. "You should cancel the appointment right away. There's a good chance he hasn't seen your name on his schedule yet."

She had started to sit forward but then sagged back as I finished my thought. "He knows my name," she said.

"I realize that. That's why I think it would be a good idea to get your name off his Monday meeting schedule."

She waved that aside. "No, I mean he heard my name today."

Malone is the one who sat forward this time. "I thought you said you didn't talk to him."

"I didn't, but I guess because I said it was personal, the secretary went and asked him about the appointment before she confirmed it with me. She had to have given him my name." She looked from one of us to the other. "He's going around killing people now? You think he's going to come after me?"

"I'm afraid that's a real possibility," I said.

"This is crazy. I can't wrap my mind around it. There might be a Portland City Commissioner gunning for me? It's fricking insane."

My partner grunted. "Best we can figure, *he's* fricking insane." She caught herself. "But this is no time for jokes. Does your house have good security?"

"No, I just live in a regular house with regular locks on the doors and windows. No cameras or motion detectors or alarm systems, nothing like that."

"Then is there another place you can stay, at least for the weekend? Maybe with your business partner?"

"I already stay with her. She's my life partner as well as my business partner."

I exchanged a quick smile with Malone. We were familiar with that concept. But none of this was helping us make a plan to protect Melody Channing.

"At the very least," I said, "you should cancel this evening's classes so you won't be heading home alone and late."

Before I finished my sentence I could tell from her stubborn expression what the answer would be. "Not a chance. That asshole screwed up my childhood but he's not going to affect my work now. Not at all." She held up a hand to stay my reply. "Lisette will stay once I've brought her up to speed on these latest ridiculous developments, so I won't be going home alone, but that's it. If that son of a bitch wants to come after me, let him come."

Given that none of the martial arts are particularly effective against a speeding bullet, her bravado wasn't very smart but I could understand it—and she clearly wasn't going to change her mind.

I stood up, reaching for my phone. "Let me make a call." I noted Malone's inquiring look. "We keep talking about using Sonny again. Now's the time."

Melody Channing rose right with me and had her hand on my arm before I could punch in a number. Very good reaction time.

"Wait a minute. Wait a minute. Who is 'Sonny' now and what does he have to do with my situation?"

I took a breath. She was right. We were hitting her with a lot of information, some of which must have sounded bizarre and all of which was upsetting. I needed to take more care. I sat down again, though I kept the phone in my hand. She stood looking down at me for a moment before she sat again.

"Sonny Sampson is another private detective that we work with," I explained as soon as Melody was settled. "*She* recently relocated here from Las Vegas and would be perfect for providing you a little extra protection until we get this resolved."

Channing grimaced a little. "You want me to hire a bodyguard?"

"Sonny would be working for us in this case. It wouldn't cost you anything—and you really should have some backup, at least short-term."

"If it helps any," Malone added, "Sonny moved to Portland to marry our friend Veronica Fortune, who owns the Pen and Pastry downtown."

Channing looked thoughtful for a moment and then went a little wide-eyed. "Veronica Fortune. Is she the woman who wrote that book about escaping life on the streets and setting up her business?"

"That's her," I said.

"I loved that book! So...are you the detective who helped her out?"

"I am."

"Wow. Okay. Let's do this."

It is good to be the hero of somebody's book. I stepped out into the lobby to make my call.

CHAPTER SIXTY-THREE

It took about ninety minutes to get Sonny to Channing's studio, where I was waiting in the lobby to escort her back to office where Malone waited with Melody. She swept in the entrance and was stopped short for a moment by all the white uniforms surrounding me. The afternoon training session had just ended and the participants were headed for their lockers.

Even though she'd helped us out with the jewelry store client, I hadn't seen our friend for several weeks. As always, she reminded me of my wife and partner: a little shorter but equally lean and fit with somewhat lighter brunette hair framing cobalt blue eyes and sharp cheekbones. This afternoon she was wearing light gray jeans with a dark red top and her usual low-heeled boots. As she paused and surveyed the lobby, she radiated confidence and competence. She smiled and made her way through the sweaty martial artists to my side.

"Hey, Clint."

"Sonny, thanks for coming."

"No problem. I have an office as of yesterday and somebody working up my website, but clients are not exactly knocking down the door yet. I appreciate the job, even if it's just bodyguarding."

"I hope that's all it is. Let's go meet your subject. Devon and I will be paying you for this one, just like the last one."

I started down the hallway toward the office and realized we were walking right behind one of the white uniforms, this one trimmed in black with a black belt and filled out by an extremely fit-looking woman with café au lait skin tone and reddish-brown hair pulled back in a short ponytail.

"Lisette?"

She stopped and looked inquiringly at the two of us. "Yes, Lisette Roth. And you are?"

"I'm Clint McCall and this is Sonny Sampson. We're private

detectives and Sonny here will be serving as a protection detail for you and your partner for a while."

She had very well-defined dark eyebrows that rose in surprise. "Oh, really? I can't wait to hear the story behind that. I assume it has something to do with Mel's past coming back around."

"Good assumption," I agreed as we all three headed on to the office.

It took another half-hour to lay out everything for Lisette and make sure she and Melody were both comfortable with Sonny and with the plan—which was simply that Sonny would stick with them until instructed otherwise by us.

It was very late afternoon by then, so Malone and I headed straight home from Gresham.

After we fed the cats and had our own dinner of pan-fried steak and microwaved frozen vegetables, we settled in the living room to enjoy a rare evening of nothing much to worry about. Melody Channing had Sonny Sampson and Sylvia Ralston had Daisy Mansfield. Everybody else was on their own.

Around mid-evening, Malone looked up from the book she was reading. "Are we going to pass Sonny's fee to Ralston? It is a result of our investigation for her."

I put down my own book, carefully since I had a cat on either side of me on the couch, and gave that some thought.

"That's a little tricky," I finally said. "It's not her responsibility that Devine might go after some other woman."

"Sonny on the job 24-7 is going to be really expensive."

I sighed. "Yeah. Yeah, it is. What do you think about splitting it 50-50 with our client? It's part of her case, but it was our idea."

Malone nodded. "That works."

We were about another half-hour into our reading and I was thinking that an early bed-time might be a good idea when my cell phone rang. I glanced at the clock on the wall. Nearly ten. Might be a casual call, but maybe not. I could just reach the phone without disturbing Stella.

"Clint McCall."

"Clint, this is Agatha. Have you heard from Daisy or Sylvia lately?"

I didn't like the sound of that and it must have shown in an unconscious reaction. My partner closed her book and both cats jumped down from the couch. "No," I answered. "Why? Should I have?"

"Beck and I were hoping. Rodney went over to Daisy's house hours ago and was supposed to be home by now. He's not answering his phone, nor is Daisy. I don't know Sylvia's number, but I'll bet she wouldn't either."

I was sitting on the edge of the couch by now and Malone had set her book aside, looking concerned. Stella and Maxine had both disappeared.

"Why do you think she wouldn't answer her phone?"

"Because we're standing on Daisy's front porch. Her car is here and the car I let Rodney use is here, but there are no lights on in the house and no one is answering the door, which is not locked, by the way. Something's wrong."

I was on my feet, as was my partner. "You haven't gone inside, have you?"

"No, I may be old and eccentric, but I'm not crazy."

"Good. Go back to your car and wait for us. We'll be there as soon as we can."

"What if we see something happening? What if a bad guy comes out? I didn't even bring my gun, damn it."

"If you see anything like that, lay low and call 911. We're on our way."

So much for nothing much to worry about.

CHAPTER SIXTY-FOUR

"I'm going to be really pissed at us if something's happened to our client," Malone muttered as I took the exit for Lake Oswego. "We get focused on protecting Melody Channing and drop the fucking ball on Sylvia Ralston."

Those were the first words spoken since I'd told her what Agatha had said.

"We don't know yet what's going on," I responded while I took the next corner at speed. "Let's save the self-recrimination for when we get there and find out."

Three minutes later I screeched to a halt behind Agatha's car in front of Daisy's home. Just as she had said: two cars in the driveway and no lights evident in the house. Given that it was full dusk by now, that was not good.

We bailed out of the Jeep, as did Agatha and Beck from their vehicle. I could see the outline of her driver, who remained in the big sedan. Apparently dealing with possibly dangerous situations was not part of his job description. The four of us gathered on the sidewalk. Agatha was wearing a green and gray-striped overcoat against the October evening chill and Beck had donned a heavy black sweater to go with her normal Goth look.

"See anything since we talked?" I asked our older friend.

"Nothing. Nobody in or out, no lights. Nothing."

"But you say the door is unlocked. It wasn't open, was it?"

"No. I tried the knob and thought about going in, but then decided to call you instead."

"Good decision. You two stay here and we'll check it out. If you hear anything like gunshots or see anybody you don't know on the property, get back in the car and call 911."

"Damn, I wish I'd brought my gun."

"Well, you didn't, so stay put, okay?"

Beck put her hand on Agatha's arm. "I'll make sure she doesn't follow you in."

"Thanks." Malone and I headed up the walk to the porch and drew our guns as we reached the front door. I opened it just enough to be able to call inside. "Daisy? Are you in there? It's Clint and Devon. We're armed and we're coming in." There was no response.

We eased through the door and closed it behind us. The house was silent but not totally dark, as it had appeared from outside. There was a faint glow coming from the direction of the big living room, most likely from the fireplace that I recalled was on the wall to the left of the archway.

Neither of us said anything but we agreed, through a combination of gesture and touch, to advance on the living room. Separating slightly, we took up positions on either side of the archway and slowly edged around into the room itself.

By then the light from the fireplace was more than adequate to survey the room. I didn't see any threats: no motion, no possible attackers crouching silently behind a couch or chair.

Malone tapped me lightly on the arm and pointed. The couch next to the fireplace was occupied by a motionless figure lying on his or her side. Blond hair glowed faintly in the firelight. Daisy.

"Time for some light," I muttered to my partner, who nodded. One more survey as I felt the wall next to the arch for a light switch. I found it and the room was suddenly bright. No one that we'd missed jumped out at us and no one appeared to be occupying any of the other furniture, so we hurried over to Daisy.

She was bound and gagged and appeared to be furious, glaring at us as we approached. I holstered my weapon and crouched beside her while Malone kept an eye on the entrances. Our friend was sputtering as I removed her gag and began to untie her.

"Slow down. What happened, Daisy? Just take it easy and I'll have you free in a minute."

"He took them, goddamn it. Got the drop on me and took them. I'm sorry."

"Who took who?" Malone asked over my shoulder, though I was sure we both knew the answer.

"Devine. It was Devine. He took Sylvia and Rodney."

"Any chance they're still in the house?"

"No. Long gone. Shit, shit, shit."

By then I had Daisy freed and sitting up. Malone holstered her gun and sat down on the couch next to her. "Are you hurt?"

"Just angry and embarrassed."

"Okay," I said as I took the nearest chair. "Tell us what happened."

She'd barely opened her mouth to respond when Agatha Pepper's voice resounded through the room from the archway. "Where the hell is my nephew?"

Beck was on her heels as she swept into the room.

"I couldn't stop her. I tried, damn it."

Halfway into the room, Ms. Pepper registered the scene around Daisy and stopped, one hand covering her mouth. "Rodney?" she asked faintly.

"We don't know where he is, Agatha," I said.

Daisy was looking a little calmer. "I'm sorry, Agatha. Ray Devine took him. Him and Sylvia. It's my fault."

Our elderly friend closed the rest of the distance and simply plopped down on the other side of Daisy, looking intently into her face. "Ray Devine? You mean the City Commissioner? He took them? Where? Why?"

I realized then that Ms. Pepper hadn't been in on any of those conversations and apparently Rodney had not been sharing what he knew. At this point, it sounded odd for anyone to be surprised. "It's a long story, Agatha, but he's a bad guy and we need Daisy to tell us exactly what happened here."

"Should I call the cops?" Beck asked. She was about two-thirds of the way into the room, but couldn't seem to decide whether she should fully join us or not.

"That's one thing I need to tell you," Daisy responded. "Devine left a message. He said that if he hears we've contacted the police he'll kill them. Sylvia and Rodney. He said he'd kill them."

"Shit," Malone said. "And, given that he's the goddamned police commissioner, he's likely to know how to find that out, even on the run."

"So that would be a no," Beck guessed.

"Not right this second, anyway," I agreed. I focused back on Daisy as Beck found a seat nearby. "Take us through it. Every detail. Especially any hints of where he may have taken them."

She squared her shoulders and took a breath. "I can tell you right off there were no hints. Rodney had come over for dinner and we were sitting around afterward when the doorbell rang. Rodney was up and answering it before I even thought to caution him. You don't expect a potential kidnapper to ring the doorbell, for Christ's sake.

"We don't hear anything for a minute and then Rodney is backing into the room with his hands up. I recognized Ray Devine from the news. He's talking before he's even fully in the room, telling us he doesn't want to hurt anyone but he will shoot if he has to. We're all supposed to sit still and be quiet. So we sat still and were quiet as he pointed to a chair for Rodney and then focused on Sylvia. That was weird. Not that the rest of it wasn't."

"What was weird about it?" asked Malone.

"It was like there was...some kind of spark between them, like they recognized each other. Sylvia looked terrified and Devine looked, I don't know, regretful? Like he was sorry to be here? It was weird."

"Okay," I said, "what happened then?"

"He told Sylvia to stand up and come with him. Rodney jumped up and said she wasn't going anywhere. Devine told him to sit down and shut up. He refused, announced that he loves Sylvia, and told Devine he'd have to shoot him."

"Rodney, you moron, good for you," muttered Agatha Pepper.

"Anyway, Devine looks back and forth between the two of them like he can't decide what to do, and then says they both have to come with him—after they tie me up. He had them use

276

the drape cords and then Rodney's handkerchief for the gag and then he gave me the message about not calling cops and took them away, leaving me hog-tied here like an idiot."

"Once he was inside with a gun on everybody, there was nothing you could do," I told her. "He said nothing about where they were going or why?"

"Not a word."

Ms. Pepper spoke up. "Will somebody please fill me in about why a Portland city official would be kidnapping my nephew and his girlfriend at gunpoint and threatening to kill them? And make it snappy. My driver's been sitting out in the car in the dark all this time. He probably needs to go to the bathroom by now, poor man."

CHAPTER SIXTY-FIVE

By the time we'd invited the driver inside to use the bathroom, brought Agatha up to speed to the extent we could about Ray Devine, persuaded her to go home rather than on a manhunt, and made our way back to the Hawthorne District, it was approaching midnight.

Only after providing the cats with a snack and ourselves with a drink did we finally settle down on the couch to catch our breaths and try to make some decisions. We were both exhausted and had exchanged only a few words as we drove home, but there was no possibility of going to sleep, at least not yet.

I could tell that Malone was even more upset than I was. I watched her grimace after taking a first sip of her beer.

"Maybe we should be having coffee," I said.

She looked up as if surprised to find me sitting right there. "What?" She studied the glass in her hand. "Oh, I'm not frowning at the beer. We fucked up. That's what I'm frowning about. We're in Gresham focused on protecting Melody Channing and her partner while our client is getting kidnapped in Lake Oswego. We talked about adding Sonny to her security, more than once, and we didn't do it." Another sip, another grimace. "I hate fucking up."

"Sonny might not have been able to stop Rodney in time, either. Once he opened the door, she wouldn't have been able to do any more than Daisy could. Devine had the drop on everyone then."

A bigger sip and a sigh. "Whatever. He's got them and we need to get them back." She looked around the room as if they might be hiding in a corner. "There's nothing we can do in the middle of the fucking night. I just wish we'd had a little more time."

"What do you mean?"

"Sylvia was starting to remember, I'm sure of it. She

recognized Devine in the photo, even if she didn't know why, and Daisy said there was that 'spark' when they saw one another this evening. If she could have retrieved some more memories, we might have gotten Devine before he got her." She sat the half-empty glass on the coffee table. "We still don't even know what happened back then, what he did or why."

"We'll find all that out when we have her—and Rodney—back safe and sound." I set my empty glass next to hers. "It wasn't that long ago that Colleen and Hoke were taken. We got them back okay. We'll do it again."

"We can't put a rescue together if we have no idea where they are." She paused, seemed to gather herself, and then offered one of her classic snorts. "I'm sorry. It's not like me to be negative or blabber like this. We need to firm up and make some decisions. For one thing, we need to decide if we're going to bring Mike in, Devine's warning notwithstanding."

I'd been thinking about that. "I don't think so," I said. "Not this time. We brought him in on the rescue of Colleen and Hoke and he wasn't very happy about that. Whatever his feelings would be this time, it would be very tricky for him to do anything to help without Melman finding out. What do you bet he's keeping a close eye on our friend?"

"Shit. You're probably right. Do you really think Melman would tip Devine? Politics is one thing; murder and kidnapping is something else."

I shrugged. "Melman probably doesn't know what Devine's been doing, so he'd still be a source of info if Devine wanted one."

"Okay. Still, we need some kind of plan."

"We also need some sleep, but I do have a thought."

"Yeah?"

"There's one thing we've talked about doing, a couple of times, and we haven't done it."

"And that is?"

I took a last swig of beer and stood, reaching down to bring Malone to her feet. "How about, first thing in the morning, we go talk to Mrs. Devine. I wonder what she thinks her husband is doing right now."

CHAPTER SIXTY-SIX

As befitted a modest and respectable Portland Commissioner, Ray Devine lived in a modest ranch-style home in a nice, middle-class neighborhood, just a couple of blocks off Sandy Boulevard in the Hollywood District.

We parked in front of the home a few minutes past nine the next morning. There were a few dog walkers and joggers about, probably typical for a Saturday morning. There was one car in the driveway, a fairly new Lexus.

"Wouldn't it be interesting," I asked my partner, "if Devine stashed them somewhere last evening and is all snug at home this morning?"

"Well, no more Miss Nice Gal if he is. Let's go see." She opened the passenger-side door and stepped out into the chilly October air. I followed suit, kind of hoping that Devine would answer the door.

But he didn't. Instead, it was opened by a petite blonde—slender, fit, attired in workout gear and barefoot, old enough to be just past cute but still working at it. She glanced from one of us to the other with a big welcoming smile. A good political wife who, my gut was already telling me, had no clue who or what her husband was.

"Yes? Can I help you?"

"Mrs. Devine?"

"Yes."

"My name is Clint McCall. This is Devon Malone. Is Ray here?"

The smile faded slightly. "No. Did he forget a meeting or something? He didn't tell me...."

"He didn't know we'd be dropping by," Malone interrupted. "Actually, we'd like to talk to you."

The smile was morphing into a very slight frown. "Me? What... What is this about?"

I pulled out my ID and showed it to her. "We are private investigators. We just have a few questions."

The slight frown was joined by a slight step back. "About what? And why?"

"We think there's a possibility your husband could be in trouble," my partner cleverly ad-libbed. I would have approved if we had planned it. "Do you know where he is right now?"

"Yes, of course, he's at the coast. What kind of trouble?"

The coast? "Can you tell us where on the coast and why he's there?"

There was no hint of a smile or welcome by now. "No, I cannot. Not unless you tell me what kind of trouble you're talking about and what you have to do with it."

"Perhaps," Malone said gently, "we could talk inside." I could tell from her tone that she'd reached the same conclusion I had: this woman had no clue.

"Let me see that ID again. Do you have one, too?"

She examined both our IDs minutely, comparing the photos to us, and finally nodded. "All right. Come in. But we start with an answer to my question. What kind of trouble?"

I suppressed a little smile as we followed her inside. I was curious myself to see where my wife and partner would go with that one. Her ad-lib, her show.

Mrs. Devine led us through an entryway into a medium-sized living room with the standard complement of couch, chairs, side table, and TV. The color scheme was predominantly blue and the wall decorations were all framed family photos. She indicated the couch and took a nearby armchair for herself.

"What trouble?" She was all business now.

"We believe there is a credible threat to your husband's welfare."

Okay, that was true enough. I would kill the son of a bitch myself if he harmed Sylvia or Rodney.

"You mean he's in danger?"

"Possibly. He asked us to look into it."

Oh, wow.

Mrs. Devine had pretty much the same reaction. "Wait a minute. You're telling me that there's some kind of possible threat to my husband and he hired two private detectives, you two, to investigate the threat? And this is the first I'm hearing about it?"

"He didn't want to worry you."

"Well, I hope you're doing a better job of investigating than you are of not worrying me."

"We don't have a choice at this point, since we don't know where he is. That's why we've come to you. Was this trip out of town unexpected? Do you have any reason to believe he might have been coerced to leave?"

"I...I...well, I don't know. It *was* sudden. He said he had to go to the coast to check on some of his properties and he left."

"That was yesterday?"

"Yes, late afternoon."

"Have you heard from him since?"

"No, but that's not unusual when he's off on a trip. Not too unusual. Have you tried calling him?"

"We've not been able to contact him."

"Well, let me try calling him." She jumped up and ran out of the room, returning immediately with a cellphone against her ear. "Ray, this is Nancy. Call me." She resumed her previous seat, holding onto the phone. "Voicemail," she said. "Is he really in trouble?"

"Possibly," I said, figuring that I'd intuited Malone's approach well enough by now that I could speak up without doing any harm. Besides, it was beginning to look like it might actually work.

"Where on the coast, Mrs. Devine, and what properties?" Malone pulled a notebook and pen from her jacket pocket and looked so sincerely concerned that I almost snorted myself. Instead, I did my own best impression of sincerely concerned.

"Tillamook. Somewhere around Tillamook. I don't know specifically. Ray doesn't share much about his business. Politics, yes. Business, no. He owns rental properties around Tillamook. That's all I can tell you. He inherited them a few years ago when his father died and I've never seen them." She looked around the room as if he might be hiding somewhere nearby. "Should we call the police?"

I caught my partner's eye. My turn. "I wouldn't do that yet. The threat is purely hypothetical at this point and we wouldn't want to embarrass him by unnecessarily involving the police. Is it unusual for him to be out of touch when he goes to the coast?"

She grimaced a little. "No, not really. Apparently some of his properties are in areas where there's no signal. I do hope he calls me back soon, though."

"I'm sure he will," I said, while hoping that he wouldn't. All we had so far was *somewhere around Tillamook, maybe so remote that there's no cell service.* We needed more time-and a lot of luck.

CHAPTER SIXTY-SEVEN

"Ray Devine does not own any property on the coast, rental or otherwise." Eleanor Ivory stood in our office doorway, looking almost as disappointed as I felt.

"You're certain?" Malone asked her.

Eleanor stepped further into the office. She was wearing Saturday-casual jeans and sweater. "It's an easy search. The man owns no real estate besides his house here in Portland. Not in his own name, anyway."

That perked me up a bit. "Which means?"

A slight shrug. "It's possible he could own property through some kind of corporate structure, but that's not a quick search. When you called me from the car, you told me to do a quick search."

We had had that thought on the way back downtown from Daisy's house and I took a chance that Eleanor might be in the office even though it was Saturday. She did have some clients she could meet with only on the weekend and sometimes she came in just to catch up on work. I lucked out. Maybe it had been a mistake, though, to emphasize "quick" so much. No question Malone and I were both feeling the urgency to find Sylvia and Rodney, but if there was a slower search that might produce results....

"I hate to ask, Eleanor, but can you stay with it and do the more thorough search? He told his wife he was checking his property on the coast and that's where he may have taken Sylvia and Rodney. I know it's a Saturday, but...."

She held up a hand. "Oh, I was planning to anyway. I just wanted to pop down the hall and give you the first update. That asshole has one of my favorite authors and I want her back just as much as you do." She turned halfway to the door and then looked back. "It is time-and-a-half on the weekend, though, even for my favorite author."

"No problem. We all have to make a living." I shooed her on out.

"Any more ideas?" my partner asked as Eleanor's footsteps receded down the hall. "There's a good chance Devine was outright lying to his wife and isn't anywhere near the coast. He could have Sylvia and Rodney any-damn-where, if he still has them."

I stood and stared down at Stark Street from our window, searching for those other ideas. "Don't even go there," I said to Malone. "They're alive. He has them. Somewhere. And we'll find them."

"Maybe," she said, "we should try to figure out what his purpose could be. I agree that they're probably still alive. He could have killed them at Daisy's house if he wanted them dead. And he left Daisy, a witness, alive so maybe he's not planning to kill them at all. But then...what? Put pressure on us to back off? It's a little late for that. And he hasn't communicated." She stood and joined me in looking down at the traffic. "It doesn't make sense, but that's par for the course with this guy."

I looked over at her. "You know what bugs me?"

She raised an eyebrow. "Besides our kidnapped client and all the dead people?"

"Yeah. What Daisy said about Devine at her house, that he seemed to be sorry about what he was doing."

"Oh, well, gee, it didn't stop him from doing it."

"It's the second time we've heard something like that, though. It's weird."

"Can you name anything about this that isn't?"

"Good point."

The agency line rang right then and I picked it up, hoping to hear more news from Eleanor. Instead, to my surprise, it was Nancy Devine.

"I just wanted you to know that I've heard from Ray and he's not in trouble. You don't need to worry about it."

I punched on the speakerphone while gathering my wits.

"You've heard from your husband? What did he say? Where is he?"

"Yes, he called me back and admitted that he'd hired the two of you, but that the trouble he was worried about turned out to be nothing. He said he'd be off the grid for a while longer, handling some urgent city business. I guess he'll get in touch with you guys when he gets back. Just wanted to let you know."

"Wait a minute." Malone was practically climbing over the desk toward the phone. "Whoa. When did he call you and did he give any indication of where he was calling from?"

"Just a few minutes ago and no, which is what 'off the grid' means."

"Well, shit."

"Sorry, but I guess that means you don't have a job, though you'll have to take my word for it for now. He said he'd officially terminate you as soon as he gets back. Just thought you'd want to know so you wouldn't be wasting your time."

She hung up and for a very long moment Malone and I just looked at each other as she slowly settled back into her chair.

"He'll terminate us when he gets back?" I finally said.

My partner threw up her hands. "Nothing like a crazed killer with a sense of humor."

CHAPTER SIXTY-EIGHT

"That was fast and clever thinking for him to agree that he'd hired us," I said. "No wonder his wife has no idea there's anything seriously amiss."

Malone cocked an eye at me over our mutual desktop. "She's a politician's wife. Part of her job is having no idea that anything's wrong."

"Yeah, I suppose so." It was only about twenty minutes since Nancy Devine had hung up on me and I was basically just making conversation, trying to think of what to do next, hoping to hell that Sylvia Ralston and Rodney Pepper were okay or at least still out there.

Lucky for me, since I couldn't think of a damned thing, Eleanor again appeared in our doorway after a quick knock. "That didn't take as long as I thought it would," she announced.

"You found something?" I gestured for her to come on in and take a seat, which she did, looking very pleased with herself.

"Turns out," she began after taking a dramatic moment to settle herself in the chair nearest me, "that Ray Devine has an LLC. He tried to make it anonymous, but...he failed." Big grin.

"And the LLC...?" Malone was making a move-along motion.

"HP Real Estate. It owns several properties right here in Portland. Still nothing on the coast, though."

"That's good news," my partner said. "It means we don't have to drive to Tillamook, but...tell me he doesn't own any warehouses. I don't want to do another damned warehouse rescue."

Eleanor frowned slightly at that, but shook her head. "No warehouses. No commercial property at all. Three single-family dwellings, all rentals as far as I can tell."

"Are they currently occupied?" I asked.

"That I cannot tell you. But I can give you the addresses and you can go look for yourselves."

"We will certainly do that," I agreed. "Good work."

She left us with the three addresses, unfortunately not all in the same part of town, and within minutes we were crossing 2nd Street to our parking lot.

"Do we want backup?" Malone asked as she settled in the Subaru's passenger seat.

"Maybe Sonny," I said as I started the car. I looked both ways and pulled into the Saturday morning downtown traffic. "Let's decide after we see what we see. If—and it's a big if—Devine has them in one of these houses, I don't want to take the time to put together a team like we had when we rescued Colleen and Hoke. We shouldn't need one, anyway. Depending on the house, the neighborhood, two or three of us should be enough."

"And Mike? Should we let Mike know, maybe at the last minute just in case?"

"Let's decide when we see what we see."

The closest of the three properties was on Gladstone, two blocks east of 39th. It was a small one-story house with tan siding and a couple of large bushes partially obscuring the porch, the yard well-mowed but going brown with the season.

The woman who answered the door was almost my height and carrying a good fifty pounds more than me. Probably in her forties, she was wearing a plain house dress and looking mildly irritated to find strangers on her porch. She glanced from one of us to the other. "I don't want any," she said, and started to close the door.

Malone caught it with her foot. "We don't have any on offer."

After glaring down at my partner's foot for a moment, she looked up at the two of us again. "Are you cops?"

"Good guess," I answered as I pulled out my ID. "Private investigators. We're looking into a case that involves your landlord. My name's Clint McCall and this is my partner, Devon Malone."

She inspected the ID. "Okay. I'm Martha Robinson. But I don't have a landlord."

"This is a rental, isn't it, Mrs. Robinson? Is it Mrs.?"

"Yeah, to both, but I mean I'm not renting from a particular person. I got this place through an agency and write the checks to some company. HP something. Except for the woman at the agency, I've never seen or talked to a person. I'm supposed to call the agency if there's a problem. There hasn't been a problem."

"What agency?" Malone asked.

"Uh, Portland Property Management. They have an office downtown somewhere."

"Okay," I said. "That's all we need, thank you, Mrs. Robinson. Sorry to bother you on a Saturday morning."

She grinned. "I can't wait to tell my husband that he missed two private eyes at the door. He's at the grocery right now."

"You have a nice day," my partner said as we turned and headed down the walkway to the car. "If there's no sign of Devine at any of these properties," she said to me, "maybe Portland Property Management will provide another lead. Maybe it's another front for Devine."

"Could be," I said as we got back in the car. I checked my phone for the other two addresses Eleanor had given us. "The next nearest place is on Holgate, near Eastport Plaza. And the third is out Highway 127 near Germantown Road, barely in the city limits it looks like, if at all. I say we go for that one next. It might be fairly isolated."

"Agreed." Malone glanced at her watch. "It's nearly noon, but I guess we'd better check that out first."

"We can grab some take-out on the way," I said with a grin. "Wouldn't want you in a weakened condition when we get there."

It was indeed way out there and isolated as well. The drive took almost a half-hour, including a quick stop for our usual burger and fries, and when we got to the indicated location we couldn't see the house, just the entrance to what looked like a road back into the woods. I pulled over a few hundred feet past the entrance.

"I guess that's the driveway," I said. "I'm thinking we should scout it out on foot."

Malone agreed and I checked my cellphone, wanting to be sure there was coverage in case we got in trouble. I had a strong signal as we walked back to the entrance. "Okay," I said. "It looks like we can stay in the brush along the side of this driveway or whatever it is. I have a hunch this is it and I wouldn't want to be caught out in the open by an armed and dangerous city commissioner."

My partner drew her Glock. "Me, neither. Let's do it."

Even better than I'd thought, we didn't have to stay *in* the brush; there was a small but clear lane between the brush that lined the driveway and the heavily wooded area. It was essentially a quarter-mile walk in the park before the house came into view.

And quite a house it was: located in a slight depression, it was a large, two-story house, dark brown siding with white trim, that from our side view looked almost like a chalet. There was a porch running the length of the front and a second-floor rustic balcony the length of the back, with a variety of dormers topping it all off.

We crept as close as we could under cover and held our position for several minutes. No sign of life, but there was a high-end SUV parked on this side of the house.

"Do we know what Devine drives?" I whispered to Malone.

"No, damn it," she muttered back and pulled out her phone. "Let me see if I can check. Maybe Eleanor...." She tapped the device a couple of times. "Uh oh."

"Uh oh?"

"I've got no service. Zero. Nada."

"That's weird." I pulled out my own phone. "I had a good signal just...." Nothing.

My partner punched my shoulder lightly. "Me too. I had

all my bars just a quarter-mile back. There has to be an illegal jammer nearby. Which means *something* is going on here."

We looked again at the house. Lots of entrances, windows, rooms.... This wasn't going to be easy.

"Let's go find a signal and call Sonny," I said.

Halfway back to the highway our bars reappeared and I called Eleanor while Malone called Sonny. By the time we reached the Subaru, we had learned that Ray Devine did own a Lexus Luxury SUV and Sonny was free to provide backup.

We settled in to await her arrival.

CHAPTER SIXTY-NINE

It took Sonny Sampson almost forty minutes to get to our location. She was dressed in black, her brunette locks covered by a watch cap and her weapon holstered at her side. We quickly brought her up to speed and walked back to the road/driveway together.

We were nearing the spot where Malone and I had crouched in the bush before when I heard a car door slam ahead of us.

"Oh, crap," my partner muttered. "If he's leaving, we'll never get back to the car in time to follow."

I lunged ahead to our spot and arrived just in time to see the front door of the house closing. I got just a glimpse of the person in the doorway, but I was sure it was Ray Devine.

"Not leaving," I whispered as Malone and Sonny joined me. "Must have gotten something out of the car."

"Was it Devine?" asked Sonny. "Did you see?"

"I did and it was."

"So should we go back to the highway and call your buddy Mike Whitehall? Now that we know for sure we have a hostage situation here?"

"That's exactly why I'd rather not call him, Sonny. This house surrounded by cops with a hostage negotiator trying to reach Devine on the landline?" I gestured up at the phone line over our heads. "Given how erratic and unpredictable Devine seems to be, he could kill Sylvia and Rodney or even himself before anybody got close. We have a better chance to get close."

She sighed softly. "Okay. I can see that. You agree, Devon?"

"We're here. We go for it."

"All right."

"How about this?" I said quietly. "We synchronize our watches and go in front and back at the same time, me in the front and you two in the back. If Devine hears one entry, the other should be able to get the drop on him." I looked at Sonny. "Did you bring the lock picks?"

She nodded and reached into her jacket pocket. "Two sets, as requested." She handed one of them to me. "What if he has high security locks and these won't work?"

"I doubt that he does. This is just one of his rental properties. He can bring a cellphone jammer with him, but he probably hasn't upgraded the locks. If he has, we rendezvous back here and call Mike. No choice, then."

It took a couple of minutes, but we managed to get two digital and one mechanical watch set to the same second.

"Okay," I finally said, "we're all set at exactly one p.m. It shouldn't take more than five or six minutes for you two to work your way around back. We're all going to have to cross a few feet of open space to get to the doors, but he probably won't be looking out a window and he probably doesn't have the hostages near one of the doors. With any luck, we'll all at least be inside before he knows anything's going on."

"Ah, yes," Malone muttered in my ear. "One of my favorite things, trusting to luck."

"You got a better idea?" I muttered back.

"Not a one. See you on the other side." She and Sonny moved off through the brush.

They would have cover nearly to the backdoor and I could work my way down to Devine's SUV without being exposed. From there, I'd be in the open for about fifteen feet to the front porch. On the bright side, all the curtains and blinds appeared to be closed and it was unlikely that Devine would choose just that moment to look outside.

The luck we were depending on held to the front door and I heard no commotion from the other side of the house, so I was assuming it held there as well. Plus, the lock on this side was not high security. I readied my lock picks and checked my synchronized watch. Three minutes to go.

It seemed to take about ten, but I made quick work on the lock, turned the knob, and eased the door open. I heard nothing, no alarm or movement, but it wasn't the silence of an empty house.

Just inside the door that I quietly closed behind me, I found myself in a large entryway with doorways to my left and right and a staircase directly ahead, with a hallway beside it that went further into the building. There was a thin rug, a simple side table, and no other furniture or decoration. The place did not look lived-in.

No surprise, since Devine probably wouldn't be using a rental property that was currently occupied. But I was seeing lots of choices and would have preferred a hint about what direction to go.

Hearing or seeing none, my best bet was to head further in, toward the back where—hopefully—Devon and Sonny were coming in my direction. If we met up without encountering Devine or any hostages, we'd make a plan from there.

I eased my way across the rug and entered the hallway. It appeared to extend all the way through the house to a kitchen or laundry room. I could see a window and a sink in the room at the far end. There were four closed doors on the right and it looked like two more hallways going off to the left. It was a big house.

I was only a few steps along when my adrenaline shot up as I caught a flicker of motion at the far end. Had someone peeked around the doorframe? Were they friend or foe? Was that Malone's Glock that I saw edging into sight? It looked like it, but I crouched against the lower left wall and took aim, anyway. There were a lot of Glocks like that in the world.

Fortunately, my partner's profile appeared above the gun as she again peeked into the hallway. I slowly stood with my hands up and she nodded recognition. A moment later she and Sonny were moving carefully in my direction. We met in the middle after checking our respective branching hallways as we passed them. I saw no one down mine and apparently they didn't down theirs.

We didn't immediately speak when we met up, but Sonny, who'd been closer to the wall on my left, pointed to her ear and that wall. She'd heard something. I gestured that we should put our heads together.

"What?" I whispered the question to her.

"A voice, male, very faint, down the hallway we just passed. Looked like a door to the room right here..." She indicated the wall again. "...is open at least a bit and that's where it was coming from."

"If the room is right here between the two hallways," Malone whispered, "maybe there's a door in this other hallway as well. I'll check." She silently moved away and a few steps into the second hallway, then returned. "There is a door, also cracked open. Didn't hear anything, though."

I looked at Sonny. "You're sure you heard the voice coming from that room."

"Ninety percent, anyway."

I nodded. "Okay, that's good. I'll take the door that you saw, Sonny, and you two take the other door. We've got a good chance to surprise whoever it is, probably Devine. I'll enter and immediately move away from the doorway so that you two aren't pointing your guns at me when you come in. If he sees me, you'll hear his reaction to trigger your entrance. If he doesn't, I'll say *now* as soon as I'm out of the line of fire."

"Roger that," Malone said as she and Sonny stepped carefully away. She looked back at me as they entered their hallway. The message was unspoken but the same both ways:

Don't get killed.

CHAPTER SEVENTY

Once they were out of sight down their hallway, I moved to mine. The slightly open door was about fifteen feet down the wall on my left. Apparently it was a very large room. As I drew closer, I could hear Devine's voice, though I couldn't make out the words.

I eased past the doorway so that I could look through the small opening. Luck was still on our side. It was indeed a large room and Devine had his back to me at the far end, near the wall. Against the wall seated on a couch, were Sylvia Ralston and Rodney Pepper.

It didn't appear that they were currently restrained in any way, except by the gun that Devine held down by his side. I was close enough now to hear him ask if they believed him.

I knew that by this time Malone and Sonny were in place to see the same scene from their side; I had watched that door open slightly. I carefully pushed my door open wider and stepped inside. I glanced across to see that they were mirroring my move.

Sylvia and Rodney were so focused on Ray Devine and his gun that they didn't react to us at all. I'm not even sure they registered our appearance, though I saw Sylvia's eyes widen slightly.

Then Devine raised his gun and yelled, "Answer me!"

That must have broken the spell because Rodney reared back and stared wide-eyed first at me and then at the two women edging down the opposite wall. We were by then just about perfectly positioned to fire without hitting each other or the hostages, so I answered Devine.

"Drop the gun, Ray."

He froze for a moment and then almost leisurely turned away from the couch, lowering but not dropping the gun as he did so. His eyes swept across me first and then took in Malone and Sonny Sampson. "Drop the gun," I repeated. "Now."

It was all the way down at his side, but he didn't drop it. "Mr. McCall. Miss Malone. And friend."

Sylvia started to edge sideways on the couch and I motioned for her to stay still. "You've got three guns aimed at you, Ray. There's no way you can get out of this."

He moved his gaze over the three of us again, his expression oddly indifferent given the circumstances.

"I know, Mr. McCall." Then he smiled, which gave me a very bad feeling. "I've said what I have to say and done more than I needed to do. It's time."

"Ray, don't...."

He swung his gun up toward Sonny and pulled the trigger.

It happened too fast to even process. We all three fired simultaneously. My ears rang with the violent sound and my nostrils were stinging from the odor of gunpowder.

Then Ray Devine and Sonny Sampson were both down.

I could see that the hostages were unharmed, though obviously traumatized. Sylvia curled across Rodney's lap as he leaned forward as if to cover her. Malone was already crouched by Sonny. "How is she?" I called over to her.

"Conscious and pissed. Doesn't look too bad."

Relieved, I stepped forward to check on Devine.

We had all three hit him. One in the shoulder, one in the chest, one in the lower side. He was very dead. We had just killed a Portland City Commissioner. We were going to have a lot of explaining to do.

I moved past him to the couch, noting that there was blood splatter on it and our friends. "Sylvia? Rodney? You two okay?"

"I think we're all right," Rodney answered, his voice rusty as if he hadn't spoken for weeks. He looked down at his lap. "Syl? You okay?"

"Yes." Her voice was muffled by his lap, but then she slowly sat upright and blearily surveyed the scene as if she had just suddenly awakened. Her eyes widened as they settled on Devine's body and then she looked over at Sonny, who was now sitting up against the wall, bleeding from her left hip and gun still in hand though resting on the floor. My partner was nowhere to be seen, which was something of a surprise.

I went over to our friend and leaned down. The hip didn't look too bad, probably a flesh wound. "How are you doing, Sonny, and where's Devon?"

She grimaced a little. "I'll live. She's looking for a landline to call 911. Are they all right?"

I glanced back at Sylvia and Rodney. "They're in one piece, as far as I can tell."

"Devine?"

"Dead."

She let the gun go. "Wow."

"Yeah."

Malone reappeared maybe three minutes later, hurrying to my side. "Paramedics are on the way. Also Mike, the medical examiner, and the crime scene guys."

"Well, you've been busy."

She shrugged. "I called 911 and Mike. I'm assuming the rest." She crouched down. "It looks like the bleeding has almost stopped already, Sonny. You'll be fine."

Sonny managed a good Malone-like snort. "I'll look forward to that. Right now it hurts like a son of a bitch."

My partner looked up at me. "You called it, Clint, or came close anyway. He didn't kill himself, but he got us to do it. Suicide by private cop."

It was only about five minutes later that the first uniformed officers arrived.

Less than fifteen minutes after that, Sonny was on her way to the hospital, Sylvia and Rodney were being treated by the paramedics for mild shock and exhaustion. A very grim Lieutenant Mike Whitehall had us on the other end of the room, listening to our story of what had happened.

"So you knew for sure that Devine was in here with two hostages, but instead of calling for backup, for, you know, an actual police presence, maybe even a proper negotiator, you came in on your own."

"Yes," I agreed.

"And ended up killing the son of a bitch."

"We didn't have a choice."

"Maybe not after you were in here, but before that...."

"It would have gone the same, either way, Mike," Malone replied this time. "Once he knew he was caught, his decision to die was immediate. The only difference, if the house had been surrounded by cops, he might have had time to decide to take Sylvia and Rodney with him."

"Maybe." Mike looked over the scene and took a deep breath. "Probably." His shoulders slumped a little as he grimaced. "You two are going to drive me to early retirement. If you still have an agency after this is over. There's going to be a fucking media storm and a very intensive investigation. You know that, right?"

We both nodded. Yes, we knew that.

He headed across the room to the couch. Apparently the paramedics had cleared the two former hostages and were packing up their gear.

My partner punched me lightly in the shoulder. "That could have gone wrong in so many more ways."

"I know. You think we made the wrong decision? That a hostage negotiator could have gotten everybody out alive and unharmed?"

She shrugged. "Given how batshit crazy Ray Devine was, probably not. We were here. We made the call. We can deal with the consequences." She pulled out her cellphone. "Meanwhile, we need to let Veronica know that her fiancé is on the way to the hospital."

CHAPTER SEVENTY-ONE

"He really was spilling his guts while threatening to shoot you?" Daisy Mansfield asked Sylvia and Rodney, who were occupying the central couch in Agatha Pepper's living room as if on display.

After a phone call from Agatha, Daisy had joined Ms. Pepper, Sylvia, Rodney, Beck, Malone and myself for the impromptu debriefing.

Mike had briefly talked to Sylvia and Rodney, quickly concluding that they were in no shape to give coherent statements on the spot, so he grudgingly gave us permission to take them to Agatha's house. In fact, he insisted that we all lay low there, avoiding media attention, until he came to get formal statements after everybody had a night's sleep. We agreed, without mentioning that we were going to stop at my house to feed and water the cats first.

Mike's plan was, for the most part, a good one. This was a very big deal and at least one or two names could leak at any time, but there was no reason to connect an elderly retired librarian with the story. Most of the focus was initially going to be on Ray Devine and what he had done, though the media would get around to the people who killed him soon enough—once it was made known that it had not been the police.

The flaw in the plan was that it didn't look likely any of us would get a good night's sleep. The adrenalin level in Agatha's crowded living room certainly didn't lend itself to even a short nap.

Despite all she'd gone through, Sylvia seemed energized as she answered Daisy's question. "Yes! He had to tell me all about what he'd done to me and why and how sorry he was…. It was like he couldn't shut up."

"Did you believe him?" asked my partner. "And did it even make any sense, given that you can't remember for yourself?"

Sylvia's eyes went wide and she practically bounced next to Rodney, who was holding her hand tightly. "But I can remember! It was like a door in my mind being kicked open. It all came back to me as he was talking." She took a breath. "Most of it, anyway. My name was Hannah! Hannah Wingate!"

I know I gasped a little at that and I think everyone else did as well. Rodney looked especially floored. Obviously his lady friend had not had the chance to share her breakthrough even with him. He sat forward and twisted to look at her. "Sylvia...Hannah...I mean...you really remember everything? That's wonderful!" He paused. "Isn't it?"

She squeezed his hand with a little smile. "Well, yes...and no. It's great to remember who I am. Not so great to remember everything that happened. It's going to take quite a while to process everything, Rodney."

"Okay."

"It'll be okay, Rod. I've been Sylvia Ralston for two decades. Nothing that I remember is going to change who I am now."

I had some doubts about that, given the probable magnitude of what she was remembering. "So you know how you ended up in that alley?"

She looked at me. "Yes, but that's more because Ray Devine told me. I can't say that I remember everything he did to me, nor do I want to. The most important thing is that I remember my childhood, my father Joe. My mother died when I was very young and even now I don't remember her. Her name was Linda, though. I remember that." She frowned a little. "It wasn't the happiest of childhoods, I guess." The frown deepened. "My dad drank a lot, I think, and wasn't a happy man. He...I guess he could be abusive." Now she looked like she was on the verge of tears. "He would hit me sometimes." Obviously the memories were still welling up and the energy had gone out of the room. Agatha Pepper looked like she might cry, as well.

"That's enough for right now," I said to Sylvia. I was dying to hear the whole story, especially Devine's part in it, but.... "You've been through a lot in the last few hours and you have a lot of memories to process. Maybe it would be best if, as Mike suggested, we all try to get some sleep and we can talk more about this tomorrow."

She exchanged a look with Rodney, then sighed. "Yes, I think that would be for the best."

Agatha pulled herself together and spent the next few minutes organizing the sleeping arrangements after Daisy took herself home, promising to return in the morning. Everybody else had a bed except Malone and me, but there were two comfortable couches we could use. Not a problem. Now that we had called a halt, I was suddenly exhausted.

CHAPTER SEVENTY-TWO

Mike was not alone when he arrived at Agatha's the next morning. Captain Horace Melman had invited himself to the party.

Within a few minutes we were all gathered in the living room again—Daisy, Agatha and Beck, Sylvia and Rodney, Malone and me—with Mike ceding center stage to his superior. He didn't look any happier about it than I felt.

In his regular detective mufti rather than his dress uniform, Melman reminded me of a pissed-off bantam rooster as he glared around the room at us.

"I am here," he announced portentously, "to take your statements in the killing of Portland City Commissioner Ray Devine. You are obliged to be fully forthcoming and truthful in these statements." He focused on me and Malone. "I understand that you two and another private investigator named Sonny Sampson, currently undergoing treatment at Providence Medical Center, are the actual shooters."

His tone made "private investigator" sound like "convicted drug trafficker."

"That's correct," I answered him politely. "We all three fired in self-defense."

He humphed. "That remains to be seen. Mr. Devine managed to threaten all three of you at once?"

"Well," Malone replied, "he shot our friend Sonny and there was no reason to believe he wouldn't keep going if we let him. We had no choice. It was his bad luck that he had three guns trained on him when he fired."

"Yes, that was indeed very bad luck," Melman observed dryly. "Not to mention extremely poor judgment. Surprising on the part of an intelligent and well-respected city official, wouldn't you think?"

"He was committing suicide." It was Sylvia who addressed

his question this time. She was seated on the couch shoulder to shoulder with Rodney.

Melman focused on her. "Ah. Miss Ralston, right? The mystery writer and supposed kidnap victim. Why would you believe he wanted to commit suicide?"

At this point I was exchanging raised eyebrows with Mike. None of this was standard protocol. We hadn't been separated, there were no recording devices in evidence, he obviously hadn't been asked to take notes, and there was no uniformed officer in the room.

Melman wasn't here to take statements. He was here to cover his ass.

"He kept trying to tell me how sorry he was. In some weird, crazy way, he genuinely regretted everything he'd done to me. Or so he said. And I think he was sorry about killing his friends."

Melman went a little wide-eyed at that. "You're saying he admitted killing Vernon Kennett and Brendan Donish?"

"Oh, yes."

"I see." Sounding as skeptical as humanly possible. "And on top of that he was apologizing for kidnapping you?"

"Not this one."

"I beg your pardon?"

"He didn't get around to apologizing for kidnapping me this time. He was talking about kidnapping, raping, and physically abusing me when I was a child. I still don't remember most of *that*, thank God."

Melman opened his mouth and for a moment nothing came out. "So...you're saying that Portland City Commissioner Ray Devine kidnapped and sexually assaulted you as a young girl and then more recently murdered two good friends of his who were also prominent Portland citizens."

"Yes."

"Don't forget," Malone suddenly chimed in, "that he also tried to murder Carl Gunther, a not-so-prominent Portland citizen. Not to mention, you know, us."

Melman gave her a look that would have killed a lesser woman. "I'm conducting this interview, Miss Malone. Please remain silent."

He ignored my partner's smirk and focused back on Sylvia Ralston. "You say you don't even remember the crimes that he supposedly confessed to committing when you were a child?"

"I said I didn't remember all of it. I remember enough. It seems that my father was a small-time crook and was working for Devine and his friends, what they called The Six. He didn't go into the details, but it was some kind of money-making scheme and they discovered that my father was skimming a lot of money for himself. When Devine found out, he came to our house to confront my father and ended up killing him. Then he took me."

"But you don't actually remember any of that, right?"

"Some of it, some of that evening anyway. I remember that I was already upset, afraid my father was going to punish me because I'd broken one of my dolls. I remember hearing a loud and violent argument, then...maybe I saw my father on the floor... After that? There was someone else there. I don't remember that it was Ray Devine or what happened, even though he told me it was him and said that he took me."

"But nothing else. You don't actually remember any of the things you claim he admitted to?"

"No, I don't. I don't remember the abuse, the rapes, much of anything else before I was found in the alley, but he admitted it all."

Melman sneered. "You really expect me to believe any of this?" He looked at Rodney. "You're the boyfriend, right? I suppose you'll claim that you heard all of Commissioner Devine's *confession*, support everything your lady friend is saying."

Rodney was sitting up straight and fierce. "I did! She's telling the truth, asshole!" Out of the corner of my eye, I saw Agatha beaming with pride.

"Yeah, right." Melman's response dripped with sarcasm. "I've heard enough."

He was just turning to Mike when Sylvia Ralston spoke up again. "I may be able to prove it."

Melman snapped back around. "What? How could you prove it? What do you mean?"

She reached into a pocket. "He didn't take my phone." She pulled it out.

Now the captain looked confused. "He let you keep your phone—and you didn't call for help?"

"No service," I interjected. "He must have had a jammer active around the house."

"Huh." Back to Sylvia. "Then what about your phone?"

"I managed to turn on the recorder app while he was talking. We can all listen to most of what he said." The corner of her mouth twitched, almost a smile. "Including his confession."

I may have been the only person near enough to Melman to make out his muttered "oh shit." Then he firmed up. "All right, Miss Ralston. Let's hear it." I could almost see him mentally crossing his fingers that it hadn't worked as she thought.

But it had.

We all sat there, enthralled, for the next forty minutes as we listened to Ray Devine's final testament. Even Captain Melman eventually sat down as it became clear that our friend had incontrovertible proof of everything she'd claimed Ray Devine admitted—and more.

Besides what Sylvia had already reported to us, we heard Ray Devine claim that he had confessed to his five friends about taking and abusing Sylvia and they had not been happy with him but willing to cover for him nevertheless. He claimed further that he regretted his actions and had done what he could to make up for them. Given what we knew about the anonymous financial support her parents had received for so many years, that appeared to be true—though difficult to understand. Not that mental illness is ever easy to understand.

Apparently, Devine lived with these impulses that he could

mostly control and regretted when he couldn't. I almost felt sorry for him. Almost.

The recording ended after the confrontation between Devine and three of us, which I knew was going to help a lot in any future legal proceedings.

There was a few moments of resounding silence in the room; then Captain Melman clapped his hands on his knees and stood. "Get everyone's statements, Lieutenant, and confiscate Miss Ralston's phone. I'll see you back downtown. We're going to have a shitstorm to deal with."

With that, he departed. The fact that he'd asked Mike to take the phone rather than taking it himself told me that he'd given up on trying to control the narrative. He was off to weather the storm as best he could.

As were we all.

CHAPTER SEVENTY-THREE

"Isn't there a rule that they aren't supposed to see each other before the wedding?" I idly inquired of Malone as we sat watching Veronica Fortune and Sonny Sampson conferring behind the counter of the Pen and Pastry.

"I think the rule says that the groom isn't supposed to see the wedding dress before the ceremony. It wasn't a problem for us because there was no wedding dress. Today, there's no groom."

"Ah."

The café was closed for the afternoon and the staff was just about finished rearranging and decorating for the upcoming ceremony—which was coming up much sooner than had been originally planned. Pre-Thanksgiving now, rather than post-New Year's. It had been nearly six weeks since our confrontation with Ray Devine and apparently there was something about being shot that lent a certain urgency to getting on with life, at least as far as our two friends were concerned.

Tempus fugit. Carpe diem. All that.

As anyone who knew the two brides might have guessed, it wasn't going to be a very traditional ceremony. For one thing, it was happening here in the closed-for-the-day and specially decorated Pen and Pastry. For another—and this was a biggie—the ceremony would be performed by none other than Reuben Keys.

Yes, the famously former prostitute was being married to her girlfriend by her famously former pimp, downloaded credentials in hand.

Perhaps the most remarkable thing about all this was that the place wasn't swarming with local media. It was a hell of a story and it looked like Alison Roberts, back on the air with her show, would have yet another exclusive since she was the only reporter in sight. Heading for our table, in fact.

"Hey, guys!" she greeted us with a big grin. She was wearing a kind of flouncy light blue dress patterned with a variety of flowers. Very colorful. She grabbed one of the few empty chairs from a nearby table and sat down, gesturing at the numerous colorful streamers hanging from the ceiling. "Isn't this a blast?"

"You're lucky to be a friend," observed Malone. "I'm surprised you didn't bring a photographer with you."

If anything, her grin got bigger as she held up her phone. "This has a very good camera. Besides, I *am* here as a friend...even though I will do a story as well." She took a picture of us and set the phone down. "*And* I'm still doing follow-ups on Ray Devine. He is definitely the gift that keeps on giving."

"What is there left to say?" I asked. For the first several weeks after Devine's death, there was little on the local news besides follow-ups, with Alison Roberts in the lead all the way. Malone and I were greatly relieved when it finally trailed off. I was hoping that, whatever Alison had left to say, it didn't involve us.

Alison poured some coffee from the pot in the center of the table. Every table had its own pot for this special occasion. Champagne was available at the counter. "I've been talking to psychologists and other mental health experts about his mental state. To me, the most interesting thing isn't what he did to Sylvia, his murdering his friends, or even that he forced you guys to shoot him; it's the twenty years when he was, as far as anyone can find out, exactly the normal, public-spirited family man and local politician that he seemed. How did that work?"

"Okay," Malone said, "you're the one who's been talking to the experts. How did that work?"

Alison took a moment. "We'll never know for sure, since he's not around to interview, but the best speculation—the best for my story, at least—is that killing Sylvia's father provoked a psychotic episode with Sylvia. He...did what he did...and then abandoned her in the alley after he came to himself.

"He claimed to regret it and that appears to be true. He anonymously contributed to her support after she was adopted; he married and lived normally, went into politics and made some real contributions as a public servant. However he was dealing with it inside, he must have thought it was all behind him for good. Then...whoops! You guys start stirring it up and he breaks all over again."

We all contemplated that for a moment or two. "Well," I finally said, "it's a theory."

"And a story." Alison's grin was back. Her eyes widened as her gaze went beyond us. "There's someone I need to talk to," she said. "Good to see you guys. And thanks again." She departed, probably on her way to another story.

My partner seemed happy to sip her own coffee and absorb the energetic atmosphere, so I relaxed and surveyed the packed room myself.

Off in a corner near the counter, Rodney Pepper and Sylvia Ralston, newly engaged, were chatting with Agatha and her young protégé, Beck. Rodney had matured quickly in the face of threats to his beloved and Beck was at least wearing colors now. She looked almost like a normal young woman as she sat next to Agatha with Morty held securely in her lap.

Our erstwhile client had chosen to remain Sylvia Ralston, leaving Hannah Wingate in the past.

Looking around further, I could see my daughter Colleen and her boyfriend Hoke. All the members of the dojang were present, most prominently Eleanor and Daisy.

I took a good swig of my own coffee. It had been a busy six weeks. Sylvia's recording of Devine's confession had saved us all a lot of grief with the authorities, but we still had to deal with much more than the usual media attention. Fortunately, that, too, was finally in the past.

Of the remaining members of The Six, neither Scott Abernathy nor Warren Macintosh were charged with any crime, but both had dropped from sight, no longer employed by the bank or the TV station. Carl Gunther was out of the hospital and still Portland's preeminent crime boss, but not fully recovered as yet.

The time arrived for the ceremony.

I was to stand with Veronica and Malone with Sonny. The two brides were wearing simple white dresses, in contrast with the colorful outfits of the waitresses who joined with us in front of Reuben. On this special occasion, he also was dressed all in white, emphasizing his coal-black skin even more than usual. He looked over the assembly and smiled.

"We all gathered here to get these two luscious ladies married, so let's do it."

Whereupon he read a short set of vows that clearly had been written by the two women. They both said "I do," Reuben announced that they were married, and they kissed—each other, not Reuben. Everyone cheered.

Less than five minutes, start to finish.

I stepped in and hugged my old friend as everyone crowded around to congratulate the couple. Veronica leaned back a bit and looked up at me. "Thanks for being here," she said.

"My pleasure," I replied with a grin. "A very nice ceremony, by the way. Reuben did a fine job."

She laughed. "I thought it was perfect, having him *and* you as part of it. The man who got me into the life, the man who got me out, and the woman I'll spend the rest of my days with. Full circle. Right here."

She planted a kiss on my cheek and bounced away to join her new wife in celebration.

Malone and I worked our way out of the happy melee and settled back at our table to visit with friends and family as they passed by. Neither of us is the party type, but it was fun to sit there and watch all the joy flowing around us.

Finally my partner and wife tapped me on the arm and I nodded in response. "Yeah," I said, "I think I've had enough." I cocked an eye over at her. "Back to the house or the office?"

The corner of her mouth quirked as she considered those choices. She leaned in. "All this wedding stuff has put me in a marital mood," she whispered. "I vote for the house."

"Nothing I like better than a moody woman," I whispered back as we rose to make a hasty departure.

The office could wait.

The End

Watch for
A Model for Murder
The tenth book in the
McCall-Malone Mystery series
Coming in 2024

It should have been a simple case. McCall and Malone are hired to identify a stalker and convince her to leave their client alone. No problem. Except the stalker can't be convinced, somebody ends up dead, and our two detectives, along with their client, find themselves in deep and deadly trouble.

Visit glennharris.us
to be notified as soon as
A Model for Murderr
is available!

ABOUT THE AUTHOR

Glenn Harris lives and writes in the middle of the Columbia Gorge National Scenic Area (Hood River, Oregon). Besides creating detective novels and short stories, he serves as staff to the same two cats that live with Clint McCall and Devon Malone. His former lives include college English teacher, private K-12 school director, graphic design business owner, weekly newspaper managing editor, corporate manager, actor, and taekwondo instructor.

Keep reading the McCall and Malone mysteries! Stay tuned for *A Model for Murder* and be sure to visit Glenn Harris' website www.glennharris.us!